# CANDY EVERYBO

After moving from Atlanta to New York City in the 1990s, Josh Kilmer-Purcell became a world-renowned drag queen by night and an award-winning advertising creative by day. 'Retiring' from drag in 2000, he became a partner in a downtown NYC ad agency and published his acclaimed memoir in 2006. He writes for *Out* Magazine and has recently completed the screenplay for his memoir, which is being produced by Clive Barker and is currently filming. Kilmer-Purcell and his partner divide their time between their Manhattan apartment and their farm in upstate New York.

Praise for Josh Kilmer-Purcell's *I Am Not Myself These Days*

'Absolutely hilarious, heartbreaking and heartfelt'
ARMISTEAD MAUPIN

'(Kilmer-Purcell's) trenchant memoir captures the mad-cap rush of the once-closeted arriviste's first brush with city life, a fall from innocence that still haunts him . . . He retells the saga . . . with level-headed grace'
*Entertainment Weekly*

'*I Am Not Myself These Days* is a glittering, bittersweet vision of an outsider who turned himself into the life and soul of the party. Kilmer-Purcell's cast is part freak show, part soap opera, but his prose is graced with such insight and wit that the laughter is revelatory'   CLIVE BARKER

Also by Josh Kilmer-Purcell

Non-fiction
*I Am Not Myself These Days*

# JOSH KILMER-PURCELL

## *Candy Everybody Wants*

HARPER

*Harper*
An Imprint of HarperCollins*Publishers*
77–85 Fulham Palace Road,
Hammersmith, London W6 8JB

www.harpercollins.co.uk

This paperback edition 2009
1

First published in the USA by
Harper Perennial 2008

Copyright © Josh Kilmer-Purcell 2008

Josh Kilmer-Purcell asserts the moral right to
be identified as the author of this work

A catalogue record for this book is
available from the British Library

ISBN: 978-0-00-730164-5

Set in Sabon by Palimpsest Book Production Limited
Grangemouth, Stirlingshire

Printed and bound in Great Britain by
Clays Limited, St Ives plc

*For my family.*

*I grant you this brief respite from memoir.*

*The media have created a new 'electronic reality,' suffused with images and symbols, which has obliterated any sense of an objective reality behind the symbols. . . . In hyperreality it is no longer possible to distinguish the imaginary from the real.*

—Kumar

*Thanks. I already turned down the part you're playing.*

—Helen Lawson

*August 1981*

# One

DALLASTY! OCONOMOWOC LANDING.
A JAYSON BLOCHER PRODUCTION
DIRECTED BY JAYSON BLOCHER
WRITTEN BY JAYSON BLOCHER
CASTING BY JAYSON BLOCHER
COSTUMES AND MAKEUP BY JAYSON BLOCHER

EPISODE III: CORNFIELDS ABLAZE!!!
SCENE 18

Open on PATRICIA EWING, and AMETHYST CARRINGTON
sunbathing on floating diving platform in skimpy
string bikinis. Patricia Ewing looks totally
sexy wearing a swirly Pucci suit, and Amethyst
Carrington also looks hot in a Lily Pulitzer
extravaganza. J. B. EWING paddles up in the
convertible Ewing-Carrington pedal boat.

PATRICIA EWING: (sarcastic) Well hello there J.B., *you jerkface*. Welcome home from work.

AMETHYST CARRINGTON: He is not a Jerkface AT ALL, Patrica! He is the father of our child! Who will one day inherit control of all of the Ewing-Carrington farmland!

J.B.: (setting drink on dock and climbing out of pedal boat) For your information, ALL OF THE EWING-CARRINGTON CORNFIELDS HAVE BEEN SET ABLAZE!

AMETHYST CARRINGTON: NO!

J.B.: YES!

AMETHYST CARRINGTON: NO!

J.B.: YES THEY HAVE!

PATRICIA: I hope my husband Robbie is out there saving the day.

J.B.: Why would he be? Your loser husband, who is my loser brother, was the one that set them on fire!

PATRICIA: (standing up and poking her finger into J.B.'s tan chest) I have had quite enough of your LIES, J. B. Ewing!

J.B. Well then maybe you should take a break . . .
IN THE LAKE! (J.B. pushes ~~Tara~~ PATRICIA off the
dock into the lake.)

AMETHYST CARRINGTON: *Sayonara*, bitch!

    J.B. WRAPS HIS STRONG ARMS AROUND AMETHYST
       CARRINGTON AND PULLS ~~HIM~~ HER AGAINST
             HIS HAIRY CHEST.

J.B.: I have wanted to do this ever since we got
our last divorce.

       J.B. KISSES AMETHYST CARRINGTON.

           \* Scene \*

'**Do we have to kiss *all the way*?**' Trey asked Jayson, dangling his legs in the unseasonably cool lake while reading over Jayson's script. The float diving dock bobbed lazily with each kick of Trey's legs.

Jayson pulled at the top half of his mother's Pucci knock-off bathing suit. Up until an hour ago it'd been a one-piece, but he'd had to cut it into two pieces in order to transform it into the 'revealing string bikini' called for in the script that he wrote earlier that afternoon.

His left water balloon tit had sprung a slow leak.

There was no time to waste on script revisions. They needed to begin shooting the scene *now*. The sun was going down and his boob was deflating at an alarming pace.

Jayson didn't feel up to an extended debate with Trey on the mechanics of the scene. It had been a long shoot day, and he was getting tired. And mosquito-bitten. But he also didn't want to risk pissing Trey off. With only himself and his neighbors – the twins Trey and Tara – playing all the roles, cast morale was of utmost importance.

Trey was always, historically, exceedingly patient with Jayson's summer vacation 'projects,' but *Dallasty!*, was by far Jayson's biggest and most complicated effort to date. A spin-off series that combined the families of the two most highly rated nighttime television dramas ever – *Dallas* and *Dynasty*. The networks loved spin-offs. And this was a spin-off squared. He and the twins had already filmed twelve of the thirteen episodes Jayson planned on sending 'on spec' to Lorimar Pictures c/o CBS Entertainment Networks. The scene they were about to film was the opening of the cliffhanger final episode of the season. If they could wrap up filming the entire episode this week, he could mail them all off to Lorimar, sign whatever contracts they came back with, and have *Dallasty!* on air as a mid-season replacement. If all went as planned, Jayson would begin his first year of high school as a celebrity – thus breaking the inexplicable curse of unpopularity he'd endured throughout middle school.

'Let's discuss this important scene,' Jayson began calmly, putting his hand on Trey's shoulder. The most important job of a director (according to what he'd read in a *People Magazine* profile of Steven Spielberg) was to keep the 'talent' relaxed and focused on their performance. 'We've established that it's a very dramatic moment with the cornfield a-blazing out at the ranch,' Jayson explained gesturing across the water toward his fictional Ewing-Carrington Dairy Farm. 'And all great TV shows mix romance with drama – *Rockford Files. As the World Turns. The A-Team.*'

Trey was silent.

'Maybe I could just *hug* you instead,' Trey asked.

Jayson set his jaw, stiffening his resolve to keep calm.

'This isn't a *kids show* we're making,' Jayson said through clenched teeth. He'd already been forced to rewrite the ending of the previous episode when Tara refused to ignite the gasoline that had been poured all over the pedal boat. It had been a long summer's work. The cast was getting short tempered.

'How about if Willie shoots it from behind so it *looks* like we're kissing, but you can't tell?' Trey asked, grasping at straws.

'Willie simply doesn't have the cinematographical expertise to film such a complicated shot,' Jayson explained. This was true. Willie, Jayson's younger brother by two years, was retarded. And not 'retarded' in the eighth grade name-calling way. He was *retarded* retarded. Willie had Prader-Willi syndrome. Which meant that he was born with a defect in the hypothalamus part of his brain which resulted in a chronic feeling of being hungry. Starving, actually. Twenty-four hours a day. Willie's ceaseless grazing, coupled with cognitive retardation and low overall muscle tone, gave Willie an appearance that many people confused with Down syndrome.

Willie's Prader-Willi diagnosis wasn't confirmed until a year after his birth. Their mother briefly considered changing William's name to something slightly less similar to the name of his affliction, but in the end decided that it was charming in an odd way. *'MY NAME IS WILLIE PRADER AND I HAVE A PROBLEM WITH THE HIPPOPOTAMUS IN MY HEAD!!!'* Willie had a habit of shouting this at complete strangers in the supermarket. *'Don't we all?'* Jayson's mom would shrug before taking advantage of the resulting confusion to cut to the front of the checkout line.

'It just seems really *gay*,' Trey finally concluded.

Tara began giggling behind them. *'Gay,'* she muttered under her breath. She was sitting on the opposite side of the floating dock with Willie, biting the toenails on her left foot.

*'Gay?'* Jayson repeated.

*'GAY!!!'* Willie added, eager to take part in whatever this repetition game was.

'I would hope,' Jayson began, trying to hold back his anger, 'that you are not making a derogatory judgment on my sexual preference.'

Jayson had decided that he was homosexual while watching a *Phil Donahue* episode on the topic eight years earlier. He'd come home early from kindergarten that day because

8

he'd gotten a stomach ache from worrying about whether his *Hee Haw* overalls were too *outré* for his peers. Jayson had been sent home from school fairly often over the years, including the first day of kindergarten when he'd become inconsolably agitated that the school wouldn't change their spelling of his name from 'Jason' to 'Jayson.' He felt very strongly that he needed the extra flair to set himself apart from the other, obviously less special Jasons in the class.

The mustachioed men on the stage of the *Donahue* program fascinated Jayson. He wasn't sure exactly why he felt such a kinship with them. Maybe it was how they deflected the barbs of angry audience members with jokes. Or maybe it was their outfits – no piece of which could be found in the Sears catalogs that Jayson was forced to shop from. Or maybe it was just that they were celebrities – put on stage in front of an audience – for no reason other than the fact that they existed. In the deepest corners of his soul, Jayson also knew that he deserved an audience. And it would be his lifetime mission to find one.

When the credits began rolling on that defining *Donahue* episode, the five-year-old Jayson had breathlessly shouted his revelation to his mother, Toni, who was out smoking on the back deck.

*Ma! I'm a homosexual!*

*And precocious!* Toni shouted back, smiling at him through the sliding glass door.

*I'm a precocious homosexual!!!*

*Yes, you are, Butter Bean. Yes you are.*

9

The many men who had played the role of Jayson's step-father during the last decade generally hadn't been as accommodating about Jayson's self-discovery. So Jayson agreed to a pact with Toni to keep this news on a need-to-know basis. She'd patiently explained to Jayson how others' jealousy of his uniqueness might sometimes, perhaps, manifest itself as anger. And/or punching, spitting, and murder.

As a result of this conspiracy, Jayson could count on his fingers how many people had been informed of what *Donahue* called his 'sexual preference.' There was his mother, the twins' parents, Willie, Phil Donahue himself (via an eloquent eight-page thank-you note), his elementary school principal, his middle school principal, a trucker he talked to once on a CB radio, the woman behind the pie counter at Pick N' Save, and, of course, Trey and Tara. Jayson and the twins knew almost everything about each other, being born within a few months of each other, and having spent their entire lives divided only by a fifteen-foot-wide strip of driveway. At the urging of both sets of parents, the twins and Jayson had been keeping Jayon's 'special difference' a secret from his classmates. Though now, as Jayson and his peers began suffering the afflictions of puberty, the secret was becoming harder to keep hidden.

Jayson stood up on the dock defiantly, and indignantly puffed forward his leaking water balloon chest.

'For your *information*,' Jayson continued, 'early Shakespearean plays were cast *entirely* with men and boys playing all the female roles. And I'm sure that Shakespeare, were he alive today, would completely concur with me that action plus passion equals *huge goddamn ratings.*' He took a calming breath, before continuing. 'Which, I think we can all agree, is *precisely* what we're after here.'

Trey sighed.

'Besides. Who else is going to play Amethyst Carrington? Tara's busy playing Patricia in this scene. I mean, I'm *sorry* that I'm not Lola Falana, but you'll just have to make do.'

Trey spit into the water and watched the gob sink.

'Alright. Whatever. I'll do it,' Trey finally said, breaking the impasse. He stood up and resignedly climbed back into the pedal boat to make his entrance. Jayson exhaled his relief.

'Who the fuck is Lola Falana?' Tara muttered to no one in particular, moving to her scene starting mark.

'Okay then! Willie, we're ready. Aim the camera over here,' Jayson instructed. 'Willie?'

Willie was preoccupied on the far edge of the diving dock inspecting the insides of a 100 Grand candybar wrapper he'd found floating in the water. Always unbearably hungry, he was scouring the inside of the wrapper for stray smears of chocolate. He licked at a piece of brownish algae.

'Willie. Buddy. Put that down. We gotta roll,' Jayson said again, tapping his husky younger brother on the head.

Willie lumbered his doughy frame into a standing position, tilting the dock at a precipitously unsafe angle.

Jayson pressed the record button on the Radio Shack cassette tape recorder which captured their dialogue.

'*. . . And . . . ACTION!*' Jayson called, taking his mark next to Tara.

Lorimar Productions was going to love this scene. It was probably the most intricately choreographed shot thus far. Episode One was good, no doubt, but it takes time to really get into the characters' development. Even *Three's Company* didn't find its ratings legs until after the first season.

Jayson worried that synching up the accompanying cassette tape soundtrack to the 16mm home movie film footage might be a bit tricky for the producers. So to help them, Jayson held up a card to the camera at the beginning of each film reel that instructed them to: '*Press Play On Tape Recorder . . . NOW.*'

'I have had quite enough of your lies, J. B. Ewing!' Tara said, opening the scene. She didn't deliver the line with quite the level of haughty anger Jayson had envisioned. But as lukewarm as Tara's performances generally were, there was no stopping once a scene was in progress. Jayson had no editing capabilities, so each scene was filmed in one take, sequentially, picking up wherever the last scene left off.

'Well then maybe you should take a break . . . IN THE LAKE!' Trey shouted.

After Trey shoved her, Tara executed an impressive wind-milling plunge into the lake and convincingly thrashed about in the water, improvising some sputtering heartfelt expletives.

As he stood on the dock watching her 'drown,' Trey theatrically 'wiped his hands clean' of her. It was a little over the top, but Jayson was pleased that Trey was exploring the boundaries of his thespianism.

'*Sayonara*, BITCH!' Jayson shouted in his best Amethyst Carrington falsetto.

All that remained was the kiss.

Suddenly, from the shore behind them, came a barrage of shouting. Adult shouting. The group on the dock turned en masse – even Willie with the camera.

'*Sayonara*, BITCH!'

It was Jayson's latest stepfather, Garth, whom Toni'd met earlier in the summer in the audience of a waterskiing show in Waukesha. He was standing in the driveway of their split-level ranch, which was painted lilac with eggplant trim and shutters. He had a suitcase in one hand and the middle finger of the other hand raised defiantly back toward the house.

'*Congratulations, motherfucker. You finally got SOMETHING up!*' Toni's voice shouted back from inside the kitchen window.

All four children stared at the domestic explosion occurring onshore. There was another brief volley of expletives before Garth climbed into his Chevy Citation and roared down the driveway in reverse, severing the sideview mirror from Toni's chartreuse Ford Maverick.

Jayson had been convinced this marriage would last at least through the summer. It had seemed more promising than the other eleven. *Twelve?* Jayson couldn't remember the exact number. His mother, Toni – for all her free-spirited ways – had one deep-seated remnant of her strict Catholic upbringing. She would never fool around with a man until she was married. Since Toni also had a deep-seated devotion to fooling around, she found herself in front of a lot of altars. Generally not Catholic, obviously.

After Garth's car sped noisily out of sight down Lake Labelle Drive, Toni emerged from the house. Jayson always thought she looked her most beautiful when she was angry. Her heavy black hair would be tousled from being pulled, and her squinting green eyes flickered with brilliant rage against her pale skin. She wasn't rail thin like most of the women on television – Mrs. Kotter, Laverne and Shirley, Vera the waitress on *Alice*. But she wasn't fat either. She had the full curves that most men truly wanted – more than the waifs they were fed on TV. She was, she always said, 'half Italian, half Russian, half black Irish, and all business.'

From their spot in the middle of the lake, Jayson, Willie, and the twins watched her march down the driveway, pick up the amputated mirror from her Maverick, and hurl it into the lake while letting loose with a primal scream. The chartreuse glinting mirror arced overhead and landed in the water with a *phloomp* only ten feet away from Jayson and his cast.

Only when it landed did Toni notice Jayson, Willie, and the twins watching from their floating island. Her mood changed instantly, as was her style. 'Fleeting' was the only constant trait of Toni's personality.

'You kids ready for hot dogs?' Toni called out to them cheerily. 'I got the kind with the cheese inside.' She planted her hands on her hips and cocked her head with incredulity. 'The cheese is on the *inside*! Can you *motherfuckinbelieveit?!?*'

Willie was still filming. He'd learned the hard way not to stop until Jayson yelled 'cut.' Jayson wasn't sure how he was going to work Toni's domestic explosion into the plot of this episode. But he'd find a way. It was good material. Very natural.

His most immediate directorial concern was finding an ending for the unexpectedly prolonged scene.

Jayson turned back toward Trey, rose on his tiptoes, pulled Trey's head toward his own, and kissed him as the original script had called for.

The water breezes kicked up as the sun set behind the houses on the far shore of the lake and Jayson lost himself in his first ever kiss.

*Never confuse yourself with your character,* Jayson reprimanded himself silently, repeating acting advice he'd heard Bette Davis offer on *Johnny Carson*.

'*Annnnd, CUT!!!*' he shouted at Willie, reluctantly separating from Trey. The twilight sky was streaked with purple, and clouds of mosquitos began swarming around them.

Tara coughed and sputtered as she pulled herself out of the water and onto the dock.

'Jesus Christ,' she hissed at Jayson, 'if you'd made out with Trey any longer, I would've fucking drowned for real.'

Trey didn't say anything. He pretended to be concentrating on gathering his belongings for the pedal boat ride back to shore. Jayson ignored Trey's discomfort. The only thing that mattered now was finishing the *Dallasty!* episodes and mailing them off to CBS.

Soon enough Jayson would be on his way to Hollywood. He would escape all of this small town nothingness. The petty domestic dramas. His insufferable unpopularity. The strangers who would stare at his strange clothes and strange brother and strange mother in the A&P.

Don't touch that dial, he thought to himself. The newest, greatest season of Jayson Blocher will premier right after these messages.

# Two

*'Jaaaaayson, I'm outta here! Come kiss me goodbye.'*

*'Jesus Jm J Bullock Christ,'* Jayson muttered to himself, putting down his pencil in the rust shag carpet of his bedroom. After one of the hottest and most humid summers on record, the carpet smelled as fetid as the slime that grew between the rocks on the shore of the lake. And it had been vacuumed about as often.

Jayson was only halfway through writing the final scene of *Dallasty*'s cliffhanger. He was farther behind schedule than he'd anticipated. The week's shooting had been frantic and stressful, with the twins' schedule being interrupted repeatedly by back-to-school shopping excursions. Jayson himself had had no such diversions. Toni had pinned a $20 bill to his bedroom door on Tuesday and told him to bicycle into town to buy what he needed. Which Jayson promptly did: four cartons of Starbursts, a box of Whatchamacallit candy bars, and thirty-six pouches of BlueBerry Blast Capri Suns.

If he could get the final scene finished today and shot sometime over the weekend, he would have the entire season of episodes ready to be dropped into the post office box by the corner of Oconomowoc High School on the first morning of classes.

*'JAYSON! I'M LEAVING!'*

Jayson slid down the front foyer steps on his ass and walked into the kitchen. In the week since Garth had left, the house had become even dirtier, which, had you asked Jayson last week, he would have sworn was impossible.

Toni was leaning against the burnt orange counter that was, poetically, pockmarked with cigarette burns.

'I didn't even know you were going somewhere,' Jayson said.

'I told you on Monday that I was going to spend the weekend at an artists' collective in Chicago,' she replied, holding her arms out for a hug.

'No you didn't. Monday you spent the entire day in the sarcophagus.'

Toni dropped her arms.

'I did?'

'You did. And I have the police citation to prove it.'

Toni had recently declared herself a 'modern artist' working out of her garage 'studio.' She announced her new vocation last spring in a press release sent to the *Oconomowoc Enterprise* that, much to her indignant disappointment, was never published. She kept a copy of it hanging on the refrigerator. By a nail. Toni had several mementos nailed to the refrigerator, since she was wary of the health effects of magnets.

## 5/21/81. FOR IMMEDIATE RELEASE

Toni Blocher, née VanSchlessor, is proud to announce a showing of her avant-garde sculptures detailing the rise and descent of woman's struggle with the modern institution of matrimony. Neither an advocate for the patriarchy, nor a traditional feminist, Blocher will exhibit her latest works in the driveway of her home at N6855 W. Lakota Dr. from April 7 to April 14. (Parking on street is strictly prohibited by the fascist Lac Labelle Homeowners Association. The artist recommends slowing to a crawl while driving by. Ms. Blocher will walk next to your vehicle and answer any questions regarding pricing of specific works. Photography is prohibited.)

To create the work for her first showing, she'd spent four days and nights in the garage attacking bolts of bridal toile with a blowtorch and cans of spray shellac. The molten plastic toile was molded into giant blobs faintly resembling historical torture devices.

The *'Pee-yes de la Raisin-stance,'* as she called it, was a working spiked sarcophagus coffin propped up against the basketball pole in the driveway in which, during certain afternoons throughout the summer she could be found writhing in imaginary pain. Completely nude. This finally did result in a write-up in the *Enterprise* this past Thursday—in the police blotter column.

'I could've sworn I'd told you about the weekend,' Toni said. 'Maybe with that motherfucking back-hair-matted limp dick pig deserting us, I got distracted.'

'Garth didn't leave, Ma. You kicked him out. Because he didn't support your *vision.*'

Toni had a way of attracting all sorts of men before ultimately eviscerating them. In Wisconsin, being 'big boned' didn't have the same pejorative meaning it had elsewhere in the country. Here, men had been trained since childhood to lust after voluptuous State Fair Dairy Queens, with their curves and – as Helen Lawson said on *MatchGame* – 'big bazooms.' The eleven (twelve?) men she'd gone so far as to marry were only the tip of the iceberg of the Titanic Toni. She'd dated hundreds of men since high school – when she had given birth to Jayson. But when looking at photos of all the different weddings, some of which he remembered and most of which he didn't, Jayson always thought that she looked less blissly marital than simply caught off guard.

Whenever Jayson asked who his father was, or Willie's father, Toni would simply point to whoever she was dating at the time and say: *'For today, he's your man.'*

Of all the things in his life, Jayson was most grateful that his mother had inherited the fully paid off, split-level lake house from his grandparents, who died when Jayson was a baby. Toni was finishing her last year of high school as a teen mother when her parents got broadsided by a milk tanker as they were exiting the Catholic Church parking lot. It was the same church in which his grandparents were too embarrassed to have Jayson baptized.

'Fuck Garth,' Toni said. 'I don't need nobody's support.' Toni puffed on a newly lit Newport. 'Except yours and Willie's.' She held out her arms again. This time Jayson assented to her hug.

'Well, until I'm of legal age, you have my undivided, custodially obligated fealty,' Jayson said.

'Thank you, Butter Bean.' She leaned over and picked up the brown paper Piggly Wiggly shopping bag she was using as a suitcase. 'And don't forget to drive the car around the block at night so the neighbors don't think I've abandoned you.'

'But you *are* abandoning us,' Jayson countered playfully.

'You know I'm only a phone call away.'

'So I should just call the operator and ask for the number of an artist collective in Chicago, then?'

'Don't be a smart ass. I was being metaphorical.'

'Then I'll be sure to only have metaphorical emergencies.'

'Perfect. Just make it look busy around here. I don't need the ASPCA dropping by again.'

'You mean Protective Services.'

'Yes. Those do-goodie-two-shoes.' Toni balanced the overstuffed bag on her hip and pushed open the screen door to the garage. 'I swear I'll burn this goddamn house down with all of us in it the next time they decide you need protection from me.'

As he watched her back the Maverick out the driveway, Jayson picked up the lit cigarette she'd left smoldering next to a pile of three years' worth of *Penny Saver* newspapers and tossed it in the sink with the other butts.

Watching over Willie wasn't as easy as his mother thought it was. Jayson had been taking care of his younger brother ever since he realized he had one. It was Jayson who took notes about Willie's care at the doctor's office. It was Jayson who put locks on the kitchen cabinets and refrigerator to keep Willie from raiding them. It was Jayson who locked Willie in his room each night in order to be sure that Willie didn't escape and forage for food in the neighbors' garbage cans alongside the raccoons.

To escape the constant stress of keeping his household running, Jayson often lay in bed at night and imagined that he was the son of one of his favorite television mothers. His most soothing fantasy was to pretend that he was the seventh member of the *Brady Bunch* – the only biological child of Carol and Mike.

Willie came around the corner into the kitchen chewing on what looked like a dog toy.

'Where'd you get that, pal?' Jayson asked him.

Willie froze. He knew that he wasn't supposed to be eating food that wasn't portioned out to him. The problem was that he only remembered this rule when he got caught.

'Hand it over, Silly Willie,' Jayson said. He held out his hand. 'And spit out whatever's in your mouth. That isn't food.'

Willie paused for a moment, his slow synapses debating whether there was a way to continue chewing on the marrow-flavored rawhide dog bone that he had found in the field out back. Concluding the inevitable, he spit out the one chunk he'd managed to soften and bite free.

'That's my boy,' Jayson said, realizing the sad parallel of addressing his brother like a pet while simultaneously holding a hunk of chewed up rawhide in his hand. 'We can have a snack later.'

Willie shuffled off into the mud room, already refocused on finding another morsel of something edible in the yard.

Jayson looked out the kitchen window at the twins' house next door. A movement caught his eye from the upstairs left window. Trey's window. A second later he saw Trey walk by the window again. He was shirtless in the late August heat.

Jayson tried not to think what he was already thinking. Trey was like a brother to him. But he'd found himself falling further and further into a crush throughout the summer. To clear his head, he went back up to his room to work on finishing the *Dallasty!* cliffhanger script.

That it contained J.B. and Amethyst Carrington's steamiest kiss yet was pure coincidence.

As Jayson breezed through the twins' kitchen later that afternoon, he called out to their mother, who was sewing daisy-patterned curtains in their dining room.

'Hiya, Terri!'

'Please call me Mrs. Wernermeier, Jayson,' she called back sternly, 'I've asked you a hundred times.'

'No probs, Mrs. Wernermeier,' Jayson responded. 'And *you* can call *me* Mr. Blocher.'

Jayson didn't even try being polite to the twins' mother anymore. Terri's main goal in life – second only to serving her LordGodJesusChristSaviorOfAllMankind – was making the Blocher family miserable. While most of the neighborhood had taken issue with one or another of the Blochers' escapades, it was generally Terri who made the first phone call to Child Services Department; the Police Department; the Fire Department; the Animal Control Department; and, in one particularly memorable accidental fish hook injury, the Hunting and Fishing Department. Toni often swore that Terri must have the government services Yellow Page ripped out and stuck to their refrigerator.

Perhaps what bothered Terri the most was her children's friendship with 'an avowed eventual sinner' like Jayson. However the twins' father, Tom, had always been more than cordial toward Jayson and his family. Like Terri, Tom had also gone to high school with Toni. As Toni had once told Jayson, he'd fingered her at Homecoming.

Trey and Tara were downstairs, sharing a green and yellow beanbag chair imprinted with a Green Bay Packers logo.

'Voila! The final script!' Jayson said, bellyflopping on the couch behind them. 'Here, I typed up two copies.' He threw them into the twins' laps. They were both engrossed in an afternoon rerun of theirs and Jayson's favorite sitcom, *Disorder in the Court*, which *TV Guide* described as 'the madcap adventures of a curmudgeonly family court judge and his six boisterously lovable inner-city foster children.' It was a blatant rip-off of *Diff'rent Strokes*, but Jayson was willing to overlook the breach of copyright ethics because the show featured Devlin Williamson. Jayson knew everything about Devlin Williamson. He ripped out every magazine article he could find about him in the library or while waiting in line at the grocery checkout. Jayson knew Devlin's favorite foods, his lucky number, his dog's name, his birthday . . . which was only three months before Jayson's. They were almost exactly the same age. Devlin was officially Jayson's first crush. Or at least the first crush that he could share with the twins. He wasn't about to admit to his newfound feelings for Trey.

Devlin Williamson played Andy Andrews on *Disorder in the Court* for the show's first season and a half. He'd become sort of a pre-teen idol for a while. Jayson had no idea what Devlin was doing currently – his star faded as quickly as it arrived. But it didn't matter to Jayson since he could still be seen on television each and every day on channel 4 from 3:00 to 3:30. Every time Devlin shrugged his shoulders, turned toward the studio audience, and impishly uttered his catchphase, *'It wuzzzzzn't me!'* Jayson's heart melted a little.

Jayson and the twins finished watching *Disorder in the Court* before the twins picked up and began reading through their *Dallasty!* scripts.

*Josh Kilmer-Purcell*

'*Another* kissing scene?' Trey asked after he'd turned the last page.

'Yes, of course.' Jayson tried to brush off Trey's concerns. 'It's the season finale. The audience will expect it to be action-packed and extra steamy.'

'What the *fuck?* I *die?!*' Tara interrupted as she reached the final page.

'As an actress,' Jayson explained, 'having your character killed off at the height of a show's popularity can be an amazing boon for your career. It frees up your contract, and most likely another network will build an all-new series around you.'

'I don't know if I feel up to it today,' Trey said, crossing his arms behind his head and sinking further into the beanbag. Jayson noticed that Trey's biceps seemed to be growing larger by the day. Jayson also noticed that he was noticing things like Trey's biceps more and more.

'Okay. No problem. We can do it after Toni gets back in town.'

'Your mother's going away?' Tara perked up. 'Where?' This was what Jayson liked best about Tara. She was remarkably lazy – until an opportunity for delinquency presented itself. What was doubly beautiful about her nefariousness was that she was so genetically innocent looking. Long straight blonde hair, a gangly athletic build, and angelic pristine blue eyes. Both of the twins exhibited a sort of prized Wisconsin Aryan-ness that excused them from blame for almost any caper. They looked like protagonists from a Disney movie, but behaved like After School Specials.

'She's heading to Chicago for the weekend. For some artsy thing,' Jayson continued nonchalantly. 'But don't say anything to your mother. I don't want to get into trouble.'

'*MOOOOOMMMMM!*' Tara turned her head and yelled up the stairs.

'*Shut up!*' Jayson mouthed.

'Yes, hon?' Terri yelled from the kitchen.

'*Jayson wants us to teach him how to pray over at his place tonight. 'Kay?*'

It was pathetically easy for the twins to deceive their mother. Terri's God might be omnipotent, but He created Terri practically non-ipotent.

Terri's head appeared at the top of the basement door, smiling widely.

'Well it's about time! May God be with you kids!'

'And may the force be with you too, Mrs. Wernermeier,' Jayson beamed back.

# Three

'Where's the booze?' Tara asked, slipping through the torn screen on the sliding glass door. Jayson was just pulling out the seventh cookie sheet of Gino's Pizza Rolls from the oven. He'd set up the kitchen island with assorted frozen appetizers, having read in *Parade* magazine about the lavish displays of food supplied by 'Craft Services' for Hollywood movie shoots. Jayson also happened to know that Gino's were Trey's favorite snack.

Trey picked up one of the pizza rolls that had just come out of the oven and tossed it into the air. It arced perfectly and plummeted square into his open mouth. Jayson had been practicing that trick for years with an appalling success rate. Trey seemed to master everything he tried.

'Holy *fuck!*' Trey yelped, opening his mouth – half spitting and half dribbling the steaming saucy puff out of his mouth onto the floor. 'These things are like a million degrees!'

'I just took them out of the oven,' Jayson apologized, suddenly worried that Trey might have burned his lips. Trey and he had four kissing scenes to film.

'What's in the bag? Bibles?' Jayson joked, nodding at the heavy case Trey had slung over his shoulder.

'Check this out.' Trey swung the case down onto the floor. Unzipping it, he pulled out his father's unwieldy new beta camcorder.

'*Ohmigod!*' Jayson squealed, instantly very conscious of the fact he was squealing. 'How'd you get that out of the house?'

'He snuck it,' Tara explained. Jayson had originally wanted to tape the entire series on the Wernermeiers' new beta camcorder since it could also record sound. But Tom Wernermeier felt that the tapes were too expensive to use for 'playing around.'

'I can't believe it! This is so perfect. I'm going to go change into costume. Who has the script? What am I wearing?'

'Worst things first, JayJay,' Tara said randomly opening the cupboards next to the pantry. 'Where's Toni keep the booze?'

Jayson opened the cabinet behind him.

'Bourbon or scotch?' he asked.

'Mix mine together,' Tara said.

'Me too.' Trey answered.

Jayson poured each of them a full, tall McDonald's glass with no ice. Jayson took every opportunity to display to the world that he'd 'collected all six' McDonaldland glasses.

'To being famous!' Jayson raised his Hamburglar glass. Tara's and Trey's Grimace and Mayor McCheese glasses clinked against his.

'And rich!' Trey confirmed.

'And bombed!' Tara chimed in.

Even at such an early age, it was easy to distinguish between their goals in life. Tara would forever be satisfied with simply having a good time, no matter where she was or whom she was with. Jayson pictured her future as one long keg party like the ones the highschoolers held out by Highway 16. Trey would always be happy as long as he had whatever the latest toy was – the latest Atari game. Or a windsurfer. Jayson predicted that as Trey aged, he would start collecting bigger toys like Corvettes and stereo systems.

Jayson's only goal, of course, was to be on TV. His first brush with fame was in kindergarten, when a traveling Frisbee troupe made up of ex-hippies came to his elementary school. During their hour-long extravaganza Jayson sat Indian-style on the gymnasium floor, enthralled by watching them use their flying discs to illustrate the safest way to cross a street and how to avoid creepy old men. This troupe of itinerant and somewhat hygienically challenged minstrels seemed to lead a far more exciting life than anyone else Jayson had ever met. Traveling around the country. Performing in front of mobs of cheering kids. For the first time Jayson felt he was a part of a 'live studio audience' and it awoke in him an all-encompassing yearning to be clapped at himself. After the show, Jayson was the only kid to hang behind and ask for the groups' autographs. He stuck around after school to wave goodbye as they drove on to the next school district in their battered VW van.

Jayson, Tara, and Trey each took a long swig of the bourbon/scotch mixture. It was vaguely sweet, and mostly bitter, like sucking on a butterscotch hard candy that had a lighter fluid center. The trio had drunk Toni's booze before, but always in furtive little sips straight from the bottle while Toni was working in her studio. Tara and Trey's parents didn't drink, of course.

Now the trio had an endless open bar weekend in front of them.

'That's *good stuff*,' Tara gasped, gravel-voiced after her first swallow.

'You sound like Helen Lawson on *Match Game 76*,' Jayson giggled.

'Let's start shooting before it gets dark,' Trey said, hoisting the bulky camcorder with his free hand. He'd been trying since Christmas to get his father to let him play with the camera, and now that he had it he wasn't going to waste a minute – even if it meant kissing Jayson again.

'As you've read, the Martini Shot – that means "final shot" in Hollywood terms,' Jayson explained, 'is a catfight between Amethyst Carrington and Christina.' Both roles were played by Jayson, so it would be a complicated effort. Without any editing facilities, the scene was a technical nightmare – requiring multiple costume changes, extreme close-ups, and body doubles played by Tara. 'I'll go get the costumes.'

Tara and Trey went out into the backyard to pick the location, and Jayson went through the upstairs walk-in closet pulling out his dead grandmother's mink coat and a taupe ultrasuede wrap dress which Toni once wore to a singles mixer at the V.F.W. From the top shelf, Jayson pulled down Toni's old platinum Lite n' Airy Eva Gabor wig, and an even older Milady II brunette cropped wig.

Stopping in the bathroom on his way back downstairs, he scooped up a handful of eyeliner pencils, compacts, and lipsticks from the pickup stick-like tangle on the back of the toilet. Now that Toni was single again, the makeup supplies had reappeared.

'You okay Willie boy?' he shouted as he passed Willie's locked bedroom door.

'Yeah. I need a snack,' came the voice from the other side, barely audible over the canned laughter of a *Love Boat* episode.

'No snacks after six, buddy,' Jayson replied. 'I'm sorry. We'll have a nice breakfast tomorrow. I promise, buddy.'

'Okay,' came the sullen reply from the other side of the door.

Tara and Trey were studying the buttons on the camera when Jayson appeared at the sliding glass door in the mink coat and Milady II wig.

'I'm going to begin the scene over here,' Jayson said, stepping into the puddle of remaining sunlight by the edge of the rusty swing set. 'Shoot me from below.'

Trey knelt in the muddy patch at the bottom of the slide. 'Okay. Ready when you are.'

'And . . . *action!*' Jayson called, instantly slipping into Amethyst Carrington's cold character.

AMETHYST CARRINGTON: *Miss Belle, there's
no way in HELL that you're going to poison
J.B. against me and our son! I'm not leaving
NorthFork Farms until I'm CARRIED OUT IN A
COFFIN!*

Trey clicked the camera off after Jayson finished his line. Jayson had to quickly change into Miss Belle's costume. Filming the dialogue between two different characters who were both played by Jayson would be a miracle of cinematography – if they could pull it off. Jayson rushed over to the swing set where he'd stashed Miss Belle's costume and began switching into the platinum wig and taupe wrap dress. There was no time to change makeup in this scene. The viewing public would just have to accept that Miss Belle and Amethyst Carrington had similar tastes in cosmetics.

Jayson rushed back to his mark. The sun was slipping fast.

MISS BELLE: *Well then, call up the funeral
home, Amethyst Carrington, 'cause you need
to get measured! Take this!*

Jayson threw the tumbler of Tab he was holding 'off screen' at the invisible Amethyst Carrington. This was meant to instigate the catfight between the two characters Jayson was playing.

With all the complications, the entire scene took nearly an

hour and a half to shoot as Jayson repeatedly changed back and forth between Amethyst Carrington and Miss Belle. Sometimes Tara – shot from the back – acted as a stunt double for the actual catfighting. It was exhausting, and by the time Jayson yelled his penultimate *Cut!*, the sun was slipping down over the lake and fireflies had begun sparkling in the background.

'We have to hurry to get the last scene,' Jayson shouted, running across the yard to the back door that led into the garage. The season's cliffhanger was to end with Trey and Jayson, as J.B. and Amethyst Carrington respectively, kissing in front of a sunset. The drama would come from Tara (Patricia) bursting out of the house with a gun aimed at one of them. A shot would ring out. Would they live? Would they die? Lorimar/CBS would have to shell out big bucks for another season of scripts to find out the answer to that one.

But first, Jayson had to find a prop that resembled a gun before he ran out of sunlight.

The garage, which doubled as Toni's studio, was dimly lit and filthy. Jayson frantically rooted around the piles of melted bridal toile and boxes of bride and groom cake decorations for something, anything, with which Tara could take aim and fire. She would be relatively far in the background, probably even a little blurry, so the gun didn't need to be *that* terribly realistic. Even the spray nozzle off a garden hose would work. In the dark he finally felt something hoselike and followed it along to the end. As hard as he twisted the nozzle wouldn't come loose, and given the dim lighting it was impossible to determine why. So he stepped down on the hose with one foot and yanked as hard as he could on the nozzle, breaking it free and nearly knocking himself over into a pile of flea market wedding dresses.

After feeling his way back to the door, he emerged from the garage, quickly passing the nozzle to Tara and running back to take his mark next to Trey. This would be his second love scene with Trey, and as much as he tried to convince himself that he was merely excited for the final scene, Jayson knew that much of his anxiety came from the anticipation of kissing Trey.

Trey propped up the camera on a splintered Teeter Totter in the overgrown grass.

'Go?' Trey asked.

'The word is *"action,"*' Jayson clarified. 'And the director says it.'

'So say it, motherfucker,' Tara shouted drunkenly from across the yard. 'My ass is glempty.' She held up her glass and tipped it upside down to illustrate her obvious point.

Jason looked through the site on the camera to be certain Tara was in frame in the background, yelled *Action*, pressed the record button, and ran to his mark in front of Trey.

*'Though you may be a common gigolo,'* Jayson recited staring up into Trey's blue eyes, *'I will always be yours.'*

With all the hurrying to finish before the sun went down, Jayson had broken out into a sweat. He could feel a trickle run under his wig and down the back of his neck. The lake mosquitos were out in full summer force and quickly zeroed in on the heat he was giving off. It felt like a dozen of them were plunging their hypodermic bloodsuckers just below his hairline all at the same moment. He resolved not to flinch. Or swat. This was the biggest moment of the whole series. The whole summer, really.

'*And I will always be there for you, Amethyst Carrington,*' Trey replied. Jayson looked deep into Trey's eyes, searching for some sign that Trey might not merely be acting. He rose up on his tiptoes and pulled the back of Trey's head down to his own. Trey hesitated for a moment before finally giving in to the inevitable. Their lips met, both warm from the hurrying about and the bourbon/scotch cocktail. As they kissed, Jayson moved his head from side to side as he'd seen all the best romantic actresses do. It was a good kiss, Jayson thought. He hoped it would read as well on screen as it was playing out in his head. And it was long.

Too long.

Where was Tara's entrance?

'*The worst thing that could happen right now,*' Trey said, pulling his face away from Jayson's, '*would be for Pamela to burst out of the house right now and shoot one of us.*'

Jayson had to admit it was pretty good ad-libbing on Trey's part. He stole a glance to the side and saw no sign of the homicidal 'Pamela.' He didn't know what to do. They needed the murder for the cliffhanger. At a loss for what to do next, he pulled Trey's face back toward his own and resumed kissing. To step it up a notch for the audience, Jayson decided to use his tongue. He hoped it would clear the censors. His tongue finally found Trey's and the two made their introductions. He was *frenching,* Jayson realized. Honest-to-God *frenching.*

'*Heya, fellas!!*'

It was Tara, stumbling through the sliding glass door. Finally.

'*Sorry for the delay,*' she continued, off script. '*But I had to get a refill. See?*' She held up the bottle of bourbon she'd brought outside to the camera to prove her accomplishment. '*Now I guess I may as well get on to killin' one of yas.*'

Finally, she was back on script.

'*No! Don't shoot!*' Jayson yelled, pulling himself closer to Trey. '*You have a beef with both of us, but I happen to know that there's only one bullet in that gun!*' Perhaps the script was a bit expository, but as Aaron Spelling told *TV Guide,* you should never overestimate the intelligence of your audience.

'*Well then, for one of you, it's your lucky day!*' Tara yelled back. She leaned down slowly to put the bourbon bottle down on the deck, nearly losing her balance. '*Whoopsie,*' she giggled before standing upright again and drawing aim at the two of them with the hose nozzle Jason had given her.

'*Prepare to meet your maker!*'

WHHHHHHHHHHHHHOOOOOOOOOOMMMM-MMMMPPPPHHH!

First came a blinding orange flash. Then the ground under their bodies bucked like a car hitting a speed bump at fifty miles an hour.

Jayson landed about ten feet from where he'd been standing. A bicycle tire pump with its plastic handle in flames came crashing down into the grass next to his head. *His* bicycle pump. From the garage.

*'JESUS FUCKING CHRIST WHAT THE HELL WAS THAT?!'* Tara was screaming from somewhere at least fifty feet west of where he'd last seen her. All of the lights in the house had gone out, but luckily, Jayson noticed, someone had helpfully lit hundreds of little candles all across the backyard.

Jayson sat up, and looked around for Trey.

*'Trey?'* he called into the darkness. *'You okay?'*

'I'm under the seesaw,' came the response. 'You okay?'

'I don't know. What happened?'

The back porch lights at the Wernermeiers' clicked on, flooding both backyards. The hundreds of candles in Jayson's yard weren't candles at all but flaming debris, being systematically doused as they fell into the dewy, overgrown weeds – flaming debris that looked suspiciously like items from Toni's garage/studio.

The garage/studio that – in the light from the Wernermeiers' porch lamps – wasn't a garage/studio at all anymore.

It was nothing.

It was an empty space, through which the trio could now see clear across the street to the moonlit lake. One by one lights up and down the backyards in both directions clicked on, like a synchronized strand of Christmas lights.

'*Are you okay?! Who's hurt!? Oh God, Where are you two?!*' Terri Wernermeier was now running across the backyards, dressed in an oversized bra and baggy cotton panties. As soon as Tara spotted her mother racing toward them, she spun around like an Olympic discus thrower and hurled the bourbon bottle in a high arc clear over the backyard, landing two yards away in the Weimhardts' pool.

Jayson kept staring at where the garage had been, trying to figure out where it had gone. From the looks of the floating pieces of fire still drifting down from the sky, it had gone, in some instances, down to the far end of Lac LaBelle Drive.

'**Jayson?** Are you out there?'

The voice was soft. Calm. Jayson could barely hear it through the persistent ringing in his ears. It was Willie, leaning on his elbows on the sill of his bedroom window. He was neither frightened, nor confused. Willie couldn't see the garage, or lack of garage, from his window. To him, it had just been a loud noise, some shaking, and his bedroom light and TV show shutting off.

He sounded simply curious. Intrigued.

'Yeah, I'm here, buddy.' Jayson said, waving up at him. 'You okay?'

'Yeah.' Pause. 'I need a snack.'

'No snacks after six, pal,' Jayson said.

Jayson picked himself up from the wet grass and made his way over to Teeter Totter where Terri was hugging both Trey and Tara.

'You *evil devil child*,' Terri hissed at Jayson. '*Jesus hates you!*'

'Well, I've never been that fond of him either,' Jayson replied, kneeling down and feeling around under their feet for the camera. He finally found it lodged next to the pile of garden gnomes that Toni had stolen from neighbors' yards over the years. She felt they were offensive to midgets.

Jayson picked up the camera and held it to his ear. It was still whirring somewhere inside its casing. Thank God. It was all on tape: the kiss, Tara's entrance, the explosion. Maybe Jesus did love him after all.

*The network suits are gonna love this*, Jayson thought to himself. He pressed the *Off* button and whispered '*Cut!*'

# *Four*

**The following Sunday night,** around 7:30, Toni's chartreuse Maverick pulled into the driveway, paused for about twenty seconds to take in the scene, then continued to pull all the way up and park on the concrete slab where the garage had stood.

The little debris that was left after the powerful explosion had been cleared by Jayson, Willie, Trey, Tara, and Tom Wernermeier. The twins' father had taken charge of the situation after his wife proved incapable of offering any help beyond hysterically screaming Bible verses at Jayson and Willie. It had taken Oconomowoc's two fire engine squads and three city policemen only about an hour and a half to deduce that the nozzle Jayson had wrenched from the hose in the garage was not a garden nozzle but the nozzle on the blowtorch that Toni used to melt down the wedding paraphernalia she used in her art. The hose, which was attached to a propane tank, had begun filling the garage with gas, which combined with the equally volatile art solvent vapors and lawnmower gasoline fumes. At precisely two minutes after 10:00 p.m. (according to the Jayson's *Dukes of Hazzard* bicycle handlebar digital

43

stick-on clock, later found down by the lake), the basement water heater had clicked to life. The minuscule electric charge pulsed through the fuse box attached to the north wall of the erstwhile garage, and ignited the soup of flammable gasses.

The resulting fireball burned so hot and so instantaneously that it used up all available oxygen in the immediate vicinity and completely burned itself out before most of the projectile debris even landed.

Whoosh.

The house itself was remarkably undamaged, except for the door that led from the garage into the kitchen. It had splintered and embedded itself in shards in the opposite pantry wall. The newly exposed wall that had previously divided the garage from the house was scorched from foundation to roofline in aesthetically appealing swirls of soot and char.

This sooty graffiti, of course, was what Toni noticed first upon swinging herself out of the driver's seat.

'Look's nice. Who did it?' she asked of no one in particular, staring up at the ascending whorls of black on the lilac melted vinyl siding.

Tara, Trey, Jayson, and Willie were sitting cross-legged at the edge of the driveway. No one wanted to answer Toni first, unsure if assuming credit would lead to further compliments or an explosion of expletives rivaling the force of the original blast.

'I didn't eat anything bad,' Willie offered up, clearing his name in the only way he knew how.

'There was an accident,' Jayson said. 'The tank on the blowtorch exploded. It was my fault. But it was an accident.'

'Well, it woulda been hard to accomplish on purpose,' Toni mused, running a finger down the sooty wall. She turned back toward the car like nothing had happened.

As she was walking around the rear of the car to unload the trunk, Terri Wernermeier burst through her front door, determinedly speed walking toward them all. She was followed by a very tall and impossibly erect man in a graying crew cut that suggested a military history not completely left behind him. Behind *him* shuffled Tom, slumped over, staring at the sidewalk. Jayson got the feeling he'd lost whatever argument might have kept them all inside.

'Are you Mrs. Blocher?' the buzz-cutted man called out curtly from halfway across the yard.

'*Ms.* to you, buddy, unless you've got a ring in your pocket,' Toni replied.

'He's Detective Unsinger with Child Protective Services,' Terri clarified, proudly. 'I called him.'

'It's about time,' Toni replied. 'You've been beating these kids up with the Bible long enough – they need a little protection.'

Tara chuckled.

'Detective Unsinger is here for Jayson and Willie,' Terri said. 'For *their* protection.'

'Thank God,' Toni sighed. 'Officer, arrest this woman for

first degree meddling and suspicion of busybodying.' Toni put one arm around both Jayson and Willie and turned them back toward the house.

'Ms. Blocher, I'm going to have to ask you to take your hands off those children.'

Toni ignored him and continued walking across the cement that used to be the garage floor.

'*Ms. Blocher,*' Unsinger repeated, before reaching out to place his hand on her retreating shoulder.

Being faced toward the opposite direction, Jayson wasn't exactly sure what happened next, and as Tara and Trey recounted it to him later, much of it was a blur to them as well. All anyone was sure of was that Detective Phillip Unsinger wound up knocked unconscious on the driveway. Apparently, he'd been cold cocked by a four-foot-eight-inch tall woman who looked like a cross between Joyce Dewitt and Charles Bronson. She'd flown out of the passenger seat of the chartreuse Maverick with her right hook pre-aimed for Unsinger's square jaw. No one had noticed her in the car when Toni arrived since her head barely cleared the cluttered dashboard.

'Terri, Tom, kids,' Toni said, ignoring the prone man at her feet and putting her arm around the tiny woman, 'this is Franck – my lover.'

Terri gasped. Tom sighed. And a second surprise guest vomited out the Maverick's door onto the driveway from his reclining position across the back seat.

'And this,' Toni continued, gesturing toward the mysterious vomiter, 'is Franck's brother, Gavin, of the infamous band: Lamb Rashes.'

'*Lamb Blisters!*' corrected the breathtakingly skinny young man wiping his mouth as he unfolded from the cramped back seat. '*Christ a'mighty. Lamb Rashes don't even make no fuckin' sense.*'

'Sorry,' said Toni.

Gavin was as tall as his sister was short. Probably six-foot-five inches, Jayson calculated. His hair was making a valiant attempt at standing up in spikes, but, it was perhaps too tired from multiple dye jobs to do much more than bristle in random, blotchy, rainbow-colored clumps. Gavin brushed by Jayson and disappeared into the house through the plywood that served as a temporary door between the missing garage and the kitchen. Jayson could tell by the smell that lingered behind that this hadn't been the first time today Gavin had vomited – though it might have been the first time he'd managed to miss his own clothes.

'Well, Franck, here's my studio I was telling you all about,' Toni said, making a sweeping gesture around the open air where the garage had stood.

Franck leaned back, propping her foot up on the front bumper of the Maverick and lighting up a Marlboro Red. Jayson liked how Franck held her cigarette butt between her thumb and forefinger, and how she winced each time she inhaled. Jayson had learned to smoke from old movies, and while he was still partial to the languid Old Hollywood method of smoking, he made a mental note to try out Franck's more masculine method one day soon.

'It's real nice, Toni, real nice.' Franck nodded. 'Got a real nice view too,' she added, giving the cotton sundress-clad Terri a sultry once-over from her head to her bare feet.

Jayson thought he heard Terri whimper, but it seemed impossible given how stiffly paralyzed she seemed.

The beleaguered Tom stepped forward and put his hand on the top of the twins' heads.

'Well, we'll be getting on home now. I think everything's okay for the immediate future, Toni,' he said.

'Thank you Tom,' Toni smiled and winked. 'And, Terri, be sure to take your trash with you.' Toni pointed toward the wincing Officer Unsinger who was rubbing his jaw while slowly regaining consciousness.

Toni went around behind the car and started emptying several beat up cardboard boxes out of the trunk. Several were torn at the sides and spilling out unfamiliar clothes . . . flannel plaids, drab army colors, black leathers.

'How long you staying?' Jayson asked Franck, who was warily watching Terri, Tom, and Unsinger cross the yard back toward their house.

'Dunno,' Franck said, pulling a cane out from the front seat. 'As long as your mother puts out, I guess.'

'So you and my mother are dating?'

'Maybe. We don't like to use patriarchal words.'

'You're a lesbian.'

'Yep, if you're into labels.'

'And so's my mother?'

'Guess so, chum.' Franck leaned her weight on the cane and sighed. She winced as if the pain of punching out a man three feet taller and a hundred pounds heavier was just catching up to her.

'What's wrong with your leg?'

'It's my hip. Dysplasia. Always been like this.'

In addition to her smoking style, Franck's cane, in Jayson's eyes, was her second redeeming quality. Ever since watching an episode of *Happy Days* where Ralph Malph broke his leg in a skiing accident and suddenly found himself the center of Mrs. C's and Joanie's sympathies, Jayson had wished for some sort of physical impairment. He'd spent an afternoon last year slamming his forearm against the kitchen counter waiting for a sickening bone snap that never came.

Franck fished a Slim Jim from inside her leather jacket and unwrapped it. Willie immediately appeared at her side.

'Want some, buddy?' Franck asked him, a wide smile spreading across her face, softening her features so that she suddenly appeared ten years younger.

'Just a little,' Willie said shyly. He really wanted a lot, but had long since realized that his luck was better when asking for a little of something than all of it. Franck put the end of the Slim Jim into his waiting mouth.

'He's not supposed to eat after six. He has Prader-Willi syndrome,' Jayson said.

'Toni told me all about it,' Franck replied, smiling widely at Willie. 'I get the willies too sometimes.' She fake shuddered from head to toe. This made Willie giggle.

She held out the jerky stick toward Willie's face. 'Now bite down and pull. Hard'

Willie did, and came away smiling, the jagged end of jerky sticking out of his mouth.

'Fwhank you,' Willie said, chewing.

'You're mighty welcome, chum,' Franck replied, putting her non-cane-using arm around Willie. The two of them followed Toni, who was carrying the boxes of Franck's clothes into the house.

Stopping just inside what used to be the door to the garage, Toni peeled the remote garage door opener off the Velcro tape that held it to the wall. She turned around, pointed it at the empty air where the overhead door used to be, and pantomimed pressing the button repeatedly with her thumb. This made Willie giggle. Which made Franck giggle. Which made Toni giggle at her own joke.

Jayson shut the driver-side car door that Toni had typically, absentmindedly left open, and followed his new Fall Season family into the house. This was undeniably a major cast-shakeup, Jayson thought. And right before school started. He wasn't certain that the big producer-in-the-sky knew what he was doing.

# *Five*

**Fortunately Officer Phillip Unsinger** was sufficiently embarrassed at being knocked flat by a four-foot-eight lesbian to decline pressing charges against her. Unfortunately, the emasculating experience stiffened his resolve to rescue Jayson and Willie from what he viewed as their depraved existence.

At Terri's urging, Unsinger filed a complaint with a Waukesha County judge which allowed Unsinger surprise visitations to the Blocher household. Unsinger took full advantage of the ruling, showing up at the Blocher house nearly every day, which, Jayson thought, sort of negated the whole 'surprise' part of the visitations. Most every afternoon, when Jayson and Willie stepped off the bus, Unsinger's brown, county-owned Buick sedan was parked in the driveway. He'd set up a kind of counseling office on the picnic table in the side yard between the Blocher and Wernermeier houses. It must have seemed like neutral territory to him. The Switzerland of Lac LaBelle Drive.

At first Unsinger tried engaging Toni in the counseling

sessions as well, but after forty-five minutes of listening to her rant about the patriarchy of uniforms, he resigned himself to focusing his therapeutic efforts on Jayson and Willie. The two brothers and he would sit at the broken picnic table for an hour of 'life lesson rap sessions.' Unsinger was partial to decade-old hippie church terminology, and Jayson frequently had to stifle his laughter. Jayson often caught Terri Wernermeier's shadowy face peering at them from behind her kitchen window screen. Tara had revealed to Jayson that Unsinger went to their church and that her mother had a secret unrequited crush on him.

The crux of Dectective Unsinger's 'therapy' consisted of scare tactics. He'd tell Jayson and Willie stories of juvenile delinquents he'd worked with in the past who, as he said, 'traded in God for Odd.' He told story after story of teen-agers running away to 'the big city' to get 'hooked on Mary Jane.' These lost souls partied in abandoned warehouses and 'violated their bodies in ungodly ways' with other 'punk hooligans.' Jayson wasn't exactly sure what body violation entailed, but it sounded deliciously edgy – very ABC Monday Night Movie-ish. It seemed to Jayson that Unsinger's profes-sional failures lived much more fulfilling lives than those he'd redeemed.

Unsinger also seemed preoccupied with offering up Trey as an example of 'clean living.' To Unsinger, Trey was the perfect young man next to whom Jayson looked like God's worst failure. Unsinger urged Jayson to spend more time with Trey, 'playing ball' and 'drinking soda pop.' If Unsinger really knew just how eager Jayson was to spend time with Trey, Jayson figured he might receive different advice.

Willie, of course, understood none of what Unsinger preached, and frequently lay down on the picnic table bench to take a nap.

The worst part of the 'rap sessions' was how they concluded. Unsinger would pull a handful of acrid, plastic-tasting, sugarless hard candies from his vest pocket and try to make Jayson and Willie 'trade in' a bad behavior in exchange for a piece of candy. 'Trade in one way,' he'd say, to which the two of them would have to reply: '*for the right way.*' Jayson had a hard time not gagging when he put the hard rubbery diabetic candy in his mouth. Even Willie, whose culinary palate included coffee grounds found in trash cans, would spit out the candy as soon as Unsinger turned his back. Under normal circumstances, Jayson wouldn't 'trade in' a case of acute poison ivy for the foul candy. But soon enough he realized that agreeing to an exchange of pretend vices for toxic candy was the only way to get Unsinger out of his yard before prime time started.

But the hassle of Unsinger's visits paled in comparison to the bad news Jayson received three weeks into the school year. Stepping off the bus one afternoon he pulled an envelope out of the mailbox with an LA return address:

10250 Constellation Blvd
Los Angeles, CA 90067

September 28, 1981

Mr. Jayson Blocher
N18975 Lac Labelle Dr.
Oconomowoc WI, 53076

Dear Mr. Blocher,
Lorimar Television does not accept unsolicited materials.
Enclosed is your unopened submission.
Please accept the enclosed autographed photo of
Charlene Tilton with our compliments.

Sincerely,
Mike Brown

It was the beginning of the end of any potential popularity he thought he might have been able to cultivate that school year. Even the grinning, bikini-posed, baby-fatted Charlene Tilton seemed to be not smiling but sneering at him.

This wasn't working out as planned. He was supposed to start school with the rumor that he 'had a project floating around Hollywood.' Then Lorimar would pick up the series, and Jayson would drop out of school immediately after the school held a huge, jealousy-fueled, goodbye rally for him.

The plan almost seemed as if it might work for the first couple of weeks. Within a matter of days, Jayson had most of the school believing Lorimar Pictures was screening his *Dallasty!* episodes. While there may have been some doubt about Jayson's story, no one was willing to write him off completely just in case he actually did become famous – *Dynomite* magazine-level famous.

Even the obvious popularity handicap of having a retarded brother seemed mitigated after the season's first ABC *AfterSchool Special* aired, entitled *Slow But Steady*. The special featured Scott Baio as a retarded kid who was adopted as a mascot by his school's cross country track team. Because of Baio's popularity with the female OHS student population, the most popular clique of girls decided to treat Willie as their own Scott Baio. Willie became more popular than Jayson. At least, Jayson had thought, until he got his Hollywood deal.

But this letter from Lorimar would bring the whole thing crashing down.

Jayson had no contingency plan. The rejection meant that he would have to resign himself to another four years of middling popularity. Over the summer, he'd had hope. More than hope. He'd convinced himself that his life was about to change. At the very least, he'd been certain that even if Lorimar *didn't* buy his scripts, someone, *someone* at the network would spot Jayson's youthful enthusiasm and fly him out to Hollywood – if only for a small segment on *Real People* about talented kids. Something. Anything to get him closer to his goal and farther away from the PBS-style drudgery of Oconomowoc, Wisconsin. He honestly didn't know how much longer he could survive here. Had anyone ever died from obscurity?

Four days after Jayson received the rejection letter from Lorimar, events took a turn from bad to unimaginable. It was like that *Happy Days* episode where Fonzie was cursed by a gypsy inexplicably passing through Milwaukee.

It was precisely at the fifty-third minute of the tenth hour of the twenty-first day of Jayson's high school career that Jayson's personal popularity ratings plummeted to the cellar after a very special episode of gym class.

Due to rain, Jayson's class was kept inside. And Jayson's gym teacher, whom Jayson had pegged as a female homosexual from the first day of class, only seemed familiar with one indoor activity: dodgeball. She announced each class of dodgeball with such excitement that Jayson wondered if she ended each evening with a rousing game of one-on-one dodgeball with her female homosexual roommate in their livingroom.

Jayson was cursed with the dodgeball double handicap of being unpopular – thus a popular target – yet having the quick reflexes that enabled him to dodge almost any throw. Being one of the last boys standing in the game yet having the most valuable bounty on his head kept Jayson in the glare of the humiliating spotlight for what seemed like hours rather than the allotted 45 minutes. Even Trey, who shared the same gym class with Jayson, had uncharacteristically turned on him, beaning him particularly forcefully right before the shower whistle was blown.

As much as Jayson dreaded public nudity, at least the shower call meant an end to hurtling orbs of rubber.

Stripping off his standard issue OHS gym T-shirt and gray shorts in the locker room, Jayson examined the growing purple welts on his stomach and chest. The biblical marks of loserdom. Glancing in the mirror that ran the full length over the sinks, he noticed his right eye was swelling shut from the memorably forceful *thwang* of red rubber hitting skull hurled by Trey.

The showers were in a roughly twenty-foot-by-twenty-foot floor-to-ceiling beige tiled vault off the locker room. There were no dividers. No curtains. Just eighteen nozzles jutting out toward the center drain. Very Auschwitz. Given the Germanic heritage of southeastern Wisconsin, and the age of the building itself, it was, in fact, very likely designed by a close relative of a concentration camp architect.

Jayson's personal Phil Donahue secret, when coupled with normal adolescent insecurities, meant that he was one of the fastest showerers in the ninth grade. He'd recently begun noticing that his genitalia were often on a different programming schedule than his brain, so the less time spent naked, the safer. Who knows what random thought might set his penis into action?

Jayson was examining a particularly angry welt on his forearm when Trey stepped up to a shower nozzle next to him. Jayson knew he shouldn't have paused under the showers.

'Hey, nice game,' Trey said. 'You were in for a long time.'

'Et tu, Bluto?' Jayson quoted from his favorite *Popeye* comic book.

'Sorry about that,' Trey apologized. 'I thought you were gonna duck.'

'Well, I thought about ducking until I spotted the four other balls heading for my crotch.'

Trey turned and looked Jayson in the eye.

'I'm really sorry. I am. I didn't mean it.'

Something about the sincerity in Trey's light blue eyes reminded Jayson of how inseparable the two of them had been during the summer months before they had to return to school and put up protective facades. Before they were forced to splinter off into different, respectively appropriate groups of friends. That was always Jayson's favorite time of year. Summer. When he had Trey all to himself. When Trey didn't have to worry about being seen with Jayson. Summer was the time when Jayson had always been happiest. It was the only time when there were no secrets, and no facades. Jayson even thought that he would probably trade in every dream of Hollywood if he could only have an eternal summer with Trey.

Jayson suddenly felt the buzzing wings of a million dragonflies brushing against the inside of his thighs . . .

*'Gayson's popped a boner!'*

Jayson didn't know who said it first. It didn't matter who said it first. What mattered was that it would be repeated, echoing across the unforgiving concrete walls of Oconomowoc High School for all of eternity.

'*Gayson.*'

The secret was out.

# Six

'So Gavin hasn't said anything at all about me?' Tara whispered, blowing a perfect smoke ring. She, Jayson, and Willie were in Willie's room watching afternoon reruns on channel 64.

'What the hell would he say about you?' Jayson replied. *'Tell me Jayson. That underage neighbour girl. Fuckable?'*

'*Shhh!*' Tara admonished, 'he'll hear.'

Tara had been obsessed with Gavin since his illustrious arrival. It was easy to understand why. Jayson was also intrigued by the hygienically challenged, punk/New Wave, anorexic giant. Gavin spent most of the day and night in the dank basement, which one of Jayson's ex-stepfathers had half-finished remodeling into a bar/rec room before he'd been shown the door by Toni. Neither Tara nor Jayson knew much about what Gavin did in his half-bar lair, but whatever it was it didn't lend itself to coherence during the few minutes a day he emerged for either a beer or a piss. Jayson didn't think he'd ever seen Gavin standing upright without holding on to something for balance. Gavin was more like a recurring guest star than a regular cast member in the Blocher family drama.

The one time Jayson had found an excuse to go into the basement since Gavin's arrival he noticed thousands of Polaroid pictures taped up on every available wall surface. When he later asked Franck about them, she explained that Gavin took a Polaroid of everyone he'd ever met. He had been doing it since he was a kid because he believed in the Native American philosophy that photographs stole people's souls, and he wanted to collect them. Jayson was growing impatient waiting for Gavin to photograph him, and began keeping a comb in his back pocket to be ready at any moment for when Gavin came after his soul.

Still Jayson liked the fact that Gavin was around. His lethargy somehow balanced out his sister's endless energy. What Franck lacked in height, she made up in stature – instituting a set of rules on the Blocher household so rigid that even Terri Wernermeier looked laidback in comparison. Of course no one paid any attention to them – especially the untamable Toni. When Franck wasn't busy painting watercolor self-portraits of her vagina, she was huffing and barking her way around the house, trying to impose some sort of structure on the Blocher chaos. Her persistence was as endearing as it was futile.

Against her mother's orders, Tara began spending most of her time after school at the Blochers', waiting for the infrequent moments Gavin made brief appearances aboveground.

She could hear his footfalls coming up the wooden steps from any corner of the Blocher house and would immediately race to the kitchen for something to drink in hopes of intercepting him.

'*Hey there*,' she would say, trying to open a Diet Squirt as seductively as possible while leaning against the sink.

At most he would grunt back at her, but usually he simply avoided acknowledgment of any kind. This didn't deflate Tara's crush in the slightest. '*Did you see that?*', she'd say later. '*He paused for a moment after dropping that beer bottle. I think he wanted to ask me to wipe it up!*'

Jayson neither indulged nor dissuaded Tara from her crush. He had too many of his own problems. Chief among them was his latest indignity. Someone had written '*GAYSON WHERE'S MAKEUP!*' on his locker in bright red lipstick. Bad spelling was one of Jayson's biggest pet peeves, so this particular insult was doubly bothersome to him.

'C'mon, Tara,' Jayson pleaded when the *Disorder in the Court* rerun broke for commercial. 'Why do you think someone wrote that?'

'Beats me,' Tara said for the third time.

'You're lying,' Jayson said, 'I can tell because you're chewing on your hair.'

Hearing this, Willie, who was lying on the bed above where they were sitting on the floor, suddenly fixated on Tara's hair, wondering if it was edible.

'If I tell you, will you promise not to get mad?' Tara

said, dropping her Newport butt into her half-empty Squirt can.

'I promise,' Jayson lied.

'It was Trey.'

Jayson nearly swallowed his Big League Chew. If his life were a sitcom, he would have done a spittake. Only Jayson's life wasn't a sitcom. It was painfully unfunny, and growing more so by the minute.

'*Trey* wrote that on my locker?'

'No . . . someone else did the actual writing. But Trey took the silly *Dalcon Crest* videotape we shot this summer to school and showed everyone the parts where you wore all the different dresses.'

'It was *Dallasty!*. Not *Dalcon Crest*,' Jayson corrected, still not able to fully comprehend the information he'd just been given. Trey had betrayed him? His oldest friend? Trey was the last person in the world he ever thought would hurt him. Ignore him, yes . . . that was just part of the ninth grade social shuffle. But to actively smear Jayson? That was incomprehensible. 'Why would he show people that?'

'Because, douchebag,' Tara answered, 'everyone was giving him shit for giving you a boner, so he thought he'd show them what a weirdo you were.'

'But why would he show people a tape with us kissing on it?'

'He didn't show *that* part, idiot. He just showed the parts with you in the dresses and wigs,' Tara answered. 'Now shut up, show's back on.'

Jayson shut up. He wondered if he would ever be able to speak again. *Trey. Trey did this to him.* He was devastated.

The boner incident had been horrible, but this episode was unsurvivable. Jayson didn't know how he would return to school knowing that everyone had seen him in a dress. He suddenly realized how silly he must have looked – like the cross-dresser on that *All in the Family* episode. Jayson was furious that he'd allowed himself to look so stupid. So abnormal. *So freakish.*

Jayson had always thought that *he* was the normal one in the circus that surrounded him. He'd always, in the back of his mind, felt that Toni, and Willie, and Garth, and Franck, and Gavin, and everyone else who'd ever found themselves part of the Blocher menagerie were the mutants, and that it was *he* who put the thin veneer of normalcy out in front of the world. But it was so clear to him now. He *belonged* in his queer family. He was *one of them*. One of the freak show.

Jayson hated that he had come to believe, he had really *believed*, in the religion that claimed that after twenty-three minutes and two commercial breaks everything would turn out okay. He believed in and worshiped that glowing blue altar which taught him when to laugh, when to cry, when to applaud, and when to love.

He had faith that even an incident as earth-shattering as a locker room boner would eventually be absolved *right after these commercial messages*. With a little 'pluck,' a little 'moxie,' a little 'gumption,' every trauma was supposed to be overcome.

But it wasn't true. It was over. He was different from everyone else – and not in a good way as he had always presumed – in a funny way. A queer way. Things didn't work out for Jayson at the end of the episode – they worked out for Trey. No one cared how Jayson's storyline resolved.

Jayson came to a soul-shattering conclusion.

*Oh God,* he thought. *I'm not the star . . . I'm the wacky neighbor!*

'I think I hear Gavin coming upstairs . . . let's go!' Tara said breathlessly, interrupting Jayson's stream of self-loathing consciousness.

'Nah,' Jayson replied. 'I don't feel so well. I think I'll hide out up here.' He listened to Tara skip away down the hall.

Jayson's funk continued to deepen in the weeks after Trey's betrayal.

'Why are you being such an ass around here?' Toni finally asked Jayson after the fourteenth consecutive dinner in which Jayson didn't utter a word.

Jayson didn't answer.

'Answer your mother,' Franck commanded.

Jayson looked down at the Beef-A-Roni mixed with La Choy Chop Suey that Toni had 'invented' for dinner. She'd called it 'Orientaly.'

Jayson remained silent.

'Is it the whole boner thing?' Toni asked. ''Cause Tara told me all about it.'

Jayson looked up from his plate and glared at Tara. Tara shrugged him off.

'These things happen,' Toni continued. 'It's completely natural.'

'She's right,' Franck affirmed. 'What you should really do, Jay-Jay, is focus your embarrassment into some sort of creative outlet.'

'Sure,' Jayson muttered. 'I'll start doing pastels of my scrotum. We can have a joint show.'

'What he's really pissed off about is that Trey showed everyone at school that video of him playing around in dresses,' Tara interjected.

*'For the last fucking time, Tara, I wasn't playing around. I was acting,'* Jayson said through gritted teeth.

'So what's wrong with that?' Toni asked. 'Didn't people like it? I thought it was a good show.' However frustrating Toni could be, the one thing that Jayson could count on from his mother was her ability to never look at a situation the way a sane person would.

'Now they're all calling me "Gayson,"' Jayson explained.

'And "homo,"' Tara said.

'Not "faggot"?' Toni asked.

'We used to say "queer,"' Franck added.

'Gay Gay Gay Gay Gay Gay Gay,' Willie started. One of the symptoms of Prader-Willi syndrome was repetitive verbalization. Willie always chose the most inconvenient times to manifest that.

'That doesn't seem like something Trey would do,' Toni said.

'After Jayson got a boner in the shower next to him, Trey started getting teased too,' Tara explained to the table. 'So he threw Jayson under the bus.'

'I'd appreciate it if everyone would stop bringing my penis up at the dinner table,' Jayson pleaded.

'Why not? It seems to come up everywhere else,' Tara joked, chortling through a mouthful of Orientaly.

Jayson stood up to clear the table. He didn't need to relive the worst moments of his life any longer.

'So what are you going to do about this?' Franck asked.

'Nothing,' Jayson replied, scraping the globs of congealed food onto one plate.

'God, you really are a little fag, aren't you? You don't have any plan on how to get even?' Franck said. From what little Jayson knew about her history, he had learned that the four-foot-eight, handicapped lesbian had solved most of life's dilemmas with her right fist. 'I guess I'm going to have to be the man around here,' she sighed.

'Well, you *do* have the mustache,' Jayson muttered.

'You're not going to punch my brother, are you?' Tara asked, suddenly a little frightened.

'I don't punch kids,' Franck clarified, defensively. 'What do you people think I am?'

'A violent, crazy dyke,' Jayson answered, rinsing off the last of the plates.

'No – a violent, crazy dyke *with a plan*,' Franck corrected.

'What are you talking about?' Jayson asked.

'You'll see soon enough,' Franck answered. She caught Gavin's dilated eye and winked.

Jayson ignored her, pouting his way through the next three hours until bedtime. He slept fitfully, waking up sometime after midnight, desperately thirsty from his two helpings of sodium-laden Orientaly. He made his way downstairs, and on his way across the darkened living room to the kitchen a voice startled him. He yelped.

'It's just me, Butter Bean,' Toni said, her voice coming from the darkness where the sofa would be.

'What are you doing in the dark?' Jayson asked. He squinted and just made out the tip of her smoldering Newport.

'Just thinkin',' came her reply. 'Come over here and sit next to me.'

Jayson felt his way across the dark room, taking small steps in order not to trip over the coffee table. When he finally felt the cold arm of the vinyl faux-leather couch, he sank down next to the warmth of his mother. She put her soft arm around him. Jayson could tell she was only wearing her bra.

'What are you thinking about?' Jayson asked. In the total darkness, he realized he could imagine his mother being anyone he wanted her to be. Mrs. Cunningham. Mama Walton. Alice the waitress. The possibilities were endless.

'I was thinking that this is the first time I've seen you unhappy.' Jayson heard the slow inhale as Toni took a final drag on her cigarette before snuffing it out somewhere in the darkness on the other side of him. 'I mean *really* unhappy.' She paused before exhaling. 'And I've realized that I'm not happy when you're not happy.'

Jayson sighed.

'You haven't been writing nothing,' Toni continued. 'Or acting, or filming . . . fuck, you aren't even singing television theme songs around the house anymore.' It was Toni's turn to sigh. 'It's hard to believe that you're this upset just because some kids didn't like your movie.'

'It was a pilot episode,' Jayson corrected. 'And they didn't just "not like it," they think I'm perverted.'

'I got news for you, Butter Bean,' Toni replied. 'You *are* perverted. I'm perverted. Willie's perverted. Franck, Gavin, even Tara is perverted. All "perverted" means is that you aren't like other people.'

'So far,' Jayson said, 'you're not helping matters.'

'Since when did you think you *were* like other people?' Toni asked. She had a point. 'You've always known you were different. I can't see why the fact that other people know it now, too, should change anything.'

Jayson got goose pimples. His mother was right.

'If you weren't different from them, how could you become a celebrity?' Toni continued. 'There's only . . . what . . . a couple hundred celebrities in this world?'

Jayson was going to correct her by pointing out that he'd just seen a special CBS presentation of *Night of a Thousand Stars*, but he didn't want to stop the soothing lull of her voice.

'And none of these other hicks around here are gonna be celebrities,' Toni continued, 'so of *course* you're perverted to them.'

Jayson listened as his mother flicked her Bic to light a fresh menthol. In the few seconds of light from the flame he looked up and saw the soft roundess of her cheeks. He wanted to lean up to kiss her, but her speech was like a lullaby and he found his eyes drooping shut.

'I don't know much about showbiz, Butter Bean,' he heard her say as he dropped off to sleep, 'but it seems to me like all you gotta do is find the applause and go stand in front of it.'

# *Seven*

**Terri Wernermeier was growing** more and more apoplectic at the increasing amount of time Tara was spending at the Blochers'. Most nights Tara fell asleep on the floor of Jayson's room, but since Terri was too terrified of Toni and Franck to knock on the front door to retrieve her, Tara wound up spending the night at the Blochers' – going to school the next day in the same clothes she'd fallen asleep in.

Eventually, no doubt at Terri's urgings, Detective Philip Unsinger started calling Tara over to the picnic table to take part in Jayson and Willie's court-mandated 'rap sessions.' The first time Unsinger included her, Tara amused herself by pretending to listen raptly to Unsinger's 'Life Lessons,' *tsk*-ing loudly whenever one of Unsinger's obviously fictional wards went from 'God to Odd,' and whose body was inevitably found 'violated and broken, face down in the gutter' of some large city. After two months of examples like these, Jayson finally asked Unsinger if any kid he'd ever worked with had actually *survived*.

After sitting and nodding along attentively to Unsinger's

rambling, Tara would try to outdo herself when the time came to 'trade in' a bad behavior for a piece of Unsinger's toxic sugarless candy. At first her trade-ins were only mildly shocking. She would convince him that she'd give up her two-pack-a-day cigarette habit for the candy. Then, over time, she upped the stakes. Unsinger never caught on to her exaggerated sins until the sixth session, when she tearfully told him that she'd 'trade-in her membership to the Lac LaBelle S&M Swinger's Club for something in a cherry flavor.'

When Unsinger caught on that Tara was mocking him, he ceased 'counseling' her. This, surprisingly, seemed to disappoint Tara. 'He was entertaining,' she told Jayson, 'in a creepy, jacking-off-in-his-car-by-the-playground way.'

Neither Jayson nor Tara saw much of Trey. His after-school athletics meant that he didn't take the bus home with them anymore. On the rare occasion he was home before supper, he would leave quickly afterwards, driven off by junior and senior level friends into nights filled with what Jayson and Tara imagined were sepia-toned high school memories in the making.

Jayson was grateful that Trey was more or less absent from his life. He wasn't sure what they would say to each other now that Trey had exposed him.

The night of the Oconomowoc High School Homecoming Dance, Jayson and Tara were sitting in their usual spot in front of the television in Jayson's room, watching an hour-long special episode of *One Day at a Time*. Jayson had long ago given up wishing he had a perfect mother like Florence Henderson or Shirley Jones. Now he'd be more happy with a sassy single mom like Bonnie Franklin. He'd even live in the ghetto with the stalwart Esther Rolle. He wasn't sure what the ghetto was, but it seemed very homey in a hardscrabble way.

Franck's head appeared in Jayson's doorway just as Ann Romano had an overly dramatic breakdown over her oldest daughter's new druggie boyfriend. '*Dammit, Julie!*' It was the first swear word heard spoken on television

'Are you coming with me to pick up Willie from the dance?' Franck asked.

'Why would we?' Jayson said. For predictable reasons, neither Jayson nor Tara had ever once given the slightest flutter of thought to attending the Homecoming Dance. However Willie's entire special needs class was required to attend. Willie's class was taught by a 1970s free-to-be throwback who insisted that all his students attend the dance to teach the rest of the school population about 'differences.'

'Let me ask again, only not as a question,' Franck said sternly. 'Get in the fucking car. Gavin's waiting.'

The mere mention of Gavin sent Tara flying into the hallway and down the steps, two at a time.

'That was unfair,' Jayson said as he rose and reluctantly followed Franck down the hall. Normally he would have let Tara go by herself, but he wasn't that interested in finding out how Julie planned on raising her child out of wedlock. He had his own problems.

'All's fair that ends fair,' Franck said. As she led him down the stairs, she put her arm around him. It was the nicest gesture she'd shown him since her arrival.

Gavin drove the tiny Maverick with Franck in the seat beside him. Tara and Jayson rode in the back. Neither Franck nor Gavin spoke during the ride to the school, so Jayson and Tara played Round 2184 of their lifelong thumbwrestling tournament. Tara was ahead, 1172 to 1012, but Jayson attributed several of her wins to the fact that she used her sharp fingernails unethically.

'Why do we all need to pick up Willie?' Jayson asked again.

'You'll see,' was all Franck replied.

'Why isn't Ma coming?' Jayson asked, digging deeper into their mysterious outing.

'I'm not sure she'd approve of this,' Franck answered.

'Of *what*?' Jayson repeated.

'You'll see,' Franck echoed.

Jayson sighed and turned his attention back to Tara's double-jointed thumb.

When they finally approached the high school they drove past the parking lot entrance where cars of parents were lining up to pick up those freshmen and sophomores without licenses or rides.

'Where are you going?' Jayson asked, tentatively.

'Just to the hill,' Franck answered, pointing ahead at the slight rise beside the gymnasium. 'The Hill' was where the worst of the pot-smoking delinquents hung out during school hours. Even Tara was too tame for their kind.

'Why aren't we heading to the dance?' Tara asked at the precise moment Gavin yanked the wheel to the right, jumping the curb and lurching the Maverick up onto the grass. Tara's head smacked against the roof of the car. Normally she would have let loose with a string of expletives, but since Gavin was the offender she let it go.

'Because we're going to a premiere instead,' Franck answered.

While normally Jayson loved words like 'premiere,' he wasn't sure that the hill behind the homecoming dance was the most promising venue for one – especially one organized by Franck and Gavin. But as they bumped across the lumpy grass, he didn't think it would be wise to question their determination.

The Maverick reached a spot directly in the center of the sloping hill, and Gavin turned the car to face the gymnasium below, shifted it into park, and shut off all the lights.

The car was silent.

'Everyone out of the car,' Franck commanded. 'And grab a good seat at the Revenge Drive-In Theater.'

Jayson had no idea what the hell Franck was talking about. Nevertheless, he and Tara crawled out of the backseat, and let Franck usher them to their seats on the hood of the car.

'Now, *no peeking*,' Franck said, smiling. 'Keep your eyes straight ahead on the screen.'

'What screen?' Jayson said, growing frustrated with all the mystery.

'Just look down toward the dance,' Franck instructed.

Jayson and Tara followed her instruction and sat watching the first of the dance goers begin exiting the gymnasium far below them. Jayson heard Franck and Gavin wrestling with some sort of equipment behind him.

'Are we all set?' Jayson heard Franck ask from somewhere behind him.

'All hooked up,' Gavin answered.

A blinding, flickering light flashed on from behind him and streamed over Jayson's shoulders, down the hill, finally splashing against the brick wall of the gymnasium. Simultaneously the loudest screeching, thumping, bass line and drums started blaring directly behind his head. The mystery was finally too much to bear, and Jayson turned around to see Franck and Gavin, standing on either side of the car, grinning wider than a Kodak commercial.

There were two huge speakers set on the roof of the car, along with the 16mm film projector that had been in the Blocher basement for decades. Gavin pointed at the speakers and then back to himself, mouthing *'This is me! . . . Lamb Blisters!'* over the deafening punk blast. After the first few cacophonous chords, the lyrics started. For someone who hardly spoke more than three words in any given conversation, Gavin had the loudest scratchiest singing voice Jayson had ever heard. The song, it turned out, was a breakneck tempo punk version of 'Make 'em Laugh': *Thought the world is so full of a number of things, I know we should all be as happy as, but are we?*

Jayson turned back to see what images were being projected onto the gymnasium wall below. At first the frames were blurry, but he could make out sparkles, and flashes, and a brilliant blue that he immediately recognized as Lac LaBelle. The sun on the lake. Rippling.

Franck fiddled with the focus knob until the movie was crystal sharp. It *was* the lake. Flashes of his and Trey's tanned legs panned by. Followed by a closeup of Tara's sandy brown shoulders. Someone was awkwardly getting the camera into position. It finally settled on Jayson as Amethyst Carrington.

*Dallasty!*

*Franck and Gavin were projecting* Dallasty! *onto the gymnasium wall!*

Jayson's initial flush of embarrassed horror quickly turned to wonder as he stared at the mesmerizing colors and action of the movie unfolding below him. There he was – two stories tall.

Even in his mother's cut-up bathing suit and ratty wigs, he decided that he looked *good* on screen. He looked like an actual celebrity. And he was in front of an audience.

It took a moment for the crowd of students below them to realize that the blinding beacon of light on the side of the hill in front of them was a film streaming over their heads onto the wall behind them. Their parents, in their cars, spotted it first — an impromptu late showing at Franck and Gavin's spontaneous drive-in.

Franck had instructed Willie when she dropped him off at the dance that he was to climb up the hill 'where the bad kids played' when the dance was over. Jayson looked down to see a lumbering, smiling Willie trudging toward them. He was oblivious to the drama unfolding around him.

The scene played out longer than he remembered. But he was surprised, even without sound, at how effective his script was. Franck, Gavin, and Tara laughed out loud when Trey pushed Tara into the water. Jayson laughed with them.

Jayson sang along with the lyrics he'd memorized since he was four. Before he had any idea what they meant: *Make 'em roar, Make 'em scream, take a fall, butt a wall, split a seam!*

For a minute or so Jayson still wasn't quite sure why Franck and Gavin had concocted this very public premiere of *Dallasty!* But as the scene drew to a close he finally put it all together.

Jayson watched the thirty-foot version of himself pull the thirty-foot version of Trey toward him. And then: the kiss.

Franck, Tara, and Gavin all sighed *'Awwwwwwww.'*

He'd forgotten how long the kiss was. He remembered it being over in a blink, but in the parking lot below him it seemed to go on forever.

The mob of teens seemed to turn away from the screen all at once to look up at the hill toward them. Even some of the parents had gotten out of their cars and were shielding their eyes while staring into the bright light.

And somewhere in their midst was Trey.

Jayson didn't want to imagine what Trey was thinking. In his heart he hoped that maybe, just maybe, Trey was watching their summer kiss with as much bittersweet fondness as Jayson was.

But Jayson knew that wasn't true. Trey must be humiliated. *Make 'em laugh! Make 'em laugh! Make 'em laugh!*

Just below the screen Jayson noticed a small group of students break away from the mob watching *Dallasty!* Three of his classmates were sprinting up the hill toward them. He recognized their jackets − their varsity jackets to be precise. They were Trey's football teammates.

'*Start the car!*' Jayson shrieked, jumping off the hood, and pointing at the advancing athletes '*Start the motherfuckin' car!*'

The others had spotted the football players too. Franck pushed the passenger side seat forward and pushed Tara into the backseat. The music was still blaring from the roof. There was no time to dismantle the projector and sound system.

'*Get in, baby! Get in!*' Franck yelled at Jayson, grabbing his sleeve and whipping him into the backseat with Tara. Gavin hopped in the driver's seat, turned the key, and gunned the engine.

'*Get Willie!*' Jayson yelled out to Franck, pointing out his slow, lumbering progress. He was still well ahead of the football players, but they were gaining rapidly.

'*Come on, pal,*' Franck yelled at Willie, smiling her encouragement. '*You can make it.*'

Willie was completely unaware of his pursuers – completely unaware of anything being amiss other than some loud noise and his family playing around on the hillside. He was only about ten feet away from the car when the first football player overtook him, pushing him down onto the ground in his hurry to reach the car.

Franck was waiting for him. Perhaps knowing that there were two more following close behind, she chose to save her famous fist and instead took out Football Player Number One with a swift arc of her metal cane across his knees. He fell into the grass, curled into a ball of pain.

Willie pulled himself upright, undeterred, and finally reached the car – panting and wheezing. He dove into the backseat, head first – all two hundred and twenty-two pounds of him landing solidly across Jayson's and Tara's laps. They momentarily had the breath knocked out of them.

Football Player Number Two was the largest, but Franck easily dispatched of him simply by knocking one of the giant 1960s hi-fi speakers off the Maverick's roof and onto his head.

Had she wanted to, Franck could've easily clambored into the front seat of the car at that point and they could have escaped without having to deal with Football Player Number Three at all.

But that wasn't how Franck operated. She finished what she started.

As Football Player Number Three approached, he slowed down – having witnessed what had just happened to his two friends. He held out his arms to his sides and crouched a little as if approaching the lineup in a game.

'*Hut one,*' Tara whispered to herself in the backseat.

'*Hut two,*' echoed Jayson.

'*Hut! Hut! Hut!*' Gavin finished, at the moment that Franck sprang toward the football player, full force, her right fist leading the way toward the player's left cheek.

He'd barely hit the ground before Franck climbed into the passenger side seat and slammed the door shut. A larger mob of people, parents this time, were making their way in quick steps up the hill toward the car. It reminded Jayson of the old *Frankenstein* movie he'd once caught on late night TV.

'Hey look,' Tara said spotting them. 'A standing ovation.'

As best he could, Jayson pretended to bow in the backseat.

'Everybody good?' Gavin asked as he gunned the engine for a quick escape.

'Yeah,' Jayson replied, smiling. 'I think I may just be better than ever.'

# *Eight*

**Trey's film debut** did not make Terri Wernermeier laugh.

Nor Philip Unsinger.

Nor the Waukesha County Family Court.

For obvious reasons, Jayson didn't return to school following Homecoming. He spent most of his days and evenings holed up watching television in what had been Gavin's basement bedroom. Much to everyone's surprise, Gavin had mysteriously vacated the Blocher home the very night they executed their caper. Tara was particularly devasted by Gavin's disappearance, even more than Jayson had expected. It wasn't as if Gavin had ever showed the smallest sign of acknowledging Tara's unrequited crush.

'He just disappears sometimes,' Franck explained to Tara and Jayson when they asked where he'd gone. 'He sometimes needs things he can't get outside of the city,' she tried to clarify, only making it all the more mysterious. In his haste, Gavin left all of his clothes and assorted sundries behind, taking only his beloved 'souls' – his Polaroids.

Trey hadn't returned to school either. The Wernermeier

household turned into a sort of funeral home for Trey's popularity. Jayson watched from his bedroom as people from the Wernermeier's church stopped by to drop off casseroles. Tom would appear at the door to take the dishes from them. Trey wasn't the only one who'd been embarrassed. Terri was too mortified to face her Christian peers, so she'd taken to her bed, refusing to see anyone but her husband. She was convinced that Jayson's homosexual demon had somehow wormed its way into her son.

Tara spent more and more time at her own house, since although no one had actually witnessed Tara at 'the Homecoming Incident,' she felt a twinge of guilt for being a party to her twin brother's tragic fall from grace. She only slipped over to the Blochers for short nighttime visits to update Jayson on news about Trey, and to see if there was any news on Gavin's whereabouts.

Six days after 'the Homecoming Incident,' Jayson was woken from his sleep on the mildewy couch Gavin had used for a bed by the phone ringing upstairs. He heard his mother answer the extension in her bedroom two flights above him, followed by approximately ten minutes of the longest string of expletives he'd ever heard come out of her mouth – a record not easily broken. After he heard the smashing of the phone's earpiece against the receiver, things were quiet except for pacing footsteps. He fell back into a fitful sleep but was awakened an hour or so later by a knock on the basement door.

'*Butter Bean?*' she called downstairs. '*I need you to come up here for a minute.*'

He looked at the Pabst Blue Ribbon clock over the bar. It was 3:45 a.m. He didn't know what Toni wanted, but it had to be important. And he presumed it had to do with the phone call. Jayson rolled off the couch and slid on his worn-out, three-year-old *Dukes of Hazzard* slippers. He found his mother on the living room couch with Franck, watching an old black and white movie on channel 18. When he appeared, Franck hugged him silently and went upstairs, leaving him alone with Toni.

Jayson curled up on his side next to his mother. Just a few days before he'd been in the same spot, curled up in her lap as she soothed him. Now *she* was the one who seemed agitated. She lit a fresh Newport directly off her old one. From her demeanor he knew she'd been chain smoking since the mysterious phone call.

'What's going on?' he asked, putting his head in her lap again, hoping it might make things better for her.

'Shh,' Toni hushed him, 'just watch the movie.'

It was a very old one. From the women's dresses he could tell that it was probably made in the late 1940s. Jayson didn't really care for any movie or television show made before 1972, but given his mother's tenseness, he didn't want to ask her to change the channel.

Even nestled into the warm lap of his mother, he felt a quiver of nervous nausea growing in his gut.

The same quiver he felt every time one of her boyfriends stormed out of the house.

The same quiver he felt at the beginning of each dreadful school year.

The same quiver he felt the summer afternoon when he first kissed Trey on the floating dock.

The quiver was – he would learn much later on in life, and only after many repetitions – a sure sign that the script was about to be rewritten by the unseen suits high up at the network. It was a sign that there might be some upcoming contract negotiations and cast shakeups – or perhaps, like *Laverne and Shirley,* a wholesale location shift. Or a network change. Maybe a 'new night and time.'

Just when he was wondering whether or not he might need to run to the bathroom to throw up, Toni spoke.

'See that man there, Butter Bean?' she asked him softly, pointing at the screen with one hand and rubbing his head with the other.

'Yeah,' he answered. She was referring to the actor who played a good-natured bank robber in the subplot of the rather silly romantic farce.

'He's your father.'

'What?!' Jayson bolted upright.

'That's your father.'

'Who is he?!' Jayson was nearly screaming. He was simultaneously ecstatic that his father appeared to be a real live movie star and livid that his mother had kept the news from him for so long. He could have been living in Beverly Hills for the past fif-teen years. Not this fucking hellhole of a tiny town.

'*Shh*. You'll wake up Willie.'

Jayson hadn't thought of Willie. 'Is he Willie's father too?'

'No,' Toni said. Jayson had never seen her struggle for words before. 'No. He's not.'

'We're not brothers?' Jayson asked incredulously.

'Yes,' Toni seemed upset by the question. 'You're both my sons, so you're brothers. Don't ever say such a thing again.'

'But who is he?' Jayson asked again, looking back toward the screen. Christ. The actor must have been ancient when he slept with his mother. Jayson quickly did the math. If he was born in 1966, and the actor looked about thirty-five in the movie . . . which had been made in the late forties . . . then the actor must have been fifty-five years old when Jayson was conceived. And now he would be *seventy*.

'Is he still alive?'

'Yes,' Toni answered. 'Yes, he is.'

'*Who is he?*' Jayson asked for a third time.

'His name is Oscar Harlande, and he made several unmemorable movies before he moved on to Broadway.'

This was all unfathomable to Jayson. Maybe because it was just after four in the morning, but it was unshakably dream-like. He didn't really believe what Toni was saying.

'How . . .' Jayson wasn't even sure what to ask. 'How did you know him?'

'He was in the touring company of *Fiddler on the Roof*

with Burt Convy. It came to Chicago, and, as you know, I've always had a crush on Burt Convy.' Jayson did not know this, and it instantly made his mother ten times more interesting. Toni continued. 'Terri Wernermeier – who was still Terri Goerlicher then – and I were both halfway through our senior year. We stole her parents' car and drove down to Chicago and waited outside the stage door.'

There were too many questions piling up in Jayson's brain.

'You and Terri Wernermeier? Stole a car? But you loathe each other.'

'Mostly because of that trip,' Toni explained. 'Go get me something to drink. A Bourbon Sour.'

Jayson got up, still nearly in a trance, and headed into the kitchen. Toni kept talking into the darkness. Jayson wondered if it was easier for her to tell the story without him around. He strained to hear her as he began mixing her drink.

'Actually both Terri and I had huge crushes on Convy. But he never came out the stage door. He always went out the front, apparently, specifically to avoid girls like us.' Jayson thought Toni sounded a little sad. She cleared her throat. 'Anyway, the only person that came out was Oscar Harlande and since I'd come all that way and all, I fucked him.'

Jayson nearly dropped the bourbon bottle. 'What?!'

'He asked me if I wanted to have a drink in his dressing room with him, so I told Terri to wait in the car around the corner and I'd be out in ten minutes. I didn't come out till the next morning and Terri, naturally, had gone and left me stranded in Chicago.' She snubbed out her Newport and took the glass Jayson brought to her. 'We've had problems with each other ever since. I, of course, later discovered I was pregnant, and I was put in a juvenile home in Milwaukee until I had you. I missed the end of my senior year. Terri married her high-school sweetheart, Tom, right after graduation and wanted nothing to do with an unwed mother when I returned home with you. Of course no one ever metioned that Terri was three months pregnant with the twins when she and Tom tied the knot.' Right then and there I promised I would never fool around again unless I was married.

'Does Oscar Harlowe . . .'

'*Harlande* . . .' Toni corrected.

'Does Oscar Harlande know about me?'

Before Toni could answer, Franck descended the stairs carrying an overstuffed duffle bag – Jayson's duffle bag. Toni nervously cleared her throat again.

'Yes . . .' Toni paused, as if about to qualify her answer, but then stopped herself and simply repeated: 'Yes, he does.'

Franck went out the garage door with the duffle bag, jangling the keys to the Maverick.

'And,' Toni said, turning her head away, 'he wants to meet you.' Was she crying?

'But . . .' Jayson began, his head full of questions.

Toni rubbed the back of her hand across her nose. She *was* crying.

'Just go brush your teeth and put your sneakers on,' Toni said, snubbing her Newport out on the bare wood of the side table. 'It's gonna be fine.' She sniffled. 'It's gonna be fine.'

To Jayson it sounded like she was trying to convince herself more than him.

# Nine

'**I fell asleep** and woke up in *Welcome Back, Kotter*,' Jayson thought as his cab crossed the Queensborough Bridge only six hours after he'd been sitting on the couch with his mother.

All he had with him was the duffle bag packed by Franck, a toothbrush, and $453 in cash that Toni had stashed in an old coffee can in the freezer. And a piece of paper – with his father's address on it.

*His father.*

The words still didn't sound legitimate. As much as he'd pried over the years, Toni had never revealed his father's identity. Whenever he asked who his father was, she'd reply: 'the guy who knocked me up.'

Of course he'd always assumed that he and Willie shared a father. Who was Willie's father? He hadn't even thought to ask during Franck and Toni's rush to the airport. And why the rush? They wouldn't answer, only tearfully telling him that 'Now was the right time to meet him' and to call as soon as he arrived at his house.

'210 E. 62nd St.' was the address written on the card in

Toni's fluid handwriting. He had no idea where that was. All he knew about New York was that Archie Bunker lived in Queens, Maude lived in Poughkeepsie, and Mr. Kotter taught school in Brooklyn. And he doubted he'd run into any of them to ask directions.

Five minutes after crossing what the cabbie had pointed out as the East River, Jason stood on the sidewalk outside a dark maroon brick townhouse, with steep front steps and glossy black double doors. He double-checked his mother's handwritten note against the numbers etched into the window glass, and climbed the steps.

To the left of the door was an intercom with a doorbell-like button on it. He took in a deep breath of early November air and pressed it. He heard chimes ring deep inside the house. It was a familiar tune. What was it? At the precise moment he realized the chimes were ringing out the tune of 'Come On-a My House,' a weathered gray face appeared behind the etched glass panes in the door. A moment later the door was opened a crack and the face spoke to him from the shadows.

'Too young. Go away,' it said before shutting the door again and flipping the deadbolt. Over the next hour Jayson walked around the block seven times, re-ringing the doorbell with each loop, trying to figure out what to do next. It was getting colder, and the sky was growing gray as the clouds seemed to drift lower and lower. The people who passed by paid no notice to him, even though he looked so completely different from all of them in a pair of purple painter's pants and a *Mork & Mindy* T-shirt that announced 'Nanu-Nanu' in large silk-screened letters across his chest. He hadn't had time to think much about an appropriate outfit before Franck and Toni drove him to the Milwaukee airport in the predawn hours. He was so preoccupied with his unexpected situation that he didn't even realize that he was freezing in the thin T-shirt until he noticed that everyone else on the street was wearing heavy black and gray suit jackets with scarves.

He considered attempting to hail a cab the way he'd seen it done in Woody Allen movies. The only sane thing to do was to head back to the airport and buy a ticket home. The last thing Toni tearfully told him was that 'if worse came to worse' he could use the $453 to buy a plane ticket home, but that he should try his hardest to get along with his father, and coming home was 'a last resort.' Why was it so dire? Sure things were bad back in Oconomowoc. But it would blow over. They'd been through worse. How long was he supposed to stay anyway?

He was just rounding the block for an eighth time when a young black man who looked about the same age as Jayson bounded up Sixty-second Street from the opposite direction and dashed up Jayson's 'father's' stairs.

'Hey! Wait!' Jayson called out, running the forty feet up to the stoop. 'Is this where Oscar Harlande lives?' he called up to the young man pulling out his keys and inserting them into the townhouse door.

The young man turned around.

It couldn't be.

It was impossible.

Jayson was convinced that this had to all be a dream, that he actually did fall asleep in his Oconomowoc basement and woke up trapped in a television.

It was Devlin Williamson.

*The* Devlin Williamson. From *Disorder in the Court*.

'Why? Who wants to know?' Devlin Williamson replied cautiously.

'*You're Devlin Williamson!*' Jayson shrieked. Devlin Williamson glanced up and down the street anxiously, as if worried that someone had heard Jayson.

'Yeah. That's me. Did you want something?'

'*It wuuuuzzzzzn't me!*' Jayson mimicked Devlin's famous *Disorder in the Court* catchphrase excitedly.

'Right. Umm. Okay. Do you want an autograph or something?'

'Yeah! Sure!' Jayson answered gleefully. He'd completely forgotten where he was and what he was doing there. The fact that he was a fifteen-year-old homeless boy on the streets of New York City, without a return plane ticket, and only a few hundred bucks in his pocket was shoved to the back of his brain in the presence of his favorite child TV star.

'Gotta pen? Paper?' Devlin asked impatiently.

'Right, Sure,' Jayson said, fumbling around in his duffle bag for a pen. Finally finding a stray purple Bic, he handed it over along with the scrap of paper in his hand.

Devlin Williamson scribbled out a close approximation to his name and handed the pen and paper back to Jayson.

'Why do you have Harley's address?' Devlin asked him, seeing what was written on the opposite side of the paper.

'Who?'

'Harley. Oscar Harlande. On the paper.' Devlin pointed at the slip of paper on which Toni had written the address.

'Oh. He's my father.'

'What?' Devlin broke out in laughter. He started to ask another question but couldn't get it out without laughing. 'Your father is . . .'

'Oscar Harlande,' Jayson repeated.

'You're kidding,' Devlin finally responded when he stopped giggling.

'My mother is Toni Blocher and they met when Oscar Harley was in the road show of *Fiddler on the Roof* in Chicago. In 1966. I just got here from Oconomowoc.'

'Where?' Devlin asked.

'Oconomowoc. Wisconsin,' Jayson clarified. Now he was growing a little impatient. 'So he *does* live here?'

'This is too good,' Devlin said, smiling again. 'I have to see this.' Devlin reached into his pocket and took out a key ring.

'You live here too?' Jayson couldn't believe his good fortune. It was thrilling enough to learn that his father had been a semi-famous movie and Broadway star. But that he lived in the same building as Devlin Williamson? It was enough to almost make him wish that he were back in Oconomowoc High School so that he could tell all his nemeses.

'Yeah. A few of us live here,' Devlin said, fumbling with the lock. *A few of us? Does that mean that it was a whole house full of celebrities?* Of course. Celebrities must clump together, Jayson thought. For protection from civilians. Jayson's heart began racing. He wasn't sure that he wouldn't faint.

Finally Devlin got the door open. Inside the foyer was nearly pitch black compared to the daylight outside. As his eyes adjusted, he started making out pieces of heavy wooden furniture lining the dark red walls. Huge movie posters – presumably Harlande's own – crowded every inch of wall space. Every surface was covered with something. With lots of somethings. Vases, framed photos, candlesticks, souvenirs, pillows, the entire front hallway looked like an impeccably organized garage sale.

'Harley?!' Devlin called out. 'You here?'

'In the kitchen, Devvie,' a gruff voice called out in a vaguely Southern accent. 'I'm making breakfast.'

'Yourself? Don't burn anything down,' Devlin called back, dropping his keys into a huge oriental bowl on the sideboard by the door. 'Someone's here to see you.'

'Lovely!' Harlande called back. 'Bring them in.'

Devlin gestured for Jayson to follow him, and they made their way down the cluttered hallway. Jayson was careful with his steps. He would be mortified if he tripped in front of Devlin Williamson. When they reached the far end,

Devlin pushed open a heavy swinging door and the two entered a bright, impossibly white kitchen flooded with light from the glass wall and skylights that overlooked the townhouse's tiny back garden.

The small gray man who had come to the door earlier was standing at an oversized gas range using a spoon to lift an egg out of a pot of boiling water. Devlin walked over to him and gave him a peck on the back of his neck. Harlande reached up behind him and patted Devlin's cheek, still concentrating on transferring the egg into an eggcup standing on the counter beside the stove.

'So, who have you brought me Devvie?' Harlande asked, turning around with the eggcup in his hand. 'Oh, you again,' Harlande said, spotting Jayson, his voice dropping into a more stern octave. 'I already said you were too young, Terribly sorry. I can't help you. What were you in, anyway?'

'High school?' Jayson half answered, not really understanding the question.

Devlin and Harlande broke out laughing. Jayson didn't get the joke.

'Look at this egg Devvie,' Harley said, changing the subject. 'What do I do wrong?' Harley had clipped off the top of his soft boiled egg with an elaborate silver scissor contraption. The inside was as clearly viscous and runny as if it had been raw.

'How long did you boil it?' Devlin asked.

'Oh, I don't know, Devvie. Thirty, forty seconds. Tops.'

Devlin took the eggcup away from Harley and tossed it into the trash.

'Here, let me make you a new one.'

'Oh don't bother Devvie. They're little heart attacks on a plate anyway. Now, child,' Harley said turning back to Jayson, 'what *show* were you in?'

'He hasn't been in anything, Harley,' Devlin answered for Jayson. 'He's your . . .' At that point Devlin cracked up again, unable to finish the sentence.

'My what?' Harlande asked, gingerly settling himself down on a modern white plastic chair like the ones Jayson remembered from the dinette set on *The Bob Newhart Show* – season four, to be exact. The table in front of Harley was set with a sparkling array of porcelain place settings. It was the most elaborate breakfast setting Jayson had ever seen, either in real life or on television. Harlande gestured for them to sit and join him.

'I'm your son,' Jayson said. He wondered why this was such a surprise to Harley. Hadn't he and Toni talked last night? Who had called so late? Jayson assumed that the call was from Harlande requesting this visit. Why was he acting so unaware?

'My *what?*' Harlande asked in the same tone that Devlin had out on the front stoop.

'Your son,' Jayson repeated. 'My mother is Toni Blocher, of Oconomowoc, Wisconsin, and you, um, impregnated her during the road show of *Fiddler* in Chicago in 1966.'

Harlande suddenly became very serious. 'I have no idea what you're talking about young man.'

'Here. I have a picture!' Jayson said remembering the Kodachrome shot of Toni that he kept in this *Little Orphan Annie* change wallet.

'You have a picture of me fucking your mother?' Harley asked. 'This I have to see.'

Jayson pulled out the shot from his duffle bag. 'It's just of my mom,' Jayson corrected. It had been taken when Jayson was three years old, and it showed a nineteen-year-old Toni standing on the shore of Lac LaBelle with Jayson sitting on her shoulders. Most of the colors had faded, so their faces were both an unappealing shade of green. But it was still Jayson's favorite photo. It looked like a photo a normal family would have. He handed it to Harlande.

Harlande studied it a second then looked up toward a corner of the ceiling as if his memories were on a shelf there. Then he looked back down at the photo again. Then back up. Then at Devlin. And finally at Jayson.

'She looks familiar,' he finally said.

'What?' Devlin asked, incredulously. 'You slept with her?'

'Times were different then,' Harley expounded. 'Plus I was likely drunk. Plus she looks quite butch, no? Look at that neck. A bit thick for a woman. Perhaps I was confused.' Both he and Devlin laughed.

Jayson was momentarily angry. He'd always considered his mother one of the most beautiful women in the world.

'She must be a dyke now, *n'est-ce pas?*' Harlande concluded.

Jayson's teeth were grinding. While Harlande may have been correct, Jayson didn't like his tone. He was suddenly overcome with an urge to flee this strange, opulent house with its snotty celebrities. He would walk back to Oconomowoc if he couldn't figure out how to catch a cab.

'Now, now,' Harlande said, reaching over to pat Jayson on the shoulder. 'I didn't mean to make fun of your mother. One should never make fun of a gay boy's mother. Each and every one of them is a saint.'

How did Harlande know Jayson was gay? Was it that obvious? In Wisconsin he'd been able to keep it a limited secret for most of his life – until Trey's betrayal, of course.

'Well,' Harlande sighed, resting his spoon on his plate. 'This is all a great deal of information for a Tuesday morning. But the most important bit is missing. What is your name, boy?'

'Jayson.'

'"Jason." Hmmm. I'm not sure I would have named you that. Very common,' Harlande mused.

'It has a "Y" in it.' Jayson added. 'J-A-Y-S-O-N.'

'Ah! A little flair!' Harlande said. 'You may have potential yet. Now if you boys'll excuse me for my morning nap.'

# Ten

While Oscar Harlande slept, Devlin took Jayson around the corner to Serendipity, a small sweet shoppe on Sixtieth street. They were shown to a booth in the back corner and while following the hostess to the rear, Jayson spotted a familiar shock of silver hair in a booth near the kitchen.

'That's Andy Warhol,' Jayson whispered excitedly to Devlin. 'From The Love Boat!'

Devlin laughed. 'The Love Boat?'

'Yes,' Jayson answered, not sure what the joke was. 'He was on an episode with Marion Cunningham from Happy Days.'

'He's probably the world's most famous living artist,' Devlin said. 'Appearing on The Love Boat was his commentary on celebrity.'

'I knew that,' Jayson lied.

Actually, there wasn't much that Jayson knew for sure anymore. It was all too much to take in. Less than two weeks ago he'd been watching a rerun of Disorder in the Court starring Devlin Williamson and now Jayson was co-starring with him while drinking something called a 'frozen hot chocolate.' Jayson wondered why everyone else in the restaurant – ladies with multiple shopping bags, teenagers dressed in designer jeans – wasn't rushing to Devlin's table for an autograph. Devlin's show had only been off the network for two years, and most UHF channels still ran reruns of it after school. Surely people still knew who he was.

'I don't get it,' Jayson asked, scooping the whipped cream off the top of the giant cup with his straw. He was trying his best to appear nonchalant. 'Why do you live here with Oscar Harlande? Why aren't you in Hollywood?'

'It's a long story,' Devlin demurred.

'I'm sure it's better than any of mine,' Jayson said.

Devlin laughed. Jayson thought it was funny to hear the same laugh he'd heard so many times on TV as a reaction to something he'd personally uttered. Devlin was even more charismatic in person, Jayson thought. The dimple on his right cheek that was made famous on the cover of *TV Guide* seemed even deeper and more endearing. Plus, he was beautiful. There hadn't been a single black person in Jayson's school, and not terribly many more in Oconomowoc as a whole. Actually, Jayson realized, this was the closest he'd been to someone not of German or Scandinavian origin in his life. And with his caramel skin and matching eyes, Devlin was even more beautiful in person than he was on television. And that dimple. . . .

Jayson found himself growing stiff. How many times had

he masturbated to fantasies of Devlin Williamson? There was no way to count, really. He made sure his napkin was loosely draped across his lap.

'Well, to make it short,' Devlin started, 'my parents got all the money I made from the show, and then divorced. What little money was earmarked for me was in a trust, and that got eaten up in legal fees and custody battles. When that started dwindling, so did their interest in custody of me.'

'But there must have been millions,' Jayson said.

'You read too much *National Enquirer,*' Devlin responded.

'I've never read that paper,' Jayson lied again, at the same moment he remembered reading a long article in it detailing exactly what Devlin was now explaining to him. Jayson remembered that there were allegations of child abuse. And that his mother had been arrested for cocaine possession, he thought.

'There may have been around a million,' Devlin continued. 'But that went quickly, and if there's anything left, I have no idea where it is.'

'But where are your parents?'

'Dunno. L.A. still, I guess.'

'Then why are you here?'

'Oscar was a guest star on *Disorder* once,' Devlin explained. Jayson vaguely remembered the episode as Devlin described it. Oscar played a homeless man in a *Disorder in the Court* Christmas Special. He showed the cantankerous judge what his life would have been like without all his mischievous-but-lovable foster children. 'After I ran out of money and got thrown out of the hotel I was staying at in L.A., I called him up because he'd said he could get me work on Broadway if I ever wanted it.'

'*Broadway?*' Jayson practically sneered. 'But you're a TV star.'

'*Was* a TV star,' Devlin corrected. 'After all the lawsuits and bad publicity with my parents I couldn't have gotten a cameo on, well, *The Love Boat*. I was a "risky hire," my agent explained before she dumped me.'

Jayson was having a hard time believing what he was hearing. He'd always had a sort of fantasy that once someone was a household name, they were always somehow taken care of. Like there was a welfare system for celebrities. Paid for out of the taxes of the currently popular stars.

'Have you been in any shows?'

'Not yet. Harley's gotten me into a couple of auditions, and some commercial auditions, but directors still won't cast me. I'm too famous to be anonymous and too anonymous to be famous,' Devlin explained. 'Harley says I just need to cool down to the right temperature.'

Jayson hated the idea of Devlin in a commercial. He was better than that.

'So, Harlande's paying for me to take cooking lessons to pass the time. He claims he was near starved to death before I showed up.'

'*Cooking lessons?* Why?'

'Because I've always wanted to learn to cook. My mother never did. When we were poor we ate fast food, and when I was working we went out to the best restaurants in L.A.,' Devlin explained. 'I'd like, for once, to live somewhere in the middle.'

Having just escaped 'the middle,' Jayson was having a difficult time imagining its appeal. But years of reading *People* had taught him that celebrities often have pedestrian hobbies to help them relate to normal people.

'And you live with Oscar?' Jayson asked.

'We call him "Harley,"' Devlin answered.

'Who's "*we*"?' Jayson asked. This was all too mysterious. He almost wished he was back in Oconomowoc measuring out precisely two cups of Count Chocula for Willie's breakfast. He'd always thought his odd little family was completely chaotic, but even Toni's eccentricities seemed to make more sense than the script he was in at the moment.

'You'll find out,' Devlin said. 'The only thing is, you can't get freaked, and you can't tell anyone.'

'I don't like the sound of that,' Jayson said. The creeping nausea he felt while lying on his mother's lap last night – Was it only last night? – was rising again. How could she have done this to him? She'd outright lied. Oscar Harlande didn't ask to see him. Oscar Harlande had no idea he even existed. Toni Blocher sent her kid to the middle of New York City with nothing but a duffle bag of outdated clothes and

107

a toothbrush. Even the bitchy stepmom on *Eight Is Enough* wouldn't do that.

'Don't worry, pal. I like you, you make me laugh,' Devlin said. 'I'll take care of you.'

The waitress came by with the check. Jayson pulled the wad of twenties that Toni had stuffed in his pocket. Devlin put his hand over Jayson's.

'I *said* I'll take care of you. I promise,' he repeated. 'I owe it to the universe. It took care of me, now I'll take care of you.' Devlin looked at the bill and started counting out his money.

Jayson refolded the money that his mother had given him. As comforting as Devlin's promise was, he was still furious at his mother.

'Don't worry, Butter Bean,' Toni had said at the gate in Milwaukee, 'Everything'll take care of itself. It always does. Call me when you get settled.'

*Sometimes things don't take care of themselves*, Jayson thought. *Sometimes people need someone to take care of them – not to put them on a plane in the middle of the night.*

'C'mon, let's go,' Devlin said. 'You should call your mother and tell her you got here safely.'

'That's okay,' Jayson answered. 'I'm not sure she really cares. And I'm not sure I care to tell her.'

'Harley' was awake when they returned. He was sitting in the ornate living room at a large desk that looked like it was carved of one solid piece of mahogany. The rest of the room was dark, with the heavy curtains that faced the sidewalk pulled closed. An immense grand piano stood in the far corner of the room, away from the windows where it was darkest.

'Devvie, come here, love,' Harley called to them. He patted the overstuffed easy chair pulled up next to the desk. 'I'm going over my list of who's doing what right now. It'll get very hectic with the holidays approaching. People coming into town and whatnot.'

Jayson sat on the velvet couch and pretended to look through a book on the gold and glass coffee table. It was full of nude photos of black men. He quickly put it down and opened another. This one was full of nude photos of white men. After picking up and putting down three more books, he realized that every single book piled on the coffee table was a photo book of nude men.

'What about Eric. How busy is he?' Harley asked looking at a list in front of him.

'He just started *The Music Man*,' Devlin answered. 'In the chorus.'

'Adam?'

'*Amadeus*,' Devlin answered. 'Not sure what he's playing.'

'Tyler?'

'Touring.'

'What about Robbie?'

'He's been in *Sugar Babies* since last year. You know that,' Devlin chuckled. 'Why do you keep asking about him?'

'Because a lot of clients keep asking about him,' Harley answered.

Jayson couldn't decipher what they were talking about. Something about Broadway actors, obviously. Was Harley a casting agent? Admittedly Jayson didn't know much about the theater except that washed-up celebrities often told reporters that they were 'happy to have a chance to get back to their beloved theater' when then couldn't land any film or TV gigs.

Jayson flipped through page after page of tasteful penises, slowly growing immune to their appeal. Devlin and Harley spent three hours recording the whereabouts and whatabouts of several hundred men.

'Oh that was tiring,' Harley said when they finished. 'I do hate running my charity.' He closed the thick green ledger with a flourish. He was still dressed in the same robe as this morning.

'Well, your charity pays for this house,' Devlin answered.

'True. True,' Harley mused. 'It really is a win-win-win for everyone involved, isn't it Devvie? Now, what should we . . .' He turned around and noticed Jayson. 'Oh! You. I'd nearly forgotten all about my long lost son, Justin.'

'Jayson.'

'Yes. Yes. With a "Y." What are we going to do about you?'

'He's tired, Harley,' Devlin said. 'I think we should let him stay here a few days.'

'Of course!' Harley said. 'I would never turn family out onto the street! He can stay in your room, Devvie.'

Devlin smiled at Jayson as if to let him know that everything was going to be fine, and Jayson desperately wanted to believe him.

Jayson *was* tired, having been up since 3:00 a.m. the night before and on a plane by 6:00 a.m., so after Devlin showed him up to his bedroom he lay down on his bed and fell asleep for nearly eight hours.

He woke at 10:47 p.m., according to the antique ivory clock on the dresser, to the sounds of raucous laughter and piano playing somewhere down below.

He was still in his *Mork & Mindy* T-shirt and painter's pants and didn't remember where he'd dropped his duffel bag. He sniffed at his armpits, decided that they weren't too offensive, and found his way to the darkened steps.

The music and singing and merriment grew louder as he descended floor by floor, peeking into each room on each floor. The townhouse seemed much larger on the inside than it looked from the outside. The clinking of glasses and crowd noises reminded him of when he would sneak to the stairway to spy on the parties Toni threw for all the women of her artists collective. Except that those were all female voices, and these were all male.

All male.

He rounded the final corner into the living room and saw dozens of men, all in suits and ties, crowded around a piano singing songs from Broadway shows. Harley was at the keyboard, leading the sing-along. It was the cliché to end all clichés, he thought. Even Jayson knew from jokes on *Match Game* and *Hollywood Squares* that homosexual men sang show tunes at piano bars. A 'fruit medley,' Charles Nelson Reilly used to call it.

Most of the men were Harley's age. Then there was a steep drop-off in demographics, leaving about a dozen men who looked to be between twenty and thirty.

'Well, well, Harley!' a short round man wearing a shocking purple jacket and matching hat exclaimed over the music. He'd noticed Jayson standing in the doorway. 'You didn't tell us you'd been to the butcher for fresh meat.'

'Stick to the ripe fruit section,' Harley shouted back, 'You know we don't serve veal here. He's not on the menu.'

Devlin looked up from the sheet music pages he was turning for Harley.

'Hey!' Devlin yelled. He turned another page for Harley and made his way through the suits and ties over to Jayson. 'Don't pay attention to the Sneezer Geezer,' Devlin told Jayson when he reached his side.

'Who?' Jayson asked.

'The Sneezer Geezer. He's the worst one here. He has a weird thing about being sneezed on.'

'Who doesn't hate being sneezed on?' Jayson asked.

'Him,' Devlin smiled. 'He pays for it.'

'*What?*'

'You were upstairs forever,' Devlin said, smiling and changing the subject. The famous dimple made a reappearance.

112

'I didn't get much sleep last night.'

'Harley thought you'd run away again.'

'I didn't run away. I was *thrown* away.'

'Well one man's trash is our new treasure.' Devlin laughed.

'C'mon, who are all these people?' Jayson asked again, as Devlin pulled him toward the door that led to the kitchen.

'They're, umm, friends of Harley's,' Devlin answered once they walked into the relative quiet and brightness of the kitchen. 'Oh what the fuck, you'll find out soon enough . . . they're clients.'

'Of his charity?'

Devlin laughed. Jayson was getting tired of not being in on the jokes.

'Stop fucking laughing at me,' Jayson snapped. He couldn't believe he was talking this way to Devlin Williamson. 'I'm homeless, broke, and I think I'm coming down with pneumonia from wandering around the block for an hour in nothing but a Mork from Ork T-shirt. Just tell me what the hell is going on.'

'I'm sorry,' Devlin said. He put his arm around Jayson and pulled him down onto the chair next to him. He pulled Jayson's chair around, with him in it, until they were face to face. 'I'm really sorry. That was shitty of me. Sometimes I get carried away with the "anything goes" vibe around this place.'

As hard as Jayson tried not to, a tear formed in the corner

of his left eye. He was — as much as he didn't want to admit it — scared.

'Hey,' Devlin said, taking both of Jayson's hands in his. 'I'm sorry. You've had a pretty fucking rotten day.'

'Just tell me the truth,' Jayson said, trying and failing to quit crying in front of Devlin Williamson. 'I don't have anywhere to go, and I don't know what I'm doing here.'

'The truth is there is no charity,' Devlin said. 'That's just what Harley calls his business.'

'What business? He charges for *sing-alongs*?'

Devlin laughed again. This time Jayson did too.

'He runs an escort company,' Devlin said. 'For old queens to find Broadway chorus boys.'

Jayson had seen an episode of *Streets of San Francisco* in which Michael Douglas's detective character went undercover to bust an escort ring. They never explained exactly what an escort ring was, so Jayson had always wondered what was illegal about paying a glamorous woman to accompany you to a nice dinner.

'Why would old men want to have dinner with young guys in plays?' Jayson asked.

'What?' Devlin asked back.

'What do the young guys escort the old men to?'

'To bed.'

'What?'

'They have sex, Jayson. The old guys pay Harley to find them a chorus boy to have sex with.'

The now familiar nausea rose in Jayson's stomach again. It was becoming chronic. There was also a *Streets of San Francisco* episode in which a teenage runaway girl was forced to become a hooker. He knew what a hooker was. There were hookers on sitcoms all the time. And pimps. Jayson didn't know what the point was of giving them a fancier name like 'escorts.'

'Why do the chorus boys do it? What did Harley do to them?' Jayson asked.

'Nothing. They do it because they get paid more to take their pants off than they do all week singing tenor in the background of two numbers. And Harley gets fifteen percent. Like he says, it's a win-win-win . . . him, the clients, and the chorus boys. Everybody gets charity.'

Jayson didn't want to ask the next question. But he had to know.

'Are you a charity case?' he asked Devlin.

Devlin's dimple appeared again as he grinned widely. He reached up his hand and brushed away one of Jayson's tears with his thumb.

'No, no, silly,' he said reassuringly. 'Harley's not like that. He's very scrupulous – at least about age. I'm just a kid. You're a kid. You're *his* kid for Christ's sake – which I still can't figure out.'

Devlin stood and pulled Jayson upright, putting his arm around him and walking him out into the hall to the stairway.

'We're not charity, pal,' Devlin said. 'We're Harley's karma insurance.'

# Eleven

'Try it one more time . . . only more aristocratically,' the director said, squinting at the fluorescent light buzzing above Jayson's head as if God were personally giving him theatrical direction tips.

'Okay. Of course,' Jayson answered. *No problem,* he thought. *I'm a kid from Oconomowoc, Wisconsin, who was dumped at a whorehouse in New York City three days ago. Aristocracy is second nature to me.*

Harley had wasted no time in getting Jayson out to an audition. A commercial auditon – not Broadway. 'There's no way I'll risk my Broadway reputation on someone who's never trod the boards,' he'd explained. Jayson surprised everyone by getting a 'callback.' What surprised Jayson was that Devlin didn't also get a callback for the same gig. Devlin claimed his feelings weren't hurt, but Jayson wondered how that was possible. Devlin had been on the cover of three *TV Guide*s, but got beaten out for a part by a kid who made home movies in his backyard. Jayson came to the callback by himself, even though Devlin offered to accompany him.

'Mmmm, yes. Aristocracy,' the younger man sitting next to the director agreed, munching on half of a bagel. He had a speck of scallion cream cheese stuck just under his nose. He was probably from the ad agency, Jayson thought. Devlin had told him that whoever was eating something in the room was most likely the advertising person.

Jayson flipped through the actor and actress rolodex in his head for a character he could copy. Nothing sprang to mind. He couldn't remember a single TV show that featured a teenage prince relishing a minty after-dinner chocolate. Devlin had tried to explain method acting to Jayson, but Jayson's best method was stealing from already famous actors.

'And . . . action!'

The graying actor auditioning for the role of the butler held out the three-ring binder that was being used as a silver tray for the purposes of the audition. Jayson was seated at a folding card table, instructed to envision that he had just finished a large multi-course meal surrounded by a table full of nobility. 'Ewww,' Jayson delivered his line while inspecting the pink pencil eraser meant to represent a chocolate mint. 'Take it back!' Jayson waved off the butler with his hand.

The butler stepped away, then turned around and presented the same binder with the same eraser that was, for the purposes of the audition, supposed to have been transformed into another, equally unappealing confection.

'Not good enough!' Jayson remarked. He was affecting

a crude cross between an English and French accent, with a surprise Italian lilt hanging around the edges.

The actor trying out for the butler, whom Jayson recognized from a Comet commercial, spun around and presented the exact same binder and eraser. Only now it was supposed to be a luscious, mouthwatering Bon Appetite! Brand-Chocolate-After-Dinner-Mint-from-the-Expert-Chocolatiers-Who-Brought-You-Cadbury-Creme-Eggs.

'What's this?!' Jayson questioned in his pan-European accent, raising one eyebrow. He picked up the eraser and inspected it between his thumb and forefinger.

'Bon Appetite, sir!' the butler wannabe drolled. Jayson felt sorry for the old man. Oscar Harlande had been successful enough to own a townhouse on the Upper East Side, while this man, roughly the same age, was still looking for his breakthrough role. Celebrity, Jayson was learning, was more complicated than it seemed from the other side of the TV screen.

'Thank you, Giles, but I asked what is it?'

'Bon Appetite, sir!'

'But what is it?' It was a stupid gag – a common phrase that was also the name of the product.

*'It's Bon Appetite! The Chocolate After Dinner Mint From the Expert Chocolatiers of Cadbury.'*

Jayson pretended to pop the eraser in his mouth and chew. Mid-fake chew, he smiled broadly.

'Mmmmm. It's Bon Appetite. The treat for the elite!'

Jayson said, as both he and the butler exchanged smiles and haughty chuckles.

'And . . . cut! Very Good. *Very Good!*' the director said, smiling. The advertising guy next to him nodded even more enthusiastically. 'Thank you very much, Mr., uhhh . . .' he looked down at his casting sheet '. . . Blocher. You should be hearing from us shortly.'

Unacknowledged, the aging actor auditioning for Giles sneered at Jayson as they left the room.

'Good luck, kiddo,' he said as they reached the door. 'It was a real *treat*,' he scowled.

Jayson walked home from the casting studio downtown rather than taking a cab or a subway. It was fifty-three blocks, but he was trying to make the money Toni'd given him last as long as he could. Harley hadn't made any generous overtures other than the roof over his head, and there was no way Jayson was going to call and ask Toni for more money. She'd dumped him like a newborn at an orphanage. Or a fifteen-year-old at a whorehouse.

It wasn't that things were all bad. He did have Devlin Williamson as a roommate. Devlin was only three months older than Jayson, but in experiential years, Jayson felt like a toddler next to him. Having nursed a crush on Devlin for going on five years made things a little awkward for Jayson – not that he'd ever mentioned it, of course. He'd learned his lesson with Trey. Having a crush on someone who didn't have a crush back was downright dangerous – especially if the crush in question was not a 'Phil Donahue guest' as well. And Devlin definitely liked girls. Although he hadn't mentioned any recent girlfriends to Jayson, Jayson remembered the long string of girlfriends that were mentioned in Devlin's old publicity articles. Jayson even read in the *National Enquirer* once that Devlin took Jodie Foster to the People's Choice Awards the year that he won for Best Teen Actor in a Comedy Series. If someone's a big enough star to date Jodie Foster, then there's no way he could be gay.

By the time Jayson reached the townhouse he was sweating underneath layers of shirts and sweaters he'd borrowed from Harley's closets. He was probably wearing an article of clothing from every decade since the 1930s. He quietly entered the front door, since it was roughly time for Harley's after lunch nap. Given the nighttime hours his charity demanded, Harley usually rose only for meals during the day and finally changed out of his dressing robe at around six at night.

But as Jayson entered the foyer he heard Harley's voice from the rear of the townhouse, in the kitchen.

'I'm not sure how many years of higher education one needs to become the operator of a telephone, but surely you must be missing at least one,' Jayson could hear Harley arguing. 'I repeat: The woman's name is "Toni Blocher" and she lives in a town with several dozen letters in Wisconsin. Something like "Okinawa." Or "OkieDokie."'

Jayson was petrified. Why was Harley trying to contact his mother? Was he going to send him back? Jayson'd made up his mind never to talk to Toni again as punishment for having deserted him. And now he was going to be sent back? He turned and tried to slip quietly back out the front door again, just as Devlin bounded down the townhouse's staircase. Jayson ducked behind the coat rack so Devlin wouldn't see him.

'I got it!' Devlin was yelling. He came running down the stairs two at a time, clutching Jayson's old gym shirt. He began spelling out the letters on the front of it loudly enough for Harley to hear in the kitchen.

'It's "O-C-O-N-O-M-O-W-O-C."' When Devlin reached the bottom stair he noticed Jayson behind the coats. *'Oh, you're home! Guess what?!?'*

Jayson couldn't possibly guess what. With the amount of real-life cliffhangers he'd endured in the last six months, he didn't want to guess what.

'I dunno. Harley's calling my mother to propose?' Jayson answered wearily.

'The casting director called! You're the Cadbury Prince!'

It didn't sink in. Devlin Williamson (TV star) was telling Jayson (mere mortal) that Jayson was going to be on TV.

'Harley's calling your mother,' Devlin continued excitedly. 'He needs a copy of your birth certificate for the contract.'

'Well, good luck with that,' Jayson said, remember his mother's filing system which consisted of twenty-six random appliance boxes in the basement, filled with loose papers and marked in lipstick on the outside: FILES!

'Hello? Is this the lovely Miss Toni Blocher?' Jayson heard Harley saying from the kitchen. '*Wonderful!* How good to hear your voice again after all these years. Still just as husky as I remember.'

Jayson pushed past Devlin and raced into the kitchen. He stood across from Harley and desperately pantomimed that he 'wasn't here.' It was bad enough that Harley was talking to Toni – Jayson certainly had no desire to. Harley looked up, nodded at Jayson, then turned back to his conversation.

'Yes, it is wonderful to have him here. We're all just *thrilled*!' Harley used every appendage when talking on the phone – as if delivering a monologue to the back row of a theater. With the same volume as well. '*We?* Well, there's myself, a lovely young man named Devvie Williamson whom I sure you know from the television, and, oh, various other friends who work for my charity.'

Jayson tried to picture Toni on the other end of the line. She was likely in the kitchen, smoking a Newport and ashing in the open dishwasher. Without anyone to monitor Willie, he was probably also nearby, sitting on the pantry floor eating every piece of junk food within reach.

'Well, yes,' Harley continued, 'he's eager to talk to you as well, but first I need a little information to help our Justin settle into his new home here … yes, "Jayson," … my mistake. I'll need to secure his numeral of Social Security as well as a copy of his birth certificate to enroll him in the world-renowned excellent New York City Public System of Higher Education.'

*School?* Harley had never mentioned anything about school. He hadn't even asked what grade Jayson was in. As if Harley had read his mind, he looked to Jayson and dismissively waved his hand to show that he was fabricating the entire story.

'Yes, yes, it is a bit of a rush. I'm very concerned that he not forget any of his mathematics or what have you. Perhaps you could get the documents into the post tomorrow?' Harley continued. 'Wonderful. Now I'll put your − ahem − *our* dear son on the line. He speaks endlessly of you day and night . . .' Harley handed the phone receiver to Jayson.

Jayson waved it away. The very last person he wanted to talk to was his mother. She'd lied to him, and sent him away with nothing more than a little cash. And now that he'd made it all work out − by himself − he wanted nothing more to do with her. Harley shoved it at him again. '*Take it!*' Harley mouthed silently and urgently. '*Take it!*'

Jayson finally realized that he had no choice but to do what Harley asked. He was, after all, a guest in his home. And his only other option was to return to the unbearable quirkiness of Toni.

'Hello,' Jayson said into the phone, as unemotionally as possible.

'*Butter Bean! How are you? Why didn't you call?*' Toni's questions came in a rapid-fire staccato. She sounded sincerely worried, but Jayson still felt no need to placate her. She continued without taking a breath. '*We were so worried! I called the number I found for Oscar Harlande but it was some 'Broadway Backdoor Charity' or something – oh, I'm so relieved. I didn't know what to say to your brother. Why didn't you call?!'* she asked again.

'Oh, I'm sorry,' Jayson replied dryly. 'I thought the fact that you put me on a plane in the middle of the night to an unknown address in the middle of the largest city in the world meant that, oh, I dunno, you didn't care whether or not I survived?'

'Jayson. I'm sorry. I really am. I didn't have a choice,' Toni's voice said.

'You didn't have a choice but to lie to me? *Harley had no idea that I even existed!*' Jayson yelled.

'You wouldn't have gone if you knew.'

'Of *course* I wouldn't have gone! Are you insane? Who would willingly take a gamble on homelessness? *I'm fifteen years old!*' Jayson was even more infuriated than he'd realized.

'I know, I know . . .' Toni tried to interrupt.

'How did you even get his address?!'

'From that old book you mail ordered that had the home addresses of the stars.'

'Jesus Christ! Almost all of those addresses are twenty years old! I never once got a letter back from Betty White, or Dick Van Patten, or even Barbara Goddamn Eden!'

'Well, at least Oscar Harlande hadn't moved.'

'Yeah,' Jayson snarled. 'I got *real* lucky.'

'I had no choice, Butter Bean! They were going to take you away from me.'

'C'mon. *They?* You sound like one of those nuts on *In Search Of,*' Jayson said.

'It was Unsinger. Unsinger and his Nazi deputies'

'Unsinger?' Jayson questioned. 'Why would Unsinger take me away?'

Toni continued her breathless explanation.

'It was the Homecoming thing. After what you and Franck did, Terri nagged Unsinger until he finally got a court order to put you into Juvenile Detention. The night before the order was going to be carried out, Tom called to tip me off that the sheriff's department was coming for you in the morning.' Toni stopped, it sounded like she was choking on something. She went on, 'You were going to Juvenile Detention in Milwaukee. I couldn't let that happen. That's where my parents sent me when I was carrying you. I couldn't let that happen. I couldn't let that happen.'

Was his mother crying again?

'I had to do something quick,' Toni continued, her voice quavering. 'When I saw Oscar on the *Late Late Movie,* I took it as a sign. I got the address out of your book. I know it was wrong. I should've figured something else out.'

'But you didn't,' was all Jayson could reply. 'You didn't.'

'When the sheriff came in the morning,' Toni went on, 'I told them that I'd sent you to your father's. They were angry. You were supposed to call. They've been trying to arrest me. I had no way to prove I hadn't abandoned you.'

Even her tears didn't soften Jayson's resentment. It wasn't a risk any normal mother would take. Not Carol Brady. Not Mrs. Partridge. Not Mrs. Cunningham. Not Linda Lavin. Not Bonnie Franklin. Not a single one of them would send their kids off to New York in the middle of the night.

'Well maybe,' Jayson said into the phone icily. 'Maybe you couldn't prove you hadn't abandoned me because, *Mother*, you *had*.' He slammed the phone receiver down and stormed past Devlin and Harley. On his way upstairs to his room he heard Harley on the phone again, already trying to smooth things over.

'Yes, they're so volatile at that age, hormones and all . . .' Harley was soliloquizing, 'I'm sure it will pass. Now you'll need my address to send those documents . . .'

# Twelve

**Jayson took his mark** next to the elaborate trompe-l'oeil marble fireplace made out of some sort of foam and adjusted his crown. It, too, was a fabricated version of the real thing, with synthetic fur around the headband and huge hunks of multicolored plastic meant to be precious jewels.

It was getting hot under the lights. And as if on cue with his thoughts, a makeup artist sprinted up to him to dab at the sweat beginning to trickle through his makeup. *A makeup person,* he thought. *I have a makeup person!*

'Okay, one more take everyone,' the director yelled. 'You're doin' great, Jay-Jay. Do it just like the last one. You're a natural.'

*A natural.* A natural actor, Jayson thought. That was one step shy of being a natural celebrity. He'd always been sure he was that, even when no one else noticed.

'Sound!' the director yelled.

'Rolling!' came the voice of the audio engineer from somewhere behind the blinding lights.

'And action!' yelled the director.

'Please, Giles, take them all away,' Jayson said in his pan-European accent, waving away all the gifts on the butler's tray. It was a different butler than he'd auditioned with. This one seemed even more bitter than the first. It was understandable, Jayson thought. They'd likely been waiting to break out all their lives, and here was Jayson, fifty years younger, just sauntering into the leading role of the commercial – on his first try.

'There *is* one more gift, master,' the butler offered with a perfect English accent. He'd told Jayson during a break that he'd performed in six different Shakespeare in the Park productions. Jayson could tell he was proud of this, for whatever reason. It certainly didn't seem like a smart career move to Jayson. The theater was for *after* you'd made your mark.

'Another gift? What is it?' Jayson responded, arching an eyebrow. He heard stifled chuckling from the sidelines of the set. They loved when he arched his eyebrow. Maybe that would be 'his thing.' Like Fonzie's thumbs up. Or Gary Coleman's stern 'Whachu talkin' 'bout, Mr. D?' Or, of course, Devlin's *'It wuuuuzzzzzn't me!'*

'Bon Appetite!'

'Thank you, Giles, but I asked what is it?'

'Bon Appetite, sir!'

'But what is it?'

*'It's Bon Appetite! The Chocolate After Dinner Mint from the Expert Chocolatiers of Cadbury.'*

Jayson took one of the perfectly unwrapped chocolate

mints off the tray. He'd seen enough candy commercials to know that this was where thay would cut away to a product shot of the chocolate being split open to reveal it's neon green mint center. He chewed thoughtfully, and arched the other eyebrow.

'Mmmmm. It's Bon Appetite. The treat for the elite!'

'Cut!' yelled the director, and the entire set broke into the laughter they'd tried to keep stifled through every take. Jayson spat the candy into the dish that a production assistant immediately provided.

'I gotta tell you, kid,' said the director, smiling widely. 'I don't see a lot of "it" in this business, but you got plenty.'

Finally, Jayson thought. Finally he'd found a place that could see what he knew all along. He had *it*. Gobs of *it*.

And there was no way in hell he was ever going back to where *it* wasn't.

The wait between filming the commercial and its first air date seemed interminable to Jayson. But in reality, it was a rush job. The Cadbury company had just switched advertising agencies and rushed the edit to get a campaign in the market before the holidays. So barely over a month after filming, Jayson, Devlin, and Harley were sitting in front of the TV on the edge of the maroon velvet divan that smelled faintly of old man cologne and not so faintly of cigarette smoke and spilled brandies. The nightly sing-along slash meat market had been delayed an hour so that the three of them could watch Jayson's television debut.

It was Thanksgiving, and Harley had a plate of turkey on his lap, left over from an early afternoon feast. After taking Jayson to the Macy's Thanksgiving Day parade in the morning, Devlin came home and put the finishing touches on the most elaborate dinner Jayson had ever seen, even better than anything on *Dynasty*. Harley had collected more crystal and silver serving dishes over the years than most royal dynasties, and he didn't seem to spare a single piece in the table setting.

It was the holiday that Jayson'd always dreamed of. Right down to the moment that the parade spectators standing around him and Devlin finally recognized 'Devlin Williamson' and inundated him with scraps of paper and pens for his autograph. One woman from Minnesota pleaded with Devlin until he finally gave in, turned to face the crowd and said, with his patented dimple: *'It wuuuuzzzzzn't me!'* The crowd exploded in laughter. Throughout the rest of the parade, Jayson watched the people around them out of the corner of his eye. They spent more time trying to see what Devlin Williamson was doing than watching the parade itself. They were tourists from all over the country, and no doubt would brag endlessly about meeting a real life celebrity to their neighbors back home. For some of them, Jayson thought, it would probably be one of the best stories of their lives. Jayson wondered how he would have reacted just two months ago when he was one of them – a mere civilian. One of the people from nowhere places with nowhere lives. Now he was practically best friends with Devlin Williamson and on the verge of becoming famous himself. Whenever Jayson got too excited about his television debut though, Devlin would remind him that as great as Jayson was, it was still just a commercial, and that Devlin had been in many, many commercials before he got his big break on *Disorder in the Court.*

But nothing could dampen Jayson's excitement.

Over two days Jayson had shot six commercials for *Bon Appetite* as 'the Picky Prince,' and they would air – one new one a week – each week until New Year's. This first one, if Jayson remembered correctly, basically set up the character of 'the Picky Prince.' He was getting impatient. He knew it was scheduled to air sometime during *Cagney and Lacey*, and the show was already almost three quarters over.

'I don't get it,' Harley said, a string of turkey meat hanging from the corner of his mouth as he stared quizzically at the television. 'These are two lady cops, and they're *not* lovers? It's simply not plausible. Back when I was on *GE Playhouse Presents,* I did a teleplay with Dinah Shore . . .'

'*Shhhh!*' Devlin hushed him, 'it's coming on soon!'

Tyne Daly's image faded to black as the show went to commercial. James Garner and Mariette Hartley's faces suddenly filled the screen as they dryly bantered back and forth about Polaroid photos. When they went to black, the ivory and gold phone on the end table next to Harley began to ring.

'Don't answer it!' Devlin instructed.

As the phone kept ringing, the television screen filled with an establishing shot of a massive stone castle in drifts of rolling snow. It was Jayson's spot! Jayson wondered where they'd filmed these outdoor bits. His part of the shoot – the castle interiors – were all shot on a soundstage in Brooklyn.

The intro music was a sort of electronic handbell version of the carol 'We Three Kings.' The exterior castle shot quicky cut to Giles entering the Prince's bedroom with his tray of offerings. Jayson wished Harley's damn phone would stop ringing.

And then, suddenly, there he was.

On the television.

Jayson.

Thinking back, Jayson realized that he'd accomplished his summer's goal even sooner than expected. He had planned for *Dallasty!* to be a mid-season replacement, and yet here he was, already on TV by the start of the holiday season. Thinking back on the silly homemade TV series he'd shot in his backyard made him cringe with embarrassment. He'd never mentioned it to Devlin. But he was sure that all the hard work and determination he'd displayed every single day of his life all led up to this moment: His face was on TV.

Devlin put his arm around Jayson and excitedly pulled him tight. Harley chuckled at Jayson's face onscreen as well.

The ringing phone went unanswered.

'Bon Appetite!' said the onscreen butler as he offered Jayson the silver tray of candy.

'Thank you, Giles, but I asked, what is it?'

'Bon Appetite, sir!'

'But what is it?'

*'It's Bon Appetite! The Chocolate After Dinner Mint from the Expert Chocolatiers of Cadbury.'*

Harley broke out in laughter when Jayson delivered the tagline.

'"The treat for the elite!"' he exclaimed. 'What a delicious tagline.'

Jayson knew the script itself wasn't that funny. But there was no denying that his odd accent and eyebrow arching were endearingly humorous.

Harley was still chuckling as he picked up the phone, which rang throughout the commercial. It was a compliment that Harley let it ring for as long as he did. He never missed a phone call. 'Charity can't wait,' he'd say, 'clients' needs can be fleeting.'

Devlin patted Jayson's thigh.

'You did great, pal,' he said, grinning. 'I'm jealous!'

Devlin Williamson was jealous of him. Devlin Williamson. As much as he was glad to have Oconomowoc behind him, he could have endured it for one more day if he could just bring his new best friend Devlin Williamson to an all-school assembly to announce that he was jealous of Jayson.

Jayson suddenly realized that a good portion of his old school had probably just seen his television debut. He wondered if they even recognized him in his costume. They'd have to have. Yes, they'd just have to have.

'Yes, yes, dear, one moment,' Harley was saying into the

phone. 'Happy Thanksgiving, by the way. *Yes* . . . just hold your horses lady,'

Harley rolled his eyes as he handed the phone receiver to Jayson, stretching the cord across Devlin's lap.

'It's your dear mother,' Harley said, 'who obviously learned English in a truck driving school.'

Toni had called several times after their last discussion, but Jayson had always refused to speak with her. Harley covered for him usually, making up excuses about his fictional schooling and equally fictional after-school activities. One time he had said that Jayson was at football practice.

Jayson wondered if she was calling because she'd seen the commercial. Franck did watch *Cagney and Lacey* religiously. But hadn't the phone begun ringing before the spot began?

'Just take it,' Devlin said. 'She is your mother and it is Thanksgiving.'

Devlin gave his advice a little wistfully. Jayson wondered if he was thinking of his own nonexistent relationship with his thieving parents. But the real reason Jayson took the phone was to gloat about his newfound fame.

'Did you see my debut, Ma?' he said. 'I guess if I could make it here I can make it anywhere,' he said snarkily.

'Jayson. I have some bad news.' Toni's voice had none of its usual *c'est la vie* flippancy.

'So you missed my debut then. That *is* bad news.'

'Trey's gone.'

'You put him on a plane to nowhere, too?' Jayson said, still angry.

'He's missing.'

Jayson was confused. She was serious.

'Missing where?' Jayson asked before realizing what a stupid question it was.

'He's run away.'

Suddenly Jayson could hear Willie's voice shouting in the background. 'Trey din't! Trey din't! Run 'way!' he was shouting determinedly with his thick tongue and slack mouth. Jayson could picture his brother perfectly. Whenever Willie was flustered, he had difficulty forming sentences and waved his hands about, seemingly uncontrollably. 'Trey din't Trey din't run 'way!' he repeated. In his anxiety, Willie ran all the words together as if they were one sentence. Toni's voice grew quieter as she momentarily turned away from the phone to calm Willie down. 'It's okay Willie. It's okay my l'il Willie Prader,' she said soothingly.

'I don't get it,' Jayson said. 'Why did he run away? Where to?'

'We don't know, nobody knows. He's been gone for three days.'

'Why would he run away?' Jayson asked. It was hard for him to imagine Trey leaving Oconomowoc. As ill of a fit as Jayson was for the small town, Trey was the opposite . . . Star athlete. Decent grades. Churchgoer.

'He ran away the night before Terri was supposed to send him to a Bible school in Mequon. They found his bike in the woods by Highway K and think he hitchhiked from there. That fucking Unsinger was on his way to a counseling session in Okachee and claims he saw someone who looked like Trey climbing into another car.'

Jayson considered the irony of it. Unsinger finally had a real chance to save a kid from going from 'God to Odd' and he just drove on past. Especially poetic since that kid was Trey – whom Unsinger had always held up as a shining example for Jayson.

'Why was he being sent to Bible school?' Jayson asked.

'Terri wouldn't let him go back to school after the "Homecoming Incident." She was convinced there would be homosexual teachers who would prey on him.'

Jayson felt a twinge of guilt. He'd inadvertantly ruined his friend's life – more than his friend. Trey was his first love.

'What about Tara?' Jayson asked, 'Is she okay?'

'She's okay. As okay as she could be, I guess. She's mostly upset that Trey didn't tell her anything about his plans.'

Willie was still protesting in the background.

'Is Willie okay?' Jayson asked.

'It was all a little scary for him. He was out foraging . . .'

'You have to keep an eye on him, Ma!' Jayson interrupted.

Toni continued, unadmonished.

'He was out foraging when Trey disappeared. At first we thought the two of them had gone somewhere together, and when the police finally found Willie they questioned him mercilessly.'

'Put him on the phone a sec.'

A second later Jayson heard his younger brother's heavy breathing.

'Hey buddy,' Jayson said in the calming voice that usually worked on Willie.

'Trey din't Trey din't run 'way!'

'It's okay pal. You didn't do anything. Trey's just out playing somewhere.'

Willie didn't respond, other than his normal, raspy, openmouthed breathing.

'Are you being good, pal?'

He still didn't answer. Jayson didn't really expect him to. Talking on the phone was a complicated concept for Willie. Jayson thought that Willie probably viewed it like the television, which he'd learned only talks at you, not the other way around.

'Be careful of snacks, pal. You know the rhyme. "Breakfast, lunch, dinner. Three meals a day and you're a winner."'

'Breakfas', lunch, dinner, fhree meals a day an' I'm a winner,' Willie repeated softly, almost under his breath.

'Hand the phone back to Ma, Willie. I love you.'

There was a rustling, then the faint familiar "psst" as Toni dropped her cigarette into a nearby open can of something.

'Are you doing okay in the city there, Butter Bean?' she asked once back on the line.

'I hope that's rhetorical.'

'Don't smartass me.'

'I wouldn't waste the energy,' Jayson replied. As soon as the shock of Trey's disappearance wore off, the grudge over Toni's abandonment quickly refilled the gap. 'Oh. I forgot to tell you,' Jayson said flatly. 'I'm famous now.'

'What?'

'Watch TV. See if you can find me.'

'What are you talking about?' Toni asked.

'Just watch the damn TV,' Jayson said in hurry to get off the phone and back to the small celebration of his newfound fame. 'And try not to lose anymore kids.'

'Happy Thanksgiving, Butter Bean.'

'Right. Thanksgiving,' Jayson repeated. 'Thanks for nothing.'

Jayson hung up the phone and passed it back across Devlin to Harley.

'What's going on?' Devlin asked with genuine concern. Jayson didn't want to go into a long explanation about who Trey was, and how Jayson had always had a crush on his best friend. After all, here he was, embarking on an entirely new, entirely better, entirely *perfect* path of his life, and his old life was trying to butt back in. It was like when the most boring storyline kept cropping back up on a nighttime soap.

'Nothing,' Jayson answered. 'Hey, did you see my eyebrow raise at the end of the commercial? I think that's going to be my thing.'

# *Thirteen*

**Whenever he and Devlin** were walking down the street – which was often since neither of them had many other obligations – Jayson could almost telepathically feel Devlin cringe whenever a random passerby recognized him and blurted out '*It wuuuuzzzzzn't me!*' Devlin was always outwardly gracious, turning to half-smile/half-wince at the unexpected fan, but Jayson knew that for Devlin, the phrase would be sort of a lifelong Chinese drip torture.

Jayson had spent the better part of his life preparing for the day a stranger might recognize him. And he knew, with his Bon Appetite commercials now airing, that that day would come soon. He'd started carrying a pen and a scrap of paper with him for autographs, just in case a hapless future fan was caught without.

He and Devlin spent most every afternoon watching movies – lots of movies. Mainstream movies, foreign films, long black-and-white art-house flicks. With Devlin's twice-weekly cooking classes as the only scheduled activity between the two of them, there was a lot of time to kill.

Jayson had finished his Christmas shopping already. He'd bought a set of chef's knives for Devlin and an antique silver chafing dish for Harley. Harley was freer with money now that Jayson was gainfully employed. Jayson had no idea how much money he was making off of his television campaign. He wasn't even that interested. With fame came fortune, not the other way around, so he was sure he was heading in the right direction. As Jayson's father, Harley volunteered his services to be his manager and agent. 'No use paying some shark ten percent,' he told Jayson. 'Family money should stay in the family.' Pretty much whatever Jayson asked for, Harley gave him, though mostly he just asked for a few bucks for movie tickets and frozen hot chocolates.

He and Devlin had just stepped out from an afternoon matinee of *On Golden Pond* at the Ziegfeld when it finally happened, the moment Jayson had always been waiting for:

'It's the treat . . . *for the elite!*'

The shouting came from across the street. He and Devlin turned and spotted a heavy-set middle-aged woman with two teenage girls. They'd no doubt come into the city from New Jersey or Long Island for holiday window shopping at those department stores where they couldn't afford to buy anything. They were pointing across the street at them. At *him*. One of them held up a camera.

It was all Jayson could do to keep himself from running across the street, pen and paper in hand, to hug them all. What a wonderful Christmas story for them, he thought. But he held back. Real celebrities stayed the course, ignoring mortals. Devlin nudged him with his elbow.

'Not bad,' Devlin said. 'You're more famous than me now.'

The campaign had been a hit. The commercials seemed to run during every show they watched. They appeared so often that both Devlin and Harley could recite the different scripts along with the television. Harley usually played Giles's part, with Devlin taking Jayson's. Devlin even perfected a mimicry of Jayson's patented eyebrow raise. Jayson would usually mock him back with '*It wuuuuzzzzzn't me!*'

He and Devlin were inseparable. They would chat long into the night from their respective twin beds in the small bedroom on the top floor of the townhouse. They knew almost everything about one another. Jayson was amazed that any two people could grow so close in such a short time. His favorite nights were when Devlin would tell him old celebrity gossip from Devlin's *Disorder in the Court* days. He told Jayson how he'd once walked in on Wilfred Bramley, the actor who played the judge, getting a blow job from Helen Lawson, who played the judge's busybody neighbor in a few guest-starring episodes. And how the judge's mysterious disappearance in the fourth season was due to a contract dispute over whether or not Wilfred could keep pieces of the show's wardrobe for his personal use. And how the oldest daughter on the show took a year off for cocaine addiction – not, as *People* had reported, because of exhaustion. Jayson loved feeling like a Hollywood insider. He considered it only a matter of time before he actually was one.

Just about the only thing the two of them didn't talk about was Devlin's love life. Or lack thereof. Devlin never once admitted an attraction, a crush, or a passing fancy toward anyone. Jayson'd spilled everything of course. His discovery of his homosexuality from Phil Donahue. His crush on Trey. 'The Kiss.' While Devlin returned Jayson's intimacy with sincere affection, Jayson felt that Devlin treated him like he was a protected younger brother – the way Jayson used to treat Willie. One thing Jayson was sure of, though, was that he wasn't going to make the same mistake he had with Trey. Devlin was straight, according to all the celebrity press Jayson had ever read. If he couldn't believe *People* magazine, well, then, there wasn't much he could believe in.

During their walk home from the matinee it began snowing. Drooping gray winter clouds had been rolling in all day, bunching up against each other like a thick down comforter pushed down to the end of a bed. As they reached the steps of the townhouse, fat, wet flakes of snow began dropping, almost in clumps, so large that they could be heard hitting the sidewalk. It was the first snow of the season and a week before Christmas. Since Jayson tended to judge events by how they would play out in the inevitable future biopic of his life, the timing of his first New York City snowfall couldn't have been more picturesquely perfect.

As soon as they cracked open the door to the townhouse,

Harley's voice rang out from the living room with the sing-songy cheerfulness that indicated that there must be a visitor with him.

'Darlings! Is that you?' he called. A second later Harley appeared in the foyer, his billowing untucked white shirt flapping behind him. He hurried up to Jayson and Devlin, whispering as he approached.

'There's a reporter here from a magazine called *Television Guide . . .*'

Jayson's heart leapt in this throat. *TV Guide*! Even more than being on TV, he'd always dreamed of being on the cover of *TV Guide*. The first words he'd ever read were from the January 13, 1970, *TV Guide* listing for the *Here's Lucy* episode entitled 'Lucy Goes on Strike.' He'd been four years old.

Jayson turned to check his reflection in the dozen mirrors that lined the foyer. *Dammit. Hat hair.*

'She's doing research for their "What Ever Happened To" column,' Harley continued breathlessly.

Wait a minute, Jayson thought. I've barely even *happened* yet.

'She wants to chat with you a little, Devvie, and to send a photographer by later if that's okay. Which I said was okay. Is it okay? Of course it's okay.'

Jayson was crushed. Devlin looked surprised.

'I don't know, Harley,' he said. 'The show's only been off the air for two years. It seems a little weird.'

'It's not weird in the slightest,' Harley protested, punctuating the word 'weird' as if it were a curse. 'You were the hottest commodity in Hollywood at one time. I know. I remember. And now you've just disappeared.'

'I didn't "disappear,"' Devlin corrected. 'I was "disappeared." No one would hire me, remember?'

'So now that they want you, you don't want them?' Harley countered. 'That's hardly polite.'

Devlin's reluctance baffled Jayson. Much of Devlin's attitude toward celebrity baffled Jayson. Devlin would skip auditions if they conflicted with his cooking class. He would change the channel over Jayson's protests whenever a rerun of *Disorder in the Court* came on. The only celebrity he seemed remotely interested in was Jayson's. And that was always in the context of Jayson's own excitement.

'It'll be easy-peasy,' Harley chirped, taking Devlin by the hand and leading him into the living room. 'You just have to answer a few of the lady's questions, smile for a picture or two, and voila! You'll be swimming in offers in no time.'

'Or drowning,' Devlin muttered, disappearing into the living room.

Jayson stood just outside the living room door and listened to Devlin's entire interview. He was impressed with how smoothly Devlin handled all the questions. His answers were pat, quotable, short, and witty. Devlin slipped back into his *Disorder in the Court* character just enough to remind the reporter, and the eventual readers, of his erstwhile appeal.

When the reporter brought up the oft-repeated rumor that Devlin had once smashed in the windshield of his father's new Datsun 280Z – purchased with Devlin's earnings – Devlin paused a moment and responded: '*It wuuuuzzzzzn't me!*'

He had the reporter swooning like his teenage fans. The photographer showed up about a half hour into the interview and took some pictures of Devlin at the piano. The reporter then asked for some photos of Harley alone. And then a few more with both Devlin and Harley. The reporter found it intriguing that Oscar Harlande, the biggest child celebrity of the 1930s, had 'adopted' Devlin Williamson, the biggest child celebrity of the 1970s. She was sure that this would somehow make it into the story, which sent Harley's voice into an even higher octave.

When he grew tired of standing outside the living room door, Jayson sat on the bottom step of the staircase to listen to the ongoing interview. He didn't dare disappear to his bedroom. At any moment he expected Harley or Devlin to call him into the living room to join in. After all, he was famous now too. Talking to 'The biggest teenage child celebrity of the 1980s' seemed like it would be the perfect triumverate scoop for the *TV Guide* reporter. But after two hours, Jayson heard the reporter wrapping up, promising to let Devlin and Harley know when the issue would be on the stands and indicating that she might be calling with some follow-up questions. Jayson ducked up the stairs before she entered the foyer to retrieve her jacket.

After she and the photographer left, Jayson skulked back down and found both of them in the kitchen.

'Hey Jay-Jay,' Devlin said, 'what do you feel like for dinner? I just got my certificate for soufflés. I could whip one up.'

'I don't care. I'm not that hungry,' Jayson answered.

'I'm not either,' Harley said. He began coughing. He'd been keeping a cold at bay for almost a week now. Devlin and Jayson had urged him to take a few days off from the charity to recover. 'I'm too busy,' he'd say. 'Places to go, people to get laid.' Harley's naps were growing longer as well. Though neither Devlin nor Jayson would ever bring it up, he seemed to be growing frailer by the day. It was if he'd delayed being an old man for so long that it was catching up to him all at once. 'I think,' Harley added, 'I may go lie down, instead.'

Devlin and Jayson looked at each other, surprised. Perhaps the excitement from the interview was too much.

'But the charity begins in an hour,' Devlin said. The holidays were, as Harley continually pointed out to them, the busiest time of the year for the charity. In just over an hour, the living room would be packed with over a dozen chorus boys and two dozen of the men who admired them. 'Sneezer Geezer' had even promised to dress as Santa for the evening, most likely hoping for some free lap action, Jayson realized.

'I think,' Harley said, 'you may have to have them entertain themselves this evening. The donation list is in the top desk drawer should there be any contentious negotiations between our patrons. You boys can handle the rest.'

148

As Harley shuffled out of the kitchen, drained of energy, Jayson was reminded of the *Disorder in the Court* episode on which Harley guest-starred as a drunken, beaten-down homeless man on Christmas Eve. By the end of the episode, after he'd shown everyone their future, Harley's character shuffled down the street under a streetlamp and disappeared into the snow.

The snow that had started falling when Devlin and Jayson left the movie theater was still falling, piling up against the bottom panes of the French doors that led to the townhouse's back garden. As Harley walked past the doors, he looked so tired and frail that Jayson half thought he might turn and exit through them – vanishing into the snowy night.

Instead, Harley turned, blew them both a kiss, and went upstairs.

# Fourteen

**Jayson and Devlin** did their best to keep the charity running during the week before Christmas as Harley lay in bed, his cough growing worse and worse. He sat upright through the night to keep the phlegm in his lungs from rattling through his nose. As much as the two pleaded with him to see a doctor, Harley stubbornly refused, believing, like all good stars, that he was merely suffering from 'exhaustion.'

For Christmas Eve, Devlin cooked a feast even more elaborate than his Thanksgiving masterpiece. Jayson and Devlin ate alone downstairs, and afterwards fixed a tray to bring up to Harley – even though they knew that he would touch none of it. Devlin set it on the nightstand next to the bed, knowing that he'd wind up picking it up from the same place, cold and congealed, the next morning – Christmas morning.

'You two are boring me,' Harley said, startling them. His eyes had been closed when they entered, and they'd assumed he was asleep. 'I'm sick of you hanging around here. It's the most wonderful time of the year, or however that milque-toast Andy Williams warbles it. Go out somewhere. Enjoy yourselves.'

By tradition – and lack of business – Harley's charity was not open on Christmas Eve.

Jayson knew immediately what he wanted to do.

'C'mon. You promised you'd take me,' Jayson pleaded with Devlin on their way back down the stairs.

'But it's not even cool anymore,' Devlin said. 'When it closed last year all the celebrities went with it. No one's come back since the reopening.'

'Yes they have,' Jayson said. 'I saw in the *Post* that Liza was there just last week.'

'They probably paid her to go.'

'*With* Bianca,' Jayson added.

'I'd pay to go anywhere Bianca Jagger *wasn't*,' Devlin said.

'C'mon. It'll be your Christmas present to me.'

'I don't think you're old enough to handle it.'

'You're only a year older than me, and you were going four years ago!'

'No.'

'Fine. I'll go by myself.'

'You won't get in.'

'I'll get in. I'm the Picky Prince.'

'They're Pickier than you.'

'Okay, Mr. "Whateverhappenedto."'

The minute the words came out of Jayson's mouth he regretted them. He knew that Devlin could care less about his own fallen celebrity status, but having Jayson use it as a weapon against him was just plain mean-spirited.

Devlin ignored the comment.

'Okay, pal,' Devlin said resignedly, 'I'll take you. But don't say I didn't warn you.'

They arrived at the club at 11:30. Even on Christmas Eve, Studio 54 had a mob of hopefuls outside its velvet rope. Jayson was wearing a silver T-shirt he'd bought with the first money that Harley gave him from his commercial earnings. As a new celebrity, Jayson wanted to be sparkly. Neither he nor Devlin was wearing a jacket, despite the six inches of snow on the ground and the frigid wind off the Hudson. Devlin recommended that they leave their coats at home to avoid the inevitable crush of drunken, high club-goers that clogged the coat check nearly all hours of the night. Devlin was wearing a T-shirt from a band named Emmy. Jayson had never heard of them and begged Devlin to wear something more current. Devlin insisted on wearing it to help promote the band's singer whom he'd met in the East Village a few months ago. She was nice, Devlin said, and really wanted to break into dance music. With a name like Madonna, Jayson thought, *good luck*.

Jayson was eager to try to exploit his new notoriety, if for no other reason than to show Devlin that he didn't need to be taken care of as much as Devlin thought he did. Jayson pushed his way through the pulsing mob of wannabes to the bouncer. He stood on the opposite side of the velvet rope from the broad Italian man dressed in a black suit and waited expectantly. And impatiently. The bouncer glanced directly at Jayson and then back over his head to scan the crowd behind him. He was being ignored. The crowd of impatient patrons ebbed and flowed toward the velvet rope like ocean waves crashing ashore. Jason nearly got caught in the undertow sweeping people away from the front of the line, when Devlin stepped in front of him.

'Heeeyyyy,' said the bouncer spotting him, '*If it iiiizzzzzzzzn't you!* Long time no see.' The bouncer chuckled at his own joke as he unhooked the velvet rope from its stanchion. Devlin patted the huge man on his bicep as he grabbed Jayson and pulled him free from the quicksand mob.

They entered the dark vestibule and pushed their way through random bodies until they reached a heavy curtain. Jayson held onto the back of Devlin's T-shirt, petrified of losing him in this pitch black crowded space that thumped with disco music that he could feel through the soles of his feet. He hadn't realized how loud it was going to be. And dark. It was already overwhelming and he wasn't even all the way inside yet.

Devlin pulled Jayson through the vestibule curtain, and his pupils nearly exploded from the brightness of the huge room in front of him. The flashing strobes and colored swirling spotlights nearly made him dizzy.

'Over here,' Devlin yelled into his ear. Jayson didn't know where 'here' was, but he held onto Devlin's T-shirt as Devlin pulled him toward a large mirrored bar under a balcony.

'What do you want?' Devlin shouted.

'I dunno,' Jayson shouted back. 'What are you having?'

Devlin turned to the shirtless bartender and ordered two rum and Cokes. When the bartender handed over the drinks Devlin held up a twenty-dollar bill. The bartender raised his hand and gestured that the drinks were on the house.

They leaned against the bar for about a half an hour watching the crowd.

'I don't see anyone famous,' Jayson said loudly into Devlin's ear.

'There are famous people here,' Devlin answered. 'You just can't spot them, because in here everyone's the same. It doesn't matter how many records you've put out, or books you've written, or movies you've been in . . . in here you're just a warm body waiting to get thrown up on by Grace Jones.'

Jayson didn't believe him. None of these people were celebrities – other than him and Devlin, of course. If there were a celebrity here, Jayson thought, he would be able to spot them immediately. They would magically stand out among the crowd of scantily dressed tourists. Otherwise there was no order to the world. There was no God. It was all just chaos.

They stood at the bar for another half hour before Devlin asked Jayson if he wanted to dance or something. Jayson was a little disappointed by how little there was to actually *do* at a nightclub. The other people looked like they were having fun, but Jayson wasn't sure what was making them laugh and smile so brightly. He wasn't sure what he was expecting, but this wasn't it. On top of it all, with nothing else to do, he'd already finished four and a half rum and Cokes and wasn't sure he could stomach finishing the one he had.

'I think I have to throw up,' he whispered to Devlin roughly a half second before he did – onto the floor, splashing against the mirror-fronted bar. 'Shit,' he muttered, his head still hanging.

'Had enough, Picky Prince?'

Devlin didn't wait for Jayson to answer. He put his arm around Jayson and led him through the sweaty crowd and out a side door onto Fifty-third Street. It was only 1:35 in the morning, though Jayson felt like they'd been inside for at least six hours. Devlin sat him down on a nearby stoop. The chilly wind felt good against Jayson's bare arms.

'Sorry,' Jayson said. 'I don't drink a lot.'

'Don't be sorry,' Devlin replied. 'You know I didn't want to come here anyway.' Devlin held up a pack of Freshen Up gum. Jayson took one.

'I don't get it,' Jayson said, his head still spinning. He couldn't fathom how Devlin could so easily leave all the trappings of celebrity behind him. Just a couple of years ago, he would've been the hottest star in the club. Now he didn't even want to go. 'It's just *weird*,' Jayson continued. 'Once you were everything. You had everything. But now you don't want it anymore? It doesn't make sense.'

'It does to me,' Devlin answered. Jayson just looked at him puzzled. Jayson was struggling to keep his eyes focused. He hadn't been this drunk since . . . when, exactly? Since he and

Trey and Tara got drunk filming *Dallasty!* and blew up the garage?

'I don't get it,' Jayson said. 'My mother used to put her little portable Zenith black-and-white television in the playpen with me . . . *in* the playpen,' he repeated for emphasis. 'If she took it away, I would scream for hours. I could sing the theme song to *Petticoat Junction* before I could sing the alphabet song.'

'Doesn't seem like a skill that's going to take you far.'

'All I've ever wanted was to be on the inside of the TV instead of the outside. I'd give up everything I own to be where you used to be.'

Devlin looked up and down the deserted street. He kicked his foot at a gray block of compacted snow by Jayson's feet. Finally he sat down next to Jayson on the cold concrete step.

'Would you give up me?' he asked quietly.

Jayson looked up. He didn't understand what Devlin was asking.

'Would you?' Devlin repeated.

'Why would you think that?' Jayson asked back.

'I don't know. I mean, you gave up on your family after you got here.'

Jayson wasn't sure what Devlin meant by that.

'I didn't give up on them,' Jayson replied, defending himself. '*They* shipped *me* off in the middle of the night.'

'They had their reasons,' Devlin argued. 'But I don't get yours.'

Jayson didn't know whether or not he should be insulted

or if Devlin was truly just curious. Of course he'd left them all behind. They deserved to be. If he was ever going to get anywhere in this world, he was going to have to jettison the dead weight. But Devlin wasn't dead weight. Devlin had saved Jayson from the streets and promised that he would take care of him. Jayson couldn't think of a better definition of a best friend. Devlin was certainly a much better friend than Trey had been – Trey, who had betrayed him so long ago. Betrayer Trey, Crazy Franck, Slacker Tara, Damaged Willie, Toni the Abandoner – all of those left behind were people Jayson was much better off without. It seemed painfully obvious to Jayson and he wasn't sure why Devlin couldn't see that.

'Why do you even care about them?' Jayson asked.

'Because I need to know if how you feel about them is how you'll feel about me one day. I need to know whether this is all worth it,' Devlin said.

'All what?'

'All that I feel about you.'

Before Jayson could react, Devlin leaned in and kissed him.

As Devlin pulled away after the kiss, he looked into Jayson's eyes. Jayson stared back. Jayson wondered if Devlin could hear the blood thumping in his ears.

'You like me?' Jayson asked.

'You vomited five minutes ago, and I still couldn't keep from kissing you. I think that means I more than like you,' Devlin said.

'Thanks,' was all Jayson could think to say. He wanted

to say more . . . so much more . . . but between the kiss and
the rum, he could barely slow his spinning brain long enough
to pull the right words out. No. He would never give Devlin
up. There was no reason he'd ever have to. They were perfect
together. It was almost impossible to believe that he had just
kissed the lips of the guy he used to pretend kiss on his old
television screen.

'I will never give you up,' Jayson finally managed to utter.
'I'm addicted.'

Jayson knew that together they would take on the world
and become the brightest stars in Hollywood.

'Merry Christmas,' Devlin said. Jayson smiled.

'This is definitely my "very special Christmas."'

'So,' Devlin said flirtatiously, 'wanna come back to my
room?'

It took almost a half an hour to find a cab so late on Christ-
mas Eve. By the time they were dropped off on the corner of
Third and Sixty-second, the clock on the dash read 4:15. It was
Christmas morning.

Jayson let himself wonder for a moment whether or not
Toni had finished her typical last-minute wrapping rush for
Willie. Or, more likely, was she still huddled under a tree dried
to a crisp from lack of water with a roll of duct tape in one
hand, a roll of wall-paper in the other, and a Newport dangling from her lips? He tried to put it out of his mind. He had
a new home, a new father, and a new boyfriend. And each one
of them rated a full three stars above what he had had before.

'What the fuck?' Devlin said when they were a quarter of the way down the block toward the townhouse. The entire front of the townhouse was roped off with yellow police tape. There was a beefy cop standing guard by their front steps who looked not unlike the bouncer at Studio 54.

'What's going on?' Jayson repeated.

'Hang back here a second,' Devlin said sternly.

'But Harley. What if he's sick?'

'There's no ambulance. The cops don't rope off half a block because someone's got a cold. Stay here.'

Jayson did as he was told, stepping back into the shadows of a neighbor's stoop. He watched Devlin approach the burly cop. At first the cop seemed to react brusquely to Devlin, but eventually Devlin's charm must have loosened him up. The two stood and chatted for about five minutes before Devlin came back and grabbed Jayson by the upper arm. Without slowing down, he dragged Jayson back toward Third Avenue and around the corner, out of sight of the cop.

'What's going on?' Jayson said, suddenly even more scared by Devlin's urgency.

'It's the charity. It's busted.'

'They raided us? On Christmas Eve?'

'The District Attorney thought it would make a bigger story.'

'But Harley . . .'

'He wasn't home. The cop said they got there and the place

was empty. You know the fat guy at the sing-alongs? With the nipple fetish?'

'Yeah,' Jayson answered.

'He's a vice detective.'

'Undercover?'

'Hell no. I saw him getting blown once in the kitchen. He must have tipped Harley off that the raid was going down.'

'Lucky for Harley. Where did he go?'

'I don't know. They don't know.'

Jayson couldn't believe what was happening. He was homeless for the second time in four months – and on the best night of his life.

'Did the cop say anything about us?'

'No. I said I was a neighbor.'

'Can we go back in and get our coats at least?'

'Are you nuts?'

'Where will we go?'

'I'm not sure. Just keep walking. I'll figure it out.'

They walked another three blocks in thoughtful silence.

'The cop didn't recognize who you are?' Jayson asked.

Devlin laughed. 'I'm black. We all look the same to cops.' He put his arm around Jayson to block the wind. 'I might as well have been Gary Coleman.'

# *Fifteen*

**Devlin checked into** the Hotel Carlyle at 7:00 a.m. on Christmas morning. It was the hotel where CBS had always put Devlin up back when they needed him for network upfronts and morning show promos. Neither Jayson nor Devlin had any cash left, having spent it all at the club and on cab fare.

Luckily one of the Carlyle's desk clerks recognized Devlin from years past, and Devlin was able to convince him that he'd just arrived on a storm-delayed red-eye from L.A. When the clerk couldn't find a reservation, Devlin explained that there must simply have been a snafu with the network's internal travel agency, and promised to clear it up the next morning. Though it was left unspoken, both Jayson and Devlin knew that the ruse could only last for a day – two at most – before they were kicked out.

Devlin snuck Jayson in a side entrance, and they both slept for a few fitful hours before dawn when Devlin snuck Jayson back out so that the hotel wouldn't notice anything suspicious – or at least anything more suspicious than Devlin's story already was. Jayson spent Christmas day wandering the empty

New York streets after having stolen a jacket from a coffee shop patron who left his chair to use the restroom. He'd never stolen anything before and was plagued with guilt, but tried to justify his actions by assuming his victim must have far more jackets at home than the homeless Jayson did. He had instructions to stay away from the hotel until 9:00 p.m. when Devlin thought it would be safe to sneak him back inside again.

As he walked block after block, Jayson grew more frustrated trying to strategize a way out of their situation. His biggest frustration was knowing he had the money from the Bon Appetite advertising campaign in some bank, somewhere. He regretted leaving Harley in charge of all his finances, having signed the papers from the production company naming Harley as his guardian and business manager. He didn't suspect any foul play on Harley's part, but neither did he expect Harley to return to the townhouse to face felony charges simply so that Jayson could get some of his cash.

Jayson tried to distract himself by pretending that he was in an ABC Movie of the Week as a homeless teen who stumbles upon a wizened old bag lady played by Ann-Margret. She would have a scruffy dog – which would turn out to be an angel. He was writing the script for *Tears for Santa Paws* in his head when he walked by a deli and saw the Christmas afternoon edition of the *New York Post*.

There it was, in seventy-two-point type on the front cover: COPS BUST MOVIE STAR & HIS HO-HO-HO'S. Just below it was a huge photo of Harley leaning against his piano.

Jayson waited until the Pakistani man behind the counter turned around to make a fresh pot of coffee before he stole a copy. Stealing was growing frighteningly easy, he thought.

Back in their illegal hotel room that night, he and Devlin pieced together the events that led up to the Christmas Eve raid. It was Devlin who recognized the lead story's byline: Janice Olmstead. She'd been the woman who interviewed Devlin − allegedly for *TV Guide*. Devlin and Jayson concluded that one of Harley's jilted customers had ratted out the aging movie star's 'charity' to the *Post* reporter, who used Devlin as her ploy to get inside and scoop a recent photograph of Harlande before handing the case to the District Attorney.

Quickly rifling through the inside-page coverage, they were relieved to find no mention of Devlin's actual name − just several mentions of 'a well-known television child star' who also lived in the townhouse. They assumed the anonymity was because Devlin was still a minor. It was tenuous legal ground for the press, as Devlin knew from his days of suing his parents, but, as Devlin also knew, it would only be a matter of time before they found a way around it.

As expected, their relief was short lived. Jayson loitered around another deli the following afternoon waiting for the next edition of the *Post*. This time the cover had a shot of both Harley and Devlin at the townhouse's piano and an inset of one of Devlin's headshots from his *Disorder in the Court* days. IT WUUUZZZZ HIM!! shouted the headline, with a subhead that read: TV TEEN LOOKER TURNED GAY HOOKER. The subhead stated: MOVIE STAR, CHILD STAR STILL ON THE LAM.

Jayson threw the paper back in the rack and started running uptown. He was nearly fifty blocks away from the Carlyle, but covered the ground in less than half an hour. As he reached the hotel's entrance, he stopped. He couldn't go inside and ask for Devlin Williamson. Surely the managers or someone on the staff had read the front page of the paper. Jayson was relieved that at least there weren't any squad cars lining Madison Avenue outside the hotel. Yet.

Jayson was unsure what to do next. He walked on to Eightieth Street with his mind racing in scattered directions. Being homeless now for the third time since summer was too surreal to contemplate. Was Devlin still inside the hotel? Had he seen the paper? Had the management called the police already? Was there a sting operation waiting for the unsuspecting Devlin to emerge from his room? Jayson didn't think he could face being alone in New York City again. A tear welled up in his left eye and ran down into the upturned collar of his stolen jacket.

'Hey, aren't you the Picky Prince?' came a voice from behind him.

He turned around.

'Devlin!' he shouted.

'Not so loud, Princess. In case you haven't heard, I'm on the lam.'

Devlin was wearing a bright orange knit hat pulled down to his eyes and a matching scarf around his mouth.

Jayson fell into his arms. Devlin hugged him briefly then took his arm and walked quickly in the direction of Central Park. In the middle of winter there wouldn't be many potential witnesses strolling around the park, Jayson realized.

'You saw it, then?' Jayson asked.

'Yep. I had a feeling it was too juicy to keep quiet for long. I waited at the newsstand for it to be delivered.'

'But you're *not* a hooker!' Jayson protested, upset at how the reporter had erroneously exaggerated her investigation.

'Doesn't really look like that from the outside, does it?'

Jayson had to agree. There weren't many credible explanations for a former child star to be receiving free room and board in a whorehouse. Other than the truth, that is.

The pair walked over to the zoo entrance of the park. It was nearly deserted in the cold. When they were underneath the Denesmouth Arch, the Delacorte Clock began its chiming. The brass monkeys rotated around the clock, banging their mallets on the bell. When Devlin had first pointed the clock out to Jayson on their way home from the Thanksgiving parade, Jayson thought it would be the most romantic spot in the world. Today, in the gray emptiness, it simply reminded him of how little time they had before nightfall – with no place to stay and no money to spend on one.

'What the fuck do we do now?' Jayson said, leaning against the arched wall under the bridge.

'This probably isn't the best idea, but it's all I can come up with,' Devlin answered. 'I'm going to take you over to Port Authority. You can hang out there till one or two in the morning without anyone kicking you out. Just stay in the busiest areas. Don't go into the restrooms unless you really need to. And don't hang out near the entrances. Just pretend you're waiting for a late-night bus. I need to take care of some business, then I'll be back to get you. I should have enough money for an SRO somewhere downtown by then.'

'What business?' Jayson asked. As much as he preferred sitcoms, Jayson had watched enough crime dramas to know that people who had unspecified business transactions outside of a nine-to-five time frame generally weren't doing something legal. And with Devlin already being wanted for a crime he didn't commit it seemed unwise for him to branch off into other illicit professions.

'*My* business, nosy,' Devlin scolded good naturedly. As if to end the discussion, he leaned in and kissed Jayson on the mouth.

**By the time** they reached the Port Authority, it was nearly 8:30 p.m. The station was surprisingly busy. The passengers rushed around him with their suitcases and bags of recently opened Christmas presents.

'Meet me right here at one o'clock, okay?' Devlin said, holding both of Jayson's shoulders so that Jayson had to look him straight in the eyes. 'And don't leave the building. Okay?'

'What's the big deal? Why can't I come with you?' On the long cold walk over, they'd discussed plans of how they would get back on their feet. Once they had a steady room and businesses were open again after the holidays, Jayson would go about tracking down someone who might know something about how he could get his commercial money. Devlin's situation was a little tougher. For the moment, they decided that he would keep his face hidden in public, and then when Jayson had his money again they would hire a lawyer to figure out what to do next. Jayson loved the conspiratorial feeling of their planning. It reminded him of the 'you and me against the world' movies-of-the-week.

Only once did Devlin come close to suggesting that Jayson call home to Wisconsin for help. But before he could finish the question, Jayson stopped him. He would rather sleep on a sewer grate than have to ask his mother for help. She'd abandoned Jayson once already. She'd have to live with whatever might happen to him.

Jayson pleaded one more time to go with Devlin while he attended his 'business.'

'No. Period.'

'Fine,' Jayson said resignedly. 'But if you're not here by one, I'm sneaking on the next bus to Hollywood.'

Devlin laughed, turned, and disappeared into the crowd.

Jayson stood for a moment, contemplating the next four and a half hours. He didn't want to pace around the vast, dirty fluorescent-lit lobby all night. He couldn't imagine what

Devlin had to do that he couldn't be a part of. If it was that dangerous, then that was all the more reason Jayson should accompany him. Jayson suddenly grew terrified of something happening to Devlin. Then he would truly be all alone.

Jayson spotted Devlin's bright orange hat and scarf one last time as he disappeared across the crowded lobby. He was heading toward the doors leading to Ninth Avenue.

*Fuck it*, Jayson thought, *I'm not staying here alone.* There was no Cagney without Lacey. No Robert Wagner without Stefanie Powers. No Karl Malden without Michael Douglas. He darted through the crowd trying catch up with Devlin. If Devlin had some sort of risky business to take care of then Jayson would help him. He would hang just behind, undetected, just in case something went wrong and Devlin needed his help.

Pushing through the battered doors, Jayson rushed out onto Ninth Avenue. Devlin had had a good hundred-yard lead. Jayson looked up and down the mostly empty street. He was about to give up when he spotted Devlin, crossing the street five blocks to the south, his orange-and-green purloined scarf waving in the winter wind. Jayson ran after him, following him for fifteen blocks, sometimes losing sight of him only to spot him again a block later.

When they reached the angled, non-grid streets of the Meatpacking District, Jayson thought he'd lost Devlin for good. Each further block he walked was populated by a different kind of hooker. It was like an archeological dig of vice.

First were the females; then the males; and then females again – or at least seemingly female. Jayson was halfway down the block when he realized that the tall and broad-shouldered women loudly making fun of his stolen camel hair jacket were not women at all. They were cross-dressers, like the one Edith Bunker made friends with on *All in the Family*. Jayson was fairly certain Edith wouldn't have been quite so chummy if she'd seen her friend out walking the Meatpacking District.

Jayson stood on the corner of Gansevoort and the West Side Highway, and pulled his jacket up around him to protect himself against the stiff winter breeze blowing off the Hudson. A constant trickle of shadowy men scuttled back and forth across the West Side Highway, disappearing among the darkened West Side Piers jutting into the Hudson. There was only one street lamp on the far side of the highway – or more correctly, only one street lamp left working. The rest had been broken by hookers and their johns trying to conceal their activities in a cloak of darkness.

Suddenly, under the light, Jayson saw a flutter of color: Orange. Without bothering to look out for the drunken drivers who rushed up and down the West Side Highway at that time of night, Jayson raced across the street. 'Devlin!' he shouted. But he'd already lost sight of him. *'Devlin!'* he called out, running past the street light in the direction he'd seen Devlin's hat and scarf heading. His eyes were having trouble adjusting to the pitch black of the piers. His voice was drowned out by the icy water lapping at the pilings somewhere below him. He didn't even know where the edge was. He was petrified. He stood in the black, listening to the waves, and the grunting sexuality all around him, and the screaming of a drug addict begging someone, anyone, for a fix. Jayson couldn't move. He was completely turned around. In the dark he couldn't even tell where he came from.

A hand clasped his shoulder.

Jayson screamed.

*'Jay Jay? Jayson Blocher?'*

Jayson turned to face the voice.

A lighter flicked to life inches from his face. He flinched, sure he was about to be set afire.

*'Well holy motherfuckin' shit, man.'*

Jayson looked up at the spookily lit face towering a foot and a half above him.

*'Gavin?!'*

# *Sixteen*

**Devlin and Jayson** tried to make themselves comfortable sitting on a pile of scratchy moving company blankets while Gavin heated up water for a packet of hot chocolate. In the dark shadows of the vast loft, lit only by the bulb in what used to be the exit sign, Jayson listened to the rustling all around him. Occasionally, someone sleeping somewhere in the shadows would talk or yelp or call out in his sleep. He had no way of judging how many people were laid out in different places across the dark floor. He had no way of judging if they *were* all people. When Gavin first sat them down on the pile of blankets he called a couch, Jayson felt a squirming underneath him that went away only when he heard the claws of a rat scampering across the wooden floor.

Devlin had heard Jayson's scream when Gavin startled him back at the piers and came running. He found Jayson collapsed in Gavin's arms, heaving, trying to catch his breath from the scare. Between Devlin and Gavin, they were able to calm him down by walking him through the deserted streets toward SoHo, to Gavin's 'loft.'

Jayson was shocked at Gavin's appearance. While he

was pale and gaunt back when he lived in the basement in Oconomowoc, now he looked like he'd died two weeks ago and had already started decomposing – and smelled similarly.

'Just tell me why you were there,' Jayson whispered into Devlin's ear as Gavin kept lighting and dropping matches trying to spark the gas hotplate. On the walk from the piers, Devlin wouldn't answer Jayson's questions. 'Why the hell were you at that place?'

'For the same reason he was, probably,' Devlin whispered back, nodding at Gavin.

'You're a junkie?' After seeing Gavin and his 'home,' Jayson finally understood what Franck had meant when she explained, months ago, that Gavin had to leave Oconomowoc because 'he sometimes needs things he can only get in the city.' He'd seen *The Panic in Needle Park* when he was nine years old when it ran as a late late movie on a UHF channel. So when Gavin ushered him and Devlin into the lobby of the abandoned building filled with squatters, and Jayson spotted half a dozen people huddled around the dim bulb over the entrance with rubber hoses around their forearms, he'd figured out exactly what it was that Gavin 'needed in the city.' Heroin.

'No,' Devlin said. 'I can't believe you just called me an addict.'

'Then what *were* you and Gavin doing there?' Jayson wasn't going to let it drop.

'I just needed money so I could get us a place to stay.'

'You sell drugs?' Jayson asked again.

'No.'

'You have a twenty-four-hour lemonade stand?' Jayson asked, frustrated by Devlin's reticence.

'No. I don't want to tell you.'

'I'm sure I don't want to hear either,' Jayson answered, growing impatient, 'but now that my personal connections have landed us in such luxury accommodations, I think you owe me.'

Gavin returned with some very weak instant hot chocolate in two deli paper cups. Even in the dim light, Jayson could make out lipstick prints on his.

'Christ, you're as dumb as I left you, Jay-Jay,' Gavin sighed, sitting down cross-legged on the floor opposite them. He'd overheard their conversation. 'Your pal Devlin was going to let some old fags suck his dick for some cash.'

Jayson turned to Devlin. Devlin looked away over the shadowy mass of junkies sprawled out across the vast empty space.

'I didn't want you to sleep outside,' Devlin said quietly. 'I didn't want you to blame me.' Devlin wouldn't look directly at Jayson.

Jayson didn't respond. He wasn't sure how to. It wasn't Devlin's fault that he was on the street. It was Toni's. She was the one who'd abandoned him. Devlin didn't owe Jayson anything. If anything, Jayson owed Devlin. If it weren't for Devlin finally introducing him to Harley, Jayson would have been living on the street months ago.

'Why would I blame you?' Jayson asked.

'Because I promised I'd take care of you, and I couldn't.'

'I don't know about that,' Gavin said. 'You probably could've made some good cash out there on the piers. Looks to me like Jay-Jay was the one who messed it all up.'

'Either way,' Jayson said, unexpectedly relieved at the truth, 'we've got a roof over our heads. I think we need to get some sleep.'

'Well lucky for you,' Gavin said, pointing at the grungy pile of blankets they were sitting on, 'the "couch" pulls out into a bed.'

Jayson wasn't sure how long he'd slept. He woke up disoriented in the strange environment, at first thinking he was back in the moldy basement on Lac LaBelle Drive. By the time he remembered where he was, he'd spotted Devlin stepping over the passed out bodies spread out like an archipelago of junkies. The loft was barely lit by a weak gray shaft of sunlight streaming in through the one window that wasn't covered by plywood. Devlin was balancing three steaming paper cups in his hands, and had a paper bag stuffed under his arm.

When he finally made it across the floor, he set down his load on the floor in front of Jayson. He pulled a toasted bialy with butter out of the bag and handed it to Jayson. Bialys were Jayson's favorite New York discovery.

'Where'd you get this?' Jayson asked.

'There's a guy with a cart over on Houston,' Devlin answered.

'And where'd you get the money?' Jayson warily asked.

'I traded my fugitive celebrity autograph for them.'

'It's only worth a couple of bialys?' Jayson joked.

'Where's Gavin?' Devlin asked. 'I got him some real hot chocolate.'

'I don't know. I just woke up,' Jayson replied, still gaining familiarity with his surroundings. He stood up, stretched, and scanned the cavernous loft. The wan sun struggling through the filthy window provided only a little more light than last night, but at least Jayson could make out individual bodies and walls. It all had a distinctly gritty, *Hill Street Blues* feel.

The space was on the top floor of the brick building. He remembered climbing up endless stairs last night. From the pipes and broken pieces of metal hanging off the walls, Jayson deduced that the building had been some sort of factory at one time. What street was it on? He remembered seeing street signs after they'd walked down Sixth Avenue and crossed over on Houston: Thompson Street, West Broadway . . . Wooster. He remembered turning on Wooster. They were on Wooster Street – between Prince and Spring. SoHo. Harley had always warned the chorus boys who were being difficult in one way or another that if they weren't more accommodating, they'd wind up 'squatting with the bohemians in SoHo.' It seemed like every time Jayson watched the local news since arriving in New York another mysterious crime had been committed in SoHo – a strange kidnapping, a drug bust involving a celebrity, a dismembered prostitute.

In its derelict state, SoHo wasn't like Harlem or Brooklyn where the poverty was mitigated by close-knit ethnic families – à la *Welcome Back, Kotter.* SoHo was a place populated by artists and junkies and junkies who called themselves artists. The factories and warehouses that made up the once-thriving neighborhood were abandoned in the 1960s and early '70s. They sat empty until the city's starving artists realized they could jack up electricity from street lamps and use plumber's tape and pipes stolen from other buildings to tap into the city's water supply. With no money down, they could have a neighborhood to call their own. And it was definitely their own. Not many people came to visit the decrepit wasteland below Houston, filled with eccentric, drug-addicted artists.

Scattered around the loft were dozens of piles of upended office filing cabinets. The wall to Jayson's left was stacked to the 18-foot ceiling with metal desks. Jayson deduced that the building must at one time have been home to an office furniture factory. Or warehouse. The only thing even slightly domesticated about the space was the tableau of thousands of Polaroid portraits that Gavin had pinned up on one wall.

'Maybe he went out,' Devlin said, referring to Gavin.

'Oh but why?' Jayson said dramatically, 'when he has all this?' He made a sweeping gesture over the junkies and piles of office furniture.

'It's more than we have,' Devlin smiled. 'Unless we decide to call it home.'

'Do we have a choice?' Jayson asked.

'There's always the piers.'

'Let's start decorating then,' Jayson replied, biting into the warm bialy. 'I'm thinking Industrial Chic.'

Jayson spent the first few days at the loft trying to gain access to his commercial money. But he was unable to reach anyone at the advertising agency which had created the Bon Appetite campaign, or at Cadbury headquarters. The only live person he was able to reach during the holiday week was a woman in accounts payable at the production company in L.A. who had produced the spots. She explained, after trying to comprehend the long complicated story that Jayson spun for her, that according to their records, the talent contract was signed by his legal guardian: 'Oscar C. Harlande.' The checks had been made out to Harlande. And all the future residual checks would be made out to him as well. If Jayson had a problem with that, he had to call his agent or business manager.

'But he *is* my agent and business manager. And he's missing,' Jayson tried to explain for the third time. 'He got caught running a whorehouse for Broadway chorus boys by a reporter researching whatever happened to my boyfriend who was the guy who use to say "*It wuzzzzn't me!*" on *Disorder in the Court.*'

There was silence for a moment on the other end of the phone line.

'Take a little tip from me and Nancy Reagan,' the accounts payable woman said finally. 'Just say "no" from now on, 'kay, hon?'

Jayson had no access to his money. Devlin finally convinced Jayson to give up the quest. 'They'll find Harley soon enough,' he said. 'And we'll get this all settled. We'll get your money back and my name cleared. Promise.'

Because of Devlin's fugitive status he had to disguise himself in a heavy scarf and hat each day. It was impossible for him to get any sort of job. He would have had to give his social security number and real name on the application anyway, which wasn't an option. Jayson, still being fifteen, was ineligible for a legitimate job as well, so the two spent their days trying to trade in on Devlin's fame – and now notoriety – with street food vendors in exchange for whatever extra food they had leftover at the end of the day.

New Year's Eve was the toughest day so far. None of the vendors were on the street. Jayson and Devlin were starving by the time the sun began to set. All the traffic on the streets was heading uptown – mostly bridge and tunnel traffic on their way to spend the next six hours trying to find a parking spot near enough to Times Square to catch a glimpse of the ball dropping.

'Let's head uptown,' Devlin suggested, his voice muffled through his ever-present scarf.

'Ugh. I'm so tired. And my stomach is starting to bloat like those kids in the Sally Struthers commercials.' Jayson protested. 'I can't deal with all those happy people,'

'I'm happy,' Devlin said.

'You are not.'

'I really am,' Devlin repeated. 'I'm happy that I have a place to sleep and someone to share it with.'

'Christ. Did I just wake up on a *Waltons* rerun?'

'Suit yourself,' Devlin said. 'But I'm going to watch the ball drop. I'm sure there'll be tons of people who brought snacks who would be thrilled to meet a fugitive teen idol has-been.'

As always, Devlin had a point. And since all his points lately had been of a life-sustaining variety, Jayson trudged along behind him as they made their way up Broadway toward Times Square.

Devlin's hunch proved correct once again. Having avoided the newspapers, Devlin and Jayson had no idea that Devlin's story had gotten so big. Nearly every tourist Devlin approached recognized him once he revealed his face. They gladly exchanged a few chips, or a pretzel, or a thermos cup full of hot chocolate spiked with brandy to be able to go home and say that they'd met the child star fugitive.

By the time midnight was drawing near, Devlin was surrounded by a new fan club that was more than happy to share whatever they'd brought with them with both Devlin and Jayson, including Champagne. A lot of Champagne. Good Champagne. Cheap Champagne. Spilled Champagne.

'I think I'm happy now too,' Jayson slurred to Devlin just as the massive crowd began chanting the ten-second countdown to 1983.

'I kinda thought you would be,' Devlin said as the crowd reached 'one.' Devlin leaned in to kiss Jayson, but Jayson pushed him away softly.

'Not here,' he said, rolling his eyes side to side to point out the crowd around them – Devlin's fans.

'Who cares?' Devlin said. 'They already think I'm a gay hooker. And they're half right.'

'I just don't think it's a good idea,' Jayson said. To be perfectly honest, Jayson was just as worried about his own reputation as he was about Devlin's. Two of the people in Devlin's impromptu fan club had recognized him as 'the Picky Prince.' When Jayson first came out to his mother so many years ago he had no idea that he had any reason to be ashamed. But years of tragic TV movies, salacious talk shows, sensationalistic tabloids, and even his own experience with Trey taught him that being publicly gay was not a good idea.

'Well, okay,' Devlin said. 'But just remember that I was named "most kissable boy" by *Tiger Beat* three years in a row.'

'Remember?!' Jayson asked, 'I went to every magazine store in town to rip out ballots and send them in.'

'With my name on them, I hope,'

'I did have to throw in a few for Robby Benson. Sorry.'

The Champagne on a mostly empty stomach hit Jayson harder than he could have anticipated. Lacking cab or subway fare, the pair had to walk all the way back downtown to the loft. By the time they turned the corner onto Wooster Street, Jayson was so tired and drunk that he could barely stay upright.

'You're a terrible drinker,' Devlin said.

'Actually, I think I'm getting quite good at it.'

When they climbed up the stoop to their abandoned furniture warehouse home, Jayson immediately sensed that something was wrong. Or more accurately, that something was *right*. The entryway and stoop had been swept clear of the used syringes and empty Carnation Instant Breakfast cans that were the junkies' primary sustenance. Someone had wired up an old plastic 'Tiffany' shaded light fixture that looked like it had come from a 1971 singles bar. Even the five flights of stairs up to the loft had been swept clean and lit with whatever junk light fixtures someone had scavenged. It was almost cheery.

'Wow,' Devlin said as they passed the fourth floor that was lit with strings of probably stolen Christmas lights. 'Looks like some junkie made one hell of a New Year's resolution.'

The random beauty of the 'remodeling' triggered something in Jayson's memory, but the clouds of Champagne rolling through his exhausted mind kept him from being able to pin down exactly what. There were only two things he was concentrating on at the moment: peeing in the coffee can they used as a urinal, and scrounging around for any leftover scraps of food to soak up the Champagne in his stomach.

When they reached the landing for their floor, the heavy metal sliding industrial door was open and a large box fan was blowing the stale, contaminated stench out of the loft in a meager effort at ventilation. Bright light streamed out from the normally shadowy loft.

Devlin and Jayson stepped over the fan and into a puddle of light. The light was shining down from a Smurfette plastic table lamp that had been crudely nailed to the beam above the door.

Jayson had the same lamp in his bedroom in Oconomowoc.

And he suddenly remembered that the plastic 'Tiffany' chandelier in the stairwell was the exact same kind that used to hang over the makeshift basement bar in his old basement.

It was too confusing for his blurry, drunk mind. Maybe Gavin had stolen the lamps when he left? He couldn't remember.

The entire front area of the loft had been meticulously cleaned up and organized. The upended filing cabinets had been tipped upright to form dividing walls in the space. Other 'rooms' appeared to branch off a filing cabinet 'hallway' that led toward the back of the loft. There seemed to be a lot of activity coming from various rooms behind the 'walls' – sounds of brooms sweeping, the clanging of a wrench on a pipe, a radio tuned to a New Wave station. There was a TV blaring on the floor on the far side of the new 'living room' area. A heavy-set man and a blonde woman were sitting in front of it with their backs to Jayson and Devlin. Again, it wasn't just *any* TV, but a Hitachi black-and-white portable TV – exactly the same model that used to be in his bedroom. . . .

Willie turned around first, and upon spotting Jayson, tried to tuck the candy bar he was eating under his thigh, crushing it. He didn't want to be caught.

Tara turned around next.

'Breakfast. Lunch. Dinner,' Willie said. 'Three meals a day makes me a winner!'

'Hey there, Pickled Prince,' Tara shouted next before turning back toward the television. 'Nice dump you got here.'

Then, from beyond one of the file cabinet walls, 'Butter Bean! Is that you?!'

Jayson simultaneously peed down his leg and vomited down his shirt as he passed out in Champagne-soaked shock.

# *Seventeen*

**For breakfast** the following morning, Toni laid out a spread of Chinese food of dubious origin on a card table that had been in their Oconomowoc attic.

When Jayson woke up, Tara, Gavin, Willie, Toni, and Devlin were already sitting down on the ancient dusty office chairs that Toni had pulled from various corners of the loft. Someone had undressed him and put him in his old Cub Scout sleeping bag. Was this a dream? He tried to will himself back to sleep, but Devlin had already caught him staring at them.

'Morning, Butter Bean,' Devlin said.

'I leave you alone for four months and you turn into a falling down drunk,' Toni teased.

Tara simply rolled her eyes at him and went back to picking out the egg bits from her pork fried rice.

Jayson struggled out of the sleeping bag, and stood up in his underwear in the middle of the loft.

'Where the hell is everyone else?' Jayson asked. The big space was eerily quiet, except for a radio playing somewhere back in the maze of filing cabinet rooms. 'And what the fuck are you all doing here?'

Gavin chimed in first.

'Ease up, Jay-Jay. You were such a mess when you got here that I called Franck to see if she could reach your mother. I didn't know she was going to pack up and move out here.'

'Lucky for all of you that I did,' Toni responded. 'Take a look around this place – I did all this in one day.'

'*We* did all this in one day,' Gavin corrected. 'You just stood and bitched at everyone.'

'Well, someone obviously had to,' Toni said. 'I've never seen a sorrier group of junkies.'

'Squatters generally aren't known for their meticulous work habits,' Gavin said, stabbing at a piece of General Tso's chicken.

'You got all this done with the junkies?' Jayson asked. 'Where are they all?'

'Well the ones that could help, helped,' Toni answered. 'You probably didn't realize this but you were living alongside two master plumbers, an electrician, and a contractor who happened to find themselves a little down on their luck. They're now going to live on the third floor.'

'And the others?' Jayson asked.

'Well, many of the others found my presence a little unnerving,' Toni answered.

'She tried to set them on fire with her blowtorch,' Gavin clarified.

'You just packed up all our shit and drove out here?' Jayson asked. There were just too many questions to sort through.

'And mine,' Tara said, matter-of-factly. 'I got thrown out.'

'You didn't get thrown out,' Toni corrected. 'Your mother just needed a break.'

'Hence her breakdown,' Tara added. 'First Trey ran away . . .'

*'Trey din't! Trey din't run away!'* Willie interrupted, spraying a mouthful of sweet and sour pork.

'Shhh, Willie Prader,' Toni patted Willie on his thick thigh. 'We know. We know. It's okay.'

'And then,' Tara continued, 'it was my turn to piss off Baby Jesus.'

'What did you do this time?' Jayson asked.

'I had a little indiscretion,' she said patting her stomach.

'Christ *Almighty*,' Jayson said. *'You're pregnant?!'* If this were a primetime soap opera, someone would walk in the door and mow them all down in a hail of bullets – not, Jayson considered, that that would be entirely unwelcome.

*'We're* pregnant,' Gavin said, putting his arm around Tara.

Jayson looked at Gavin, then Tara, and then Gavin again. Then Devlin.

'I got the whole story last night,' Devlin said, 'the night of your Homecoming Incident, Gavin and Tara hooked up down in your basement.'

Jayson shuddered at the idea of Devlin getting chummy with his family. And at the idea of Gavin sleeping with Tara.

'Then I freaked out and ran off,' Gavin finished. 'I didn't realize I'd left someone behind.' Gavin swallowed another mouthful of Chinese food, and stood up. 'Okay everyone . . . time for my first clinic appointment.'

'Good luck,' Toni said. 'Maybe they'll give you a sucker.'

After Gavin left, Toni explained that one of the concessions Toni had wrought while wielding her blowtorch was a promise from Gavin to get on methadone. It would 'make him a better father.'

'And where's Franck?' Jayson asked as he stood marveling at the sink someone had installed in the new kitchen-like area.

'In Waukesha,' Toni answered. 'She's fulfilling her lifelong dream of becoming a cop.'

'That fits,' Jayson said, thinking of her constant rule-making and propensity to settle problems with her fists. 'So you're splitsville?'

'Guess so. As much as any lesbians ever are,' Toni answered. 'You gay boys have a much better attitude toward hooking up.' Toni nudged Devlin. 'I like your boyfriend. He's the kind you'd want to take home to your mother − if your mother hadn't brought your home to you.'

Seeing his mother so friendly with Devlin infuriated Jayson. Why didn't anyone acknowledge how incredibly crazy this all was?

He exploded. The sudden outburst even surprised himself.

'What the fuck are you all doing here?! I don't need your help. You put me on a plane to a whorehouse, which, if *that* wasn't bad enough, got shut down – and I was thrown out on the street. I found this place on my own. It's *mine*. Mine and Devlin's and Gavin's.' Jayson's jaw was clenched so tight he worried he might crack a tooth. 'I don't want your help. I don't need your help. I don't need *you*!'

The loft filled with silence after his tirade.

'Well, Butter Bean,' Toni said, calmly standing up and scraping everyone's leftovers onto one plate, 'Did you ever think that maybe, just maybe . . . we needed *you*?'

Devlin stood up.

'Put on some jeans and let's go for a walk,' he instructed Jayson.

It was frigid out on the street. *On the street . . . on the street . . . why do I spend nearly all my time out on the damn street?* Jayson thought.

'What's your problem with them?' Devlin asked when they reached the corner of Wooster and Spring.

'You can't see it?' Jayson asked. 'They're freaks!'

'They've been nice to me.'

'Of course they have,' Jayson sighed, exasperated. 'They need fresh blood to survive.'

'Your mother cleaned up the loft, brought you a sleeping bag, and bought breakfast for us. I don't see what's so horrible about that.'

'You'll find out soon enough.'

'She said that she'd always wanted to move to New York to pursue her art,' Devlin said.

'Her *art*?' Jayson said incredulously. 'Have you *seen* her art?'

'Can't be any worse than the rest of the stuff in the galleries around here.'

'I just don't understand,' Jayson said sitting on the stoop of another abandoned heroin shooting gallery and pulling Devlin down next to him. 'I was getting somewhere. I had the commercials. I was getting famous. People recognized me. And now it's all going backward – at top speed.'

'I think you're confusing "getting somewhere" with "getting famous,"' Devlin said. 'And I think I'm all the proof you need that those two things aren't mutually inclusive.'

It bothered Jayson when Devlin was so self-deprecating. The idea that celebrity didn't mean anything to Devlin was number one on Jayson's 'turn off' list.

They were interrupted by an outburst of screaming expletives coming from down the street, in the vicinity of their building.

Squinting, Jayson could just barely make out a group of three shouting junkies, running down Wooster, trying to get away from a madwoman wielding a blowtorch.

'Just give it a little while,' Devin said. 'It's not like we can't use the help.'

'You'll regret saying that,' Jayson replied. 'This might be new to you, but to me, this episode is a rerun.'

# Eighteen

By the end of January, Jayson's life was back to a dismal 'normal.'

Toni had enrolled both him and Tara in P.S. 144, which was filled with a mix of Asian, Puerto Rican, and black students. Jayson's brief flirtation with celebrity came back to haunt him on the second day of school when a girl in his homeroom recognized him from the Bon Appetite commercials. He was christened with his new nickname, 'The Dicky Princess.'

He was fairly immune to the taunting, and at least he had Tara to look out for him. While her blonde hair and Nordic features were the norm in Oconomowoc, they were exotic to the ethnically diverse boys at P.S. 144. She quickly cultivated a fan club of upperclassmen. No one noticed her pregnancy. Being only four months pregnant, as well as naturally petite, she was able to hide her swelling stomach under the collection of heavy black sweaters that she favored.

That left Toni, Devlin, and Willie to hang around the loft together almost all day and night. Toni and Devlin grew so close that she began calling him 'the grateful son I never had.'

After rehabbing the loft space as much as she could, Toni used whatever leftover scrap metal and wood there was for her art. She was presently completing a sixteen-foot-tall scrap-metal wedding dress that had nails welded to it with the points facing outward. It looked like a medieval torture device. She planned on shipping it to Charles and Diana in honor of their recent royal nuptials. She had a bad feeling about their future together.

Devlin spent most of his free time cooking. Unable to attend formal classes due to his fugitive status, he made a commitment to studying the craft at home. Since they had almost no money, Devlin had to be very creative with whatever scraps his loftmates could forage. Gavin, Jayson, Tara, and Toni began a routine of stopping at every grocery store or deli that they passed to duck inside to steal at least one food item – whatever caught their eye. It was then up to Devlin to make some sort of edible sense out of the selection of sundries lined up on the counter each afternoon. Sometimes the results were inedible, such as coconut fried chicken livers, but more often than not they were amazingly palatable, like this evening's pickle-brined lamb shank braised in V8 juice.

'Don't forget your vitamins,' Jayson reminded Tara, as he did at every meal. Without any money for prenatal doctor's appointments, they were putting all their faith for a healthy baby in handfuls of children's vitamins.

Tara balked. 'I can't chew anymore of those things,' she said. 'They're disgusting.'

'Come on,' Gavin urged. 'I promised methadone, you promised Flintstones.'

'If I chew one more of those fuckers, I'm going to squeeze out Betty fucking Rubble,' Tara muttered.

As always, Tara finally gave in, chewing one of each member of the Bedrock community. No one in the loft knew if there was any difference in nutrition between the different vitamin characters, so it was resolved that Tara should chew one of each color at every meal.

When Tara first came to Toni back in Oconomowoc and explained that she was nearly certain about being pregnant with Gavin's baby, Tara pleaded for help to get an abortion. Toni who usually could make Gloria Steinem seem like Phyllis Schafly, disagreed with Tara's pro-choice choice. It was another remnant of her Catholic upbringing.

Toni's argument against having the procedure, while perhaps illogical, was authentically Toni: 'What the hell better do you have to do than create a life?' she asked Tara. When it was put that way, Tara couldn't come up with a counterargument. In fact, she found herself in complete agreement with the flawed reasoning. 'What the hell else *did* she have to do?' she explained later that evening to her mother and father.

Terri, predictably, flew into a rage. She blamed everything on Toni since Toni had been an unmarried teen mother herself. Because abortion went against every one of Terri's religious convictions, she took to praying – out loud and in Tara's presence – for a miscarriage.

Tara marched straight back over to the Blochers' house and began camping out on the same foldout sofa where she'd been impregnated. While Tom Wernermeier was concerned about his daughter, he also had his hands full with his wife. The combination of Trey's disappearance and Tara's pregnancy tipped Terri into full-blown religious delusions. She soon became convinced that Jesus lived in her kitchen appliances, and that the devil spoke to her through the electric organ in the living room. Terri sat by herself, every afternoon, listening to the organ's pre-programmed rumba beat.

Tom was heartbroken when Tara announced that she was going to New York with Toni, but was in no position to argue. Terri wouldn't even step out to the driveway to wave goodbye to her daughter.

'Blech,' Tara gagged, washing down a grape Bam-Bam with the last swallow of her watered-down Capri Sun. 'I deserve a joint. Anyone care to join me on the veranda?'

Tara had nicknamed the roof of the warehouse building 'the veranda,' and it was a rare evening that she went to bed without getting stoned. Her many admirers at school kept her amply supplied with pot.

'Fine, let's go,' Jayson agreed. He, Devlin, and Tara pulled on random layers of the sweaters and jackets that littered the loft. They knew better than to ask Gavin. He was nearly three weeks 'clean.'

'Me too!' Willie asked, bending over and trying to pull

on an old 'Billy Beer' sweatshirt Toni had found behind the building.

'Not tonight, pal,' Jayson said. 'Stay here and help mom clean up.'

The trio climbed the rusty fire escape. Jayson had never been afraid of heights but the rickety fire escape attached to the abandoned warehouse always seemed like it could give at any moment.

When they reached the roof, the three continued climbing up the narrow steel ladder mounted to the side of the water tower. There was a slim beam on which the wooden tower rested. They'd discovered that the three of them could just fit on the beam, dangling their legs over into the open air and leaning back against the wood soaked with years of tar.

Tara took a joint out of the front pocket on her black jumper.

'Lighter,' Tara demanded, as dispassionately but urgently as an operating surgeon. Devlin always had a lighter on him. As the loft's cook, he was the one who lit the burners and oven on the abandoned stove they'd rigged up to the building's gas line.

'C'mon, I'm fucking tense tonight,' Tara said. 'Hand it over. Trey.'

Jayson and Devlin registered her slip first.

*Trey.*

The name hung there in between them while Tara lit her

joint. It didn't seem like she noticed her mistake. Trey's disappearance was a topic avoided in the loft. If someone merely mentioned the words 'run away,' Willie would flip out. '*Trey din't Trey din't run 'way!!*'

Tara inhaled from the joint deeply, held the smoke in for a seemingly biologically impossible time, and exhaled with a slight cough. Her breath crystallized in the frigid late January air. She held the joint out for Jayson.

Trey's name still hovered over the group like the puff of smoke from Tara's lungs.

'*Okay. So I said his name,*' Tara finally acknowledged, breaking the silence. 'Boogeyman! Boogeyman! Boogeyman!' she yelled, waving her hands in Devlin's face. 'See,' she continued looking out over the skyline, 'nothing happens.'

A plane flew overhead, directly up the center of Manhattan. The red lights on the tips of its wings looked liked they would barely clear the Empire State Building.

'Why, I bet ole Trey's getting raped by some sicko perv *as we speak*,' she continued.

'Christ, Tara!' Jayson gulped, coughing out the smoke he'd just inhaled. 'That's sick. He just ran away!'

'That's what *you* say,' she said flatly. 'That's what you *all* say. But it's not true.'

'What do you mean?' Devlin asked, surprised to hear Tara finally talking openly about her brother. Trey was rarely discussed, even more rarely by Tara.

'I had dreams about him when he first disappeared,' Tara said. 'Bad dreams. No one would listen to me, but he didn't run away. I can just *tell*.'

'Come on,' Jayson said, hoping she'd change the subject. Jayson still harbored some guilt over the events that led to Trey's running off. 'You've been watching too much *In Search Of. . . .*'

'Trey and you were twins, right?' Devlin asked.

'*Are* twins,' she corrected. 'I mean, unless you think he's dead.'

'No, no . . .' Devlin quickly clarified.

'I mean what would you call one half of twins anyway?' Tara asked.

'A "twin"?' Devlin offered.

'Makes no sense,' she countered, waving smoke out of her face. 'A twin of what? Nah. It's gotta be a matching set or it doesn't exist at all.' She swung her legs contemplatively. 'It makes no sense.'

'Like your dreams,' Jayson said.

'I don't know,' Devlin countered. 'Twins are supposed to have a weird bond. Maybe Trey's sending her a message.'

'You too?' Jayson asked Devlin. 'Maybe we should call *That's Incredible*.'

'I don't know,' Tara said, uncharacteristically serious. 'Devlin might be on to something.'

'I think you're both wackos,' Jayson said. 'Trey ran away because he didn't want to go to Bible school. Period.'

'He wouldn't do that to me,' Tara said. 'He wouldn't do it to you either,' she added, looking at Jayson.

'Of course he would,' Jayson said. 'I was the whole reason he had to go.'

'Yeah,' Tara chuckled. 'But he still wouldn't have disappeared without giving us some clue – he loved you too, queerboy. Just not how you wanted him to.'

Jayson flushed. He didn't want to talk about Trey that way in front of Devlin. It all seemed so childish now – his unrequited crush. But somewhere deep inside he knew Tara was probably right. Trey would have told Jayson and Tara where he was going. Or at least give them some sort of hint. But unlike Tara, Jayson didn't like to think about what might have happened. It was easier to believe that Trey had run away. There was a motive, and evidence.

'So I'm not your first love?' Devlin asked. 'I'm crushed,' he joked.

'You'll get over it,' Jayson said. 'You're a much better kisser anyway.'

198

# Nineteen

'**And where were you** last night?' Jayson asked as his mother slid open the heavy fire door to the loft. She was out of breath after climbing the five flights of stairs to the apartment.

Jayson was feeding Willie his breakfast of leftover broiled ham hocks in apricot jelly sauce while trying to pull together a clean outfit for school. Neither Tara nor Devlin was up yet.

'I had a date,' Toni answered, collapsing into one of the vinyl chairs with decorative daisies that used to sit around their kitchen table in Oconomowoc.

'Who's the unlucky woman?' Jayson asked.

'Sal Castellari,' Toni said.

'That's an awfully butch name,' Jayson said, reaching out to stop Willie from eating the gobs of pig fat on his plate. 'Can't you bring me home a more femme second mommy?'

'Sal is a *he*,' Toni clarified.

'You're going back to men?' Jayson asked.

'I suppose,' Toni sighed. 'They're just so damn persistent.'

'Sexuality is not a choice,' Jayson said, echoing a line he'd read on a T-shirt in the West Village.

'Everything's a choice, Butter Bean. Even "all of the above."'

'So how'd you meet this sucker?' Jayson said, packing up his backpack.

'On the street. He was down here looking for a space for a new gallery. He's an art dealer.'

'Please say you didn't show him your "art,"' Jayson said. 'If he's got any money I'd like him to stick around for a bit.'

'As a matter of fact,' Toni said, 'I did bring him up here yesterday while you were at school. He called my pieces "An important look at positing Foucauldian ideas as an apotheosis of post-structuralist binaries."'

'And you took that as a compliment?' Jayson finished tying his shoes and yanked open the door that Toni had just shut. He had no interest in sticking around to hear anymore about his mother's latest conquest.

Jayson took the long way to school. He'd worked so hard at being invisible to his classmates that no one usually noticed if he didn't make it to class until mid-morning. His notoriety as the 'Dicky Princess' wore off fairly quickly, since the ad campaign stopped running after the holidays. He was slipping back into the old, familiar role of 'nobody,' and as frustrating as it was, he was at least growing numb to it now.

Jayson arrived at school in the middle of third period. Rather than interrupt the class, he opted to wait on the back steps until the bell rang signaling a new period. He sat watching a group of kids hanging out at the far side of the basketball court. They were joking with each other and passing a joint around. To Jayson, they looked like alien beings. He'd never be able to simply walk over and hang out with regular civilians. He was just different. He didn't fit in a small town. He didn't fit in a big city. The only place he really fit was in front of an audience.

His moment of zen self-pity was interrupted by the electronic tone that signaled an upcoming PA announcement. He could barely hear the static-y, muffled voice through the doors behind him.

'Jayson Blocher to the main office. Blocher to the main office.'

Fuck. Was he finally going to get in trouble for his chronic tardiness? He wasn't sure he could handle being chastised. He looked across the drab playground and considered getting up and walking away for good. But the thought of trying to explain dropping out to Toni was more onerous than simply sitting and listening to someone lecture him on the importance of timeliness.

He dragged himself inside and across the school to the main office. He walked up to the counter and announced his presence to the receptionist. She didn't look up. Just pointed the pencil with which she was doing a crossword puzzle toward the principal's door. Jayson walked behind the front desk and made his was over to the heavy wooden door with ancient gold letters that had been peeled off and rearranged from PRINCIPAL to CRAP LIP.

Inside, Jayson took the seat opposite the desk and waited for the principal to finish up a phone call about his wife's car repair. When he finally hung up, Mr. Frommer, a weary, middle-aged man with a pot belly and age spots covering his bald head, ruffled through a stack of papers before finally looking up and realizing that someone was in his office.

'You need something?' Frommer asked.

Jayson briefly considered letting loose with a litany of frustrated desires.

'You called for me. Jayson Blocher.'

'Right, right.' Frommer leafed through the stack of papers again, looking for something specific. 'You were in some candy commercial, right?'

'Bon Appetite,' Jayson answered.

'What?'

'Bon Appetite,'

'I don't get it.'

'Bon Appetite,' Jayson repeated for the third time, exactly as the script had four months ago. *'The treat for the elite.'*

'Oh right. You were some king or something.'

'Sure. Right.' Jayson couldn't imagine where this was going. Did he want an autograph for his kid or something?

'I've got something for you. A message.' Frommer picked up another stack of the papers that littered his desk. 'Ah. Here it is. Some company out in L.A. called every school in New York looking for you.' He handed the phone message slip to Jayson. The scrawled handwriting read: 2/3/82, Kidz

Kasting, Los Angeles, 'Picky Prince,' commercial, Jason Blocher. URGENT.

That was all that was written. The message itself was a week old. Jayson could feel his pulse quicken in his fingertips as he held the yellow slip of paper.

'What's this about?' Jayson asked Frommer.

'Beats me. I don't answer the phones around here.'

'Can I use your phone?' Jayson asked, his voice starting to shake.

'These phones don't call long distance.'

'But this says "urgent."'

'Take it up with the taxpayers, kid.'

Jayson stood up and turned to walk out the door. It was all he could do to keep from breaking into a sprint. He walked quickly back through the front office, down the hallway to the front door, and down the front steps. It wasn't until he hit the sidewalk that he couldn't hold back any more. He ran full-speed down Houston toward the loft, jumping over the homeless people and junkies who littered the streets of SoHo even during daylight hours.

When he burst into the loft, Toni, Devlin, Willie, and a junkie who used to work for the NYC sewage department were working on rigging up a makeshift shower.

'What are you doing home?' Toni asked him, wiping a blob of caulk off her forehead.

'Gimme a quarter. A bunch of quarters, Dimes. Nickels. Whatever . . .' Jayson said between gasping breaths.

'Slow down, Butter Bean, what's going on?'

'I need some money for a phone call.' He bent over with his hands on his knees trying to catch his breath. 'To L.A. Someone needs to talk to me.' He handed over the yellow slip to Devlin.

'I know these guys,' Devlin said reading the cryptic message from Kidz Kasting. 'They're big.'

'Quarters! I need quarters!' Jayson pleaded.

'I don't get it. What's going on?' Toni asked again, taking the slip and reading it over.

'Sounds like a casting company is trying to reach Jayson,' Devlin explained.

'Is that good?' Toni asked. The only phone messages Toni ever got had been from overdrawn banks and collection agencies.

'I don't know,' Devlin said. 'Let's go find out.'

Toni, Devlin, Willie, and Jayson launched a scavenger hunt around the entire loft space for stray coins to use in the payphone outside on Wooster Street. When they'd collected $5.78 from various crevices, pockets, and befuddled junkies, they climbed down the five flights of stairs and gathered around the battered, graffiti-covered pay phone.

*Please God let it work today*, Jayson thought of the often broken phone. It was just after noon, so the office in L.A. would have just opened. He grabbed the phone and started force feeding coins into the phone's slot.

'Hang on, Picky,' Devlin said, gently taking the receiver out of Jayson's tight grip.

'What are you doing?!' Jayson asked.

'You shouldn't call yourself. They're expecting you to have an agent.'

Jayson realized that they'd probably been unsuccessfully calling Harley's old phone number before launching their search of area schools. *Harley.* Just the thought of him on the run somewhere with his money enraged Jayson.

'I don't *have* an agent,' Jayson said, reaching for the phone back.

'Now you do,' Devlin said, starting to dial.

It seemed like hours to Jayson as they all stood around in the frigid February air watching Devlin listening to a phone ringing somewhere across the country.

'Uh, hello,' Devlin finally said. 'I'm returning your call on behalf of Jayson Blocher. I'm his representation, William Devlinson.'

Jayson rolled his eyes.

Devlin's part in the conversation consisted mainly of 'yes's and 'I'll check with Jayson's and 'Can you give me more detail?'s. It only lasted for three minutes or so before Devlin ended with: 'A number? I can be reached, at, um, ah . . .'

They hadn't thought this completely through. Of *course* they needed a phone number to reach him. *Fuck,* thought Jayson. *Fuck Fuck Fuck.*

'You can reach my office at . . .' Devlin read the barely

legible phone number that was printed on the pay phone '212-785-8375 . . . Thank you very much . . . Goodbye.'

'What's going on? What did they want?' Jayson felt faint with anticipation.

Devlin smiled at him with his patented dimple.

'We'll have to steal a suitcase from somewhere,' Devlin grinned. 'It'll look funny for you to arrive in Hollywood with a trash bag.'

# Twenty

**Jayson's life suddenly seemed** to be moving simultaneously in fast and slow motion – like on *Six Million Dollar Man* when they counterintuitively illustrated Lee Majors's supersonic running speed by slowing down the film. Jayson was to be flown to L.A. in just over a week for pilot season – more specifically, to appear in a sitcom pilot entitled *Lights Out!* for CBS.

During subsequent calls with L.A., 'William Devlinson' got more information on how Jayson had gotten the part. Kidz Kasting had been given the casting bid for the show with the lead role already set. The series had been conceived as a vehicle for Helen Lawson, the aging film star turned game show regular turned variety show guest turned *Love Boat* comic relief character. She was one of Jayson's favorite celebrities. The show called on Helen to play against type. She was best known for her legendary bawdy ripostes, but in *Lights Out!* she would be cast as an Amish spinster who finds her teenage nephew from New York City on her Pennsylvania doorstep one morning. The premise's backstory was that the nephew's rich parents had died in a yachting accident, and Helen Lawson's spinster character was his next of kin.

Devlin learned that Helen Lawson had been sent the pilot script over the holidays. Coincidentally, she'd been captivated by Jayson's comedic timing in the Bon Appetite commercials which were running at that time during her soaps. She decided that the role of the world-weary, fish-out-of-water, spoiled teenager could be played by none other than 'the Picky Prince.' Without Helen, the show had no traction at the network, and without Jayson there would 'be no Helen "La" Lawson,' she told the director – calling herself by her favorite nickname. So the casting agent was ordered to find 'the Picky Prince.'

The agent first tracked down an executive at Cadbury who tracked down the ad agency producer who tracked down Jayson's name and old address at Harley's – which had obviously been a dead end.

At Helen's stubborn insistence, the casting director grew desperate enough to call every school in Manhattan.

Ever since that first call to L.A., Jayson had kept the front loft window nearest to the street open in order to hear the pay-phone when it rang. The show's production office called six more times during the week, and each time 'William Devlin-son,' Jayson's official new agent, bolted down the warehouse stairway, generally reaching the phone on the seventh ring. For the first time Jayson was glad Devlin was a fugitive – at least he couldn't go out anywhere and miss an important call.

Most of the calls from L.A. regarded random business questions: Jayson's social security number, his new address, if he preferred to leave on the 1:45 or 2:55 flight to L.A. – first class of course. Even though Jayson wasn't part of the union yet, Devlin was savvy enough from his own experiences to negotiate for every perk possible.

Jayson lay awake, unable to sleep for the eighth night in a row.

'Can we close the window yet?' Devlin asked sleepily. 'You leave tomorrow. They're not going to call you at two a.m. the day before you leave.' He nodded his head toward the window, open to the February night. 'It's actually snowing *inside* now.'

As on every night of the previous week, Devlin and Jayson were sleeplessly curled up together, watching TV on the futon Toni had foraged from the street somewhere in Chinatown. It smelled not so faintly of cabbage and seafood, but it was far more comfortable than the wooden floor.

'Uh, *no*,' Jayson said. 'What if my flight changes? What if they need to give me limo information? What if Helen Lawson is in the middle of a drunken binge and just wants to chat with her new costar?'

Helen Lawson's drinking was legendary. One of the most memorable stories was about an incident that occurred during an appearance at the Dean Martin roast for Lucille Ball. Having lost her notes somewhere while stumbling to the podium, Helen pulled the cigar from Milton Berle's mouth, lifted up her skirt, and inserted it into her panty-less vagina. She then informed the audience, 'This is only the second Cuban I've had inside me – but it's the first one that isn't married to a redhead.'

Devlin confirmed that many of the rumors were well founded. Helen Lawson once did a six-episode stint on *Disorder in the Court* playing the judge's sister. As usual, she was hilarious, and as usual, she stopped showing up for work just as it began looking like she might be added as a regular cast member. 'I've made a career out of career suicide,' she explained to Devlin.

Jayson folded himself across Devlin's lap on the grimy futon as Devlin flipped through TV stations. Their options were limited to three snowy VHS stations and one blizzardy high-on-the-dial UHF channel. On about the fourteenth rotation through the four stations, a familiar theme song sprang though the static on channel 55. Devlin hurriedly clicked past.

'No leave it,' Jayson begged, sleepily.

'I don't think so.'

'C'mon. I'm the star in the house now. What I say goes.'

Devlin threw his head back and groaned.

'*You can tell it to the judge,*' Jayson began softly singing along with the theme song. '*You can tell it to the jury. But when it's time to grow up, there's no need to worry. All for one and one for all, no time to sort. We're sentenced to love . . . and the mercy of the court!*'

Devlin buried his face in the futon pillows when the twelve-year-old version of himself on the television entered the show's living room set to a riotous round of studio applause.

'Oooo, it's one of my favorite episodes,' Jayson said. 'It's the one that ends with the judge having a heart attack.'

'He was having a contract dispute with the producers. They wanted to scare him into thinking the show could go on without him. He was a real dick.'

'Really? God. You ruin everything.' Jayson laid his head down in Devlin's lap.

'You nervous about the shoot?' Devlin asked.

'No. Should I be?'

'If you're not, you're not.' Devlin shrugged.

Jayson closed his eyes and listened to the television. This episode had each of the foster kids getting into more and more mischievous trouble, with seemingly hilarious consequences, but by the end the judge was so overwhelmed that he clutched his chest and dropped to the floor. Jayson remembered the swelling cello music that swelled at the cliffhanger ending. He remembered being taken completely by surprise, sitting in the Wernermeiers' basement with Trey and Tara, expecting the episode to wrap up with the usual shrug and '*It wuuuuzzzzzn't me!*' from Devlin's character. Instead, he was thrown into a several week-long funk waiting to see if the lovable judge would recover.

Jayson thought about Devlin's question. He truly *wasn't* nervous. Anxious, yes. He was anxious to begin moving forward again after the little pit stop of Harley's disappearance and his mother's reappearance. He was anxious to have this particularly annoying commercial interruption of his life over so that his show could go on.

The exhaustion finally caught up to Jayson and he nodded off with his head resting on Devlin's well worn Levi's. In the first moment of sleep after he closed his eyes, he drifted halfway across the continent back into the Wernermeiers' basement. His head was on Trey's lap instead of Devlin's. Jayson felt a quick, light kiss on his neck. He blinked his eyes open and looked up at a smiling Devlin.

'G'night, star,' Devlin whispered.

Jayson closed his eyes again, and just before drifting off for good smelled the sweet scent of Diet Squirt. The same sweet smell that had been on Trey's breath the first time they kissed on the dock in the lake.

'G'night, me,' Jayson murmured.

# *Twenty-one*

**The captain explained** that they'd be circling for another twenty minutes at least, due to poor visibility. Jayson looked down at the greenish brown cloud that hung above what he assumed was L.A. Years ago he'd seen a Jessica Savitch NBC News Special Report about the deadly effects of Los Angeles smog, and had always pictured it to be like dirty, warm cotton candy.

Somewhere down there, underneath the killer smog, was the place Jayson had always been destined to wind up.

The first class steward came by his seat and asked him if he'd like another drink.

'Do you have Orange Crush?' Jayson asked.

'Of course,' the steward said, reaching behind into the galley and grabbing a can and a cup. 'You look familiar,' he continued. 'Are you on TV?'

'Sort of,' Jayson smiled. 'I was in some commercials.'

'You're the Picky Prince!' he exclaimed. 'I love those commercials. Do the line for me.'

Some of the other first class passengers had overheard him and turned around to see Jayson.

'Oh, I dunno,' Jayson said coyly.

'C'mon. Do the line. Just once.'

In his best nonsensical pan-European accent, Jayson complied.

'Bon Appetite. It's the treat (pause) *for the elite!*'

The cabin around him burst into laughter.

'Are you here to film some more commercials?' The blond-highlighted steward asked. He had that too-perfect vanilla look of an extra, and Jayson supposed that he had probably come to L.A. to chase his own dream of stardom at one point. Jayson wondered what quirk of fate had put himself in the first class seat and this guy in the jumper seat. But deep down he knew that some people were born stars and others just could never light the spark. Jayson looked up at the steward with something just short of pity.

'Actually,' Jayson answered, 'I'm here for pilot season.'

'Really?' the steward replied. 'That's fantastic! Congratulations.' The steward took a step forward to take the drink order of the passenger seated in front of Jayson.

'Yes, I'm staying at the Beverly Hilton tonight,' Jayson continued, forcing the steward to listen to the rest of Jayson's story. 'And I shoot a pilot tomorrow.'

The steward continued helping the passenger in front of Jayson pull out his tray table.

'That's wonderful, kid. Good for you.'

'It's a Helen Lawson vehicle,' Jayson continued.

'Who?' the steward asked, barely listening anymore.

'Helen "La" Lawson,' Jayson clarified. How could someone not know Helen Lawson? 'From *Match Game*? *Love, American Style*? She guest stars on almost everything. Was *huge* on Broadway.'

'I'm sure I'd know her if I saw her face,' the steward said, turning his attention back to the next passenger.

'*Ladies and gentlemen, we've been cleared for landing at LAX,*' the captain announced over the intercom. '*Please extinguish all cigarettes and fasten your seatbelts for landing.*'

*Oh, you'll know her soon enough,* Jayson thought, *especially now that we're a team.*

The plane descended through the smog until a monotonous beige patchwork of low-slung buildings, pavement, and traffic was visible – interrupted only by the occasional straggly palm tree. From up here it looked nothing like the Technicolor episodes of *The Beverly Hillbillies*. It didn't even look as vibrant as the black-and-white episodes. But the unexpected drabness didn't dampen Jayson's enthusiasm. By the time the wheels touched the runway, he was convinced that he and Devlin would soon call this place home, and he could finally put his freakish family behind him for good.

An hour later, stuck in traffic, Jayson peered out the windows of the limo the studio had sent to the airport to take him to his hotel. He was still having a hard time reconciling the colorful L.A. of the later *Laverne and Shirley* episodes with the rundown neighborhoods leading away from the airport. He expected the limo's CB to crackle out: '*One Adam 12,*

*One Adam 12 . . . diminished expectations in progress on La Cienega.'*

Jayson spent his first afternoon and evening in L.A. mostly in his hotel room – taking the occasional break to walk around the pool on star-sighting missions. The only two people he recognized were the 'third Chrissie' from *Three's Company* and Nell Carter. As much as he wanted to rush around all the famous Hollywood landmarks he knew from television – *The Brady Bunch* house, the *Dragnet* building, the *Chico and the Man* garage – he had no idea how to get around the city. When he asked the front desk about directions to the subway the concierge could barely contain his chuckling. Besides, he liked the idea of hanging out by the pool in a hotel paid for by someone else. *Guests of the Merv Griffin Show stay at the sumptuous Beverly Hilton Hotel. . . .*

He spent the night in restless anticipation, switching among the thirty television channels offered at the hotel. *Thirty.* He vowed he would never live anywhere without cable television again in his life.

The same production assistant that had dropped him off at the hotel was back to pick him up and bring him to the studio the next morning.

He was picking out his breakfast at the craft service table when he heard a familiar voice behind him.

'Was that the last bran one?'

He turned around and was looking Helen Lawson square in her craggy but well-moisturized face. Jayson put the bran raisin muffin he was holding back down on the platter and turned around toward the familiar whiskey-cigarette voice.

'Um. Yeah. But that's okay. I'd rather have a cranberry one,' Jayson stuttered.

'Well, I don't want that one after you've *fondled* it.'

Helen breezed ahead of Jayson, grabbed a banana off the fruit plate, turned on her heels and headed back to her dressing room.

Jayson wasn't sure what to do next. He stared around the set, at the dozens of grips and production assistants, amazed that no one else seemed to react to Helen's brief appearance. She was a legend and yet no one paused even to glance at her.

Jayson didn't see Helen again until the cast and writers assembled around a long table on the set for their second, and final, script read-through before the taping that afternoon. Helen, wearing a silk floral blouse and butter yellow pants, was the last one to seat herself, across the table from Jayson.

'What are we waiting for?' she said. 'The sooner we start, the sooner this crapfest gets canceled.'

The read-through started off fine, if the reactions of the assembled writers and director were any judge. Personally, Jayson thought that the jokes were a little sitcom cliché, mostly revolving around the modern technology that his orphaned character introduced to the Amish community. A bit about Helen's character refusing to listen to Jayson's character's Walkman seemed to go on forever.

'You should run, *man*, not *Walk-man* away from such

Devil noise!' was Helen's final punch line in the scene. She delivered it in her familiar baritone rasp, and the entire table cracked up – except Jayson.

'You don't find that line funny, Jayson,' Helen said as the laughter died down – not asking, but telling.

'It's funny,' Jayson said. 'Everyone laughed.'

'Not everyone. Not you.'

'I'm sorry, I was concentrating on my next line.'

'People don't laugh at concentration,' Helen chided, 'your reaction to a joke is just as important as its delivery.'

Jayson didn't know what to say.

'The real reason you didn't laugh,' Helen continued, 'is because that joke is flatter than Betty Bacall in a tube top.'

The writers began furiously scribbling notes in the margin of the script as Helen finished out the scene.

Helen only appeared in the first and final scenes, with the rest of the show devoted to Jayson meeting the other Amish neighbors. Helen stood up after her lines were over and went back to her dressing room, followed by her beleaguered personal assistant and a wardrobe girl.

The rest of the read-through continued smoothly, with the writers occasionally interrupting with slight line changes. In the hours between the read-through and the taping, Jayson sat in the makeup room, gossiping with crew members. He didn't have his own dressing room like Helen, only an area he shared with the other lesser-known cast members.

A half hour before the taping began, a production assistant

whispered in Jayson's ear that Helen wanted to see him. Privately.

Jayson knocked on the half-open door and Helen swirled around in her chair, wrapping up a phone call. She motioned for him to come in and sit down. She was already dressed in her black Amish garb, its drab plainness comically contradicting her overly made-up face. Jayson waited as she finished a heated phone conversation with, he deduced, her agent. He sat, staring down at his feet, trying to feel like he belonged there. It was three in the afternoon and Helen's voice was already slurring.

'Hey, Half-pint,' she said stubbing out a cigarette butt in the amber glass ashtray on the counter, 'you want a candy?' She slid a glass bowl of candy across the makeup table toward him. 'Sorry they're sugarless. Goddamn diabetes. I save my sugar allowance for booze. I'm probably gonna lose a limb before long. Good thing I'm not a hoofer.'

Jayson looked at the bowl of candy. They were the same horribly acrid candies that Unsinger used to offer him. 'Trade in one way for the right way,' Jayson remembered Unsinger lecturing. He smiled to himself. He wondered what Unsinger would think of him now. Jayson had traded in most everything from those days – for this! He was standing in the dressing room of one of the most legendary performers of the century. Jayson wished he had Unsinger's phone number so that he could call him directly from Helen's dressing room.

'So, Half-pint,' Helen continued, 'that thing I said earlier … forgeddaboutit.'

It took Jayson a moment to remember the scolding she gave him over not laughing.

'You were right. I wasn't paying attention,' was all Jayson could think to say.

'It's just a fucking pilot. And a crap one at that,' she went on. 'I know crapfests. I've been in more of them than Nancy "Trash Talker" Walker. But the audience doesn't know crapfests. They're just waiting to see if those guys on the screen are having a good time. *That's* what makes a hit in this business – an audience who gets caught up in watching actors who think their shit doesn't stink.'

Jayson didn't know how to respond.

'So just go out there, feygeleh, and fart up a flower garden, got it?'

'Okay.'

'Toss me that lighter on your way out. And don't suck this afternoon.'

Jayson took the purple Bic off the side table next to him and walked it over to Helen as she picked up the phone receiver and started punching at its numbers with the tips of her long fingernails.

Jayson walked out and sat in a hard wooden chair on the set, waiting on the sidelines for the taping to begin.

**The show went well,** overall. Since it was a pilot, there was no studio audience, and without any crowd reaction the actual taping seemed barely different from when he used to act out

220

scenes from his favorite shows in his bedroom. Except with better lighting and not having to play all the roles himself.

It seemed to be over before it began. Everyone complimented Jayson on his timing, which was unique in the business, they said. 'A *real professional*.' Helen was the most complimentary, loudly taking credit for her 'discovery' and her insistence on his casting. There was a sustained round of applause from the cast and crew as the director toasted each actor, one by one, after the taping. Helen downed her plastic cup of Champagne in one swig, smiling pleasantly but looking vaguely bored.

As Jayson sat in the makeup chair, having his makeup wiped away with tissues and cold cream, Helen walked up behind him. She was already on her way off the set, bag over her shoulder, with her garish makeup untouched. As the makeup woman worked on Jayson's face it was impossible to swivel the chair around, so he stared at Helen's reflection in the mirror.

'Just wanted to tell you that you did a good job, Half-pint.'

'Thank you.' Jayson said. 'I had a good time.'

Helen laughed.

'Well, I guess that's all that matters,' Helen chuckled. Jayson wasn't sure if she thought Jayson's response was truly funny or whether she was mocking him. 'If – God forbid – the show gets picked up, I guess I'll see you back here.'

'I hope so.'

'Be careful what you wish for,' Helen said, still chuckling. 'Where are you from anyway?'

'Oconomowoc.'

'Ocon-*what-the-fuck*? What the hell kind of place is that? Sounds like an Indian reservation that had to pawn off its consonants.'

'Oconomowoc. It's in Wisconsin. But I live in New York now.'

'Ah, New York.' Helen's face relaxed. 'I love New York. Broadway. That's what counts. You do a lot of theater?'

'Not yet.'

'Well, do some theater, Half-pint. I'll get you some names. I've had some success on Broadway. Your family in New York?'

'Mostly,' Jayson said.

'You have a boyfriend back there?'

Jayson blushed. Was it that obvious he was gay? Jayson had been growing increasingly nervous about revealing his homosexuality. The closer he got to actual fame the more he had an instinctual feeling that he should cover it up. He'd never read about any gay celebrities. But it wouldn't hurt if Helen knew, would it?

'Yeah,' he said. 'Sort of. I think you know him.'

'Ah, Christ. Did I sleep with him? I've slept with a lot of fags.'

'No,' Jayson laughed. The thought of the seventy-something Helen Lawson sleeping with Devlin was far more hilarious than anything in the script they'd just performed. 'His name is Devlin Williamson. He was the oldest kid on *Disorder in the Court.*'

'You're gay *and* dating a colored?' Helen asked, raising her eyebrows. 'Well, they say anything goes nowadays. At least I don't have to beard so much anymore. Between Merv and Tab and Harley, I was the only person who didn't get laid during the sixties.'

Jayson wondered if he heard correctly. It couldn't be. Then again, they were both in the theater at about the same time. 'Oscar Harlande?' Jayson asked.

'Closet Hard-on we used to call him,' Helen confirmed. 'He was my very first fag.'

'Oscar Harlande is my father,' he told her.

'Don't kid me, Half-pint. I'm a drunk, not retarded.'

'Seriously. Oscar Harlande is my father,' Jayson repeated. 'I just found out a few months ago.'

'God damn. That old fruit's gotta be pretty ripe by now. What's he up to?'

'Haven't you read the news?' Jayson asked.

'I only read the obits and the comics, and sometimes I don't know which is funnier,' Helen said.

'He was running a prostitution ring out of his townhouse in New York and it was raided,' Jayson explained. 'But he was tipped off and ran off before the cops arrived.' Jayson left out the part about how Harlande had absconded with all his money.

'Well shit on my shoes,' Helen said. 'That Harley always did have the luck.'

'Can you tell me anything more about him?' Jayson asked.

'If I wasn't late for a meeting with my bartender, I'd fill up your entire afternoon with sordid Harley stories.'

'You don't have any idea where he might be, do you?' Jayson pushed.

'I can probably make a few calls and get a few leads. Harley can't stay out of the gossip loop for too long. He gets the shakes.'

'Really? Could you do that?' Jayson asked hopefully.

'For a complete stranger like you? Of course, love,' Helen said. Jayson wasn't sure if she was being facetious or funny.

Helen turned around and walked away, leaving a cloud of hovering scotch.

The most shocking thing about his trip to Hollywood was that it was over so quickly. And it felt very over, very quickly. Jayson wasn't sure what he'd expected it to be like after the filming, but he definitely hadn't envisioned sitting in the back of a town car heading back to LAX within forty-five minutes of the director yelling 'cut.' Where were the crowds of autograph seekers? Where were the paparazzi? As he sat stuck in traffic on La Cienega, a bleak depression settled over him.

He hadn't imagined it would be like a job. Like any other job. But it *was* just a job to everyone else on the set. Even during the farewell toasts the crew was busy taking down lights and piling props into large rolling gray bins. They had wives and kids they were trying to get home to. It wasn't all make-believe after all.

The pretend life he'd been living for the past day and a half disappeared even faster than one of Toni's life-changing whims. When his character disappeared, Jayson felt that he did as well. Sitting in the backseat of the limo he wasn't sure who he was supposed to be anymore. Wisconsin Jayson was long gone, and New York Jayson felt very distant now, too.

Jayson wondered what would happen if he instructed the driver to turn around and head back up into the hills. Maybe he could crash at Helen's house for a few days to relax and unwind. He would pour two scotches, hand one to her, laugh, and say he was 'suffering from exhaustion.'

But he knew he couldn't. He wasn't a full-fledged citizen of celebrity until *Lights Out!* got formally picked up by a network. There were hundreds of actors around town in the same position he was in. Probably some of them were also in limos on the way back to their old lives right now.

He tried to find something positive about his return to New York. He had three months before he'd learn if the network liked the show enough to put it in the fall schedule. He was sure they would. It was a Helen 'La' Lawson vehicle, after all.

Jayson imagined slipping into bed tomorrow morning after his plane landed at six a.m., and Devlin pulling him next to him and kissing his ear. He tried to imagine how nice it would feel. That it would be comfortably familiar, and reassuring.

But his mind kept wandering. He didn't want the familiar. He wanted everything new. *An all-new cast on an all-new night and time!* There was no way his extended freak show of a family – which now included a fugitive has-been child star – could ever be a part of Jayson's Hollywood future.

He tried not to think of what Devlin had asked him that first night they kissed – when Jayson said that he'd give up everything to become famous.

'Would you give up me?' Devlin had asked.

Jayson stared out the window as the sun went down over the highway. He was afraid of the answer.

He'd make the best of the short wait until the network upfronts, he vowed. It was only three months. He was an actor, after all.

When the car pulled up to the TWA Terminal, the driver turned and handed Jayson his card.

'If you come back you call this number and I will drive you,' the young Pakistani driver said in stilted English.

'*When* I come back,' Jayson answered, handing over a celebrity-worthy ten-dollar tip.

# *Twenty-two*

**By the time the cab turned** onto Wooster Street, Jayson's mood had soured further. He hadn't slept at all on the red-eye flight, instead spending the time mentally reliving his short but glamorous Hollywood debut.

The sight of his trash strewn SoHo street brought all his conflicted thoughts to a head. He felt like he was stepping into a rerun. This particular scene was supposed to be finished, why hadn't someone yelled 'cut'?

His plane had landed at 5:30 a.m. and, without any traffic, he'd made it home from JFK by 6:15. He didn't think anyone would be up yet. As he reached the final flight of stairs up to the loft, the zipper broke on the overstuffed *Lights Out!* duffel bag that had been handed out to the cast and crew. His dirty laundry spilled down the stairway.

'*Fuck it all.*'

When he slid open the loft door, Devlin was just inside, having heard Jayson's footsteps in the stairwell. Devlin grabbed Jayson in a hug and lifted him off the ground, spinning him around.

'Hello, star!' Devlin said, smothering his neck with kisses.

Tara, Toni, and Willie were also up, seated around the kitchen table that was loaded with celebratory foodstuffs cooked by Devlin. Willie was busy sneaking pinches of food while everyone's attention was focused on Jayson.

'Look, Devvie, a real live Hollywood celeb in our crappy little home!' Tara said.

'Ow,' Jayson said. 'You're crushing my new bag.'

Devlin set Jayson down gently.

'Sorry,' Devlin said, smiling. 'Didn't mean to manhandle the star.'

'Look!' Willie shouted excitedly, pointing wide-eyed at all the food on the table in front of him. 'A party!'

'Mother*fucker*, that flight was long,' Jayson said.

'Did you sleep?' Devlin asked.

'Not at all. I'm beat,' Jayson answered, looking for a quick escape to bed so that he wouldn't have to pretend to be over-joyed to be back in New York.

Jayson walked over to the food-laden table.

'Is this all for me?' Jayson asked, trying to feign a modicum of enthusiasm.

'Mostly, yes, but it's also a double celebration,' Devlin said. Jayson was surprised and a little pissed at having to share his homecoming. As much as he didn't feel celebratory about his (hopefully) temporary return, he certainly didn't want to share his party.

'Let me guess,' Jayson said wearily. 'Tara's joined AA, Ma's decided that she's a transsexual, Willie's taken up the violin, and you've taken a job as a short-order cook.'

An awkward silence fell over the group. The edge in Jayson's voice made it unclear to everyone whether or not he was joking.

Jayson himself wasn't sure where his venom came from. But it was there. And there was no shaking it. He tried to change the subject.

'Where's Gavin?' he asked.

'Gavin broke our little deal,' Toni said. 'I caught him shooting up in the back of the loft so I kicked him out.'

Jayson looked at Tara.

'Can't say that he was going to be the best father figure anyway,' Tara shrugged. Jayson decided that if they weren't concerned about Gavin's absence then there was no reason for him to be.

'Look, guys, I'm really beat,' Jayson said. 'I'm going to go lie down.'

'Devlin went to a lot of effort here,' Toni said. 'It took us days to shoplift all this.'

Jayson sighed.

'Well, the least you could do before you crawl into bed is toast your mother,' Toni yelled over the filing cabinets.

'For what? Did you get a paying job? Find us a real house? Bake my first birthday cake?'

'She's engaged!' Devlin said, excitedly, trying to break the

229

tension. It didn't work. Toni's engagement only made things worse. This was another step backward. They weren't making this easy on him. He wasn't sure he could fake his way through the next few months with them – but he *knew* he couldn't feign any sort of enthusiasm for a new cast member in the freak show.

Jayson walked away into the 'bedroom' that he shared with Devlin without acknowledging his mother's announcement. He began unpacking the three outfits he'd brought to L.A. When he unzipped the bag, he swore he could smell the sunshine. 'Don't worry,' Toni shouted over the filing cabinet walls. 'According to Emily Post you have a year to buy me a present.'

Tara stuck her head around the filing cabinet doorway.

'The new guy's pretty cool,' Tara said. 'I helped him pick out the ring. Plus, he's loaded.'

'Great,' Jayson replied. 'Did you catch his name, or don't they know each other that well yet?'

'It's Sal, stupid. The art dealer. The guy she's been dating.'

' . . . for two weeks,' Jayson felt compelled to add.

'I think it's more like three,' Tara clarified.

'So where is my new father?'

'He lives uptown somewhere. Toni's not moving in until after the wedding,' Tara explained.

'Just like a good little Catholic,' Jayson responded. He really didn't want to discuss this any longer. He just wanted to go to bed and sleep the next three months away.

'She's going to take Willie with her,' Tara explained. 'So it'll be just you me and Devlin.'

'How cozy.'

'Why are you being such a dick?'

'Because,' Jayson began, 'because I'm sick of this. I'm sick of pretending that I live a normal life. I'm sick of squatting in an abandoned building with a patchwork of wires and plumbing and gas lines that could explode at any minute.'

Devlin joined Tara in the doorway.

'Why don't you lie down for a bit,' Devlin said calmly.

'Don't patronize me.' The blood was rushing to Jayson's head.

'I'm not. I'm telling you to take a break,' Devlin said.

'Well you should know all about breaks,' Jayson said. 'How long have you been out of work?'

Devlin was silent for a moment, but then took Jayson's hand and led him over to the sleeping bag they shared. 'I'm so sick of all of this,' Jayson muttered.

'Then leave,' Tara said from the doorway. 'What the fuck is keeping you here?'

'I *should* go,' Jayson said. 'I should run away from all of you just like Trey did.'

Willie, on cue, started yelling from the other room. '*Trey din't! Trey din't run 'way! Trey din't! Trey din't . . .*'

'*WOULD YOU SHUT THE FUCK UP YOU GODDAMN FUCKING RETARD!!!*' Jayson shouted, losing every last ounce of self-restraint.

The loft fell into silence.

The only noise any of them could hear was a truck driving through the slush far below on Wooster Street. It sounded, to Jayson, like the static after a TV channel went off for the night.

# Twenty-three

**The three months** between the filming of the pilot and the network upfronts went by uneventfully. After Jayson's initial outburst, most everyone gave him a wide berth, going on with their lives almost as if he'd already left for L.A. Toni spent ever more time at Sal's townhouse on the Upper East Side. Willie went with her. The two of them only stopped back at the loft to pick up changes of clothes and art materials for Toni. Toni told Jayson that he had an open invitation to come meet Sal, but that she wouldn't put up with any 'celebrity attitude.' Jayson politely told her that he'd stop by 'one of these days' but never did. There was no reason to. His life was simply on pause. Soon enough, Toni would be nothing more to him than a sidebar in his *People* magazine profile. The network upfronts were now only two weeks away.

With Toni and Willie gone, Jayson dropped out of school. Tara stayed enrolled, even after her pregnancy had progressed too far to be hidden. She'd made friends with her inner city classmates. It was probably the first time she'd been social in her life. Consequently, Jayson and Devlin had the loft mostly to themselves.

As the days began to grow warmer in March and April, Devlin was forced to spend most of his time inside. His disguises consisted mainly of hats and scarves, and they began to look more and more out of place with the spring thaw. Without the scarf to disguise his dimple, he would've been recognized on the street in an instant.

'Why don't you just go out and get it yourself,' Jayson said to Devlin after Devlin asked him to go steal some rosemary for a lamb dish he was cooking. 'No one's even talking about the whole mess anymore.' Jayson was tired of having to do all the errands. 'I don't understand why you don't just come clean. It hasn't been in the news for months. Besides, you didn't even do anything wrong.'

'I will come out of hiding, eventually,' Devlin said. 'I just want to have money to hire a lawyer. Who knows how messy it could get?'

'Like *PM Magazine* is really going to park a satellite van outside your door anymore.'

Devlin had gotten so used to Jayson belittling his ex-child-star status that he let such comments completely wash over him.

Jayson turned back the to the ten-foot-tall episode of *The Ropers* that he was watching on the projection TV he'd bought with the $5000 he received for the *Lights Out!* pilot. Jayson hadn't even considered lending the money to Devlin to hire a lawyer, and Devlin had never brought it up.

He was just about to take a before-dinner nap when the loft's huge metal door slid open with a bang behind them. Both Jayson and Devlin turned around with a start.

'Hey, faggots! I'm home!'

It was Gavin.

He looked worse than ever, which Jayson would have thought impossible. His dirty clothes were torn at all the seams, exposing flesh the same pale gray color as the pigeons that lived on the fire escape. His hair, which had always been long and straggly, was now falling out in large patches, and his face was covered with sores. His normally thin six-foot-four frame was now skeletal. Jayson was surprised that he'd actually been able to roll the heavy loft door open. They were both speechless.

'I'm kidding. Don't worry,' Gavin said, laughing a phlegmy laugh through his mostly toothless mouth. 'I'm not staying long. I'm just swinging by to pick up the last of my stuff.'

When Gavin fell off the wagon and Toni chased him out, he'd left almost all of his belongings behind in the loft. Not that there was much. Just some blankets, cassette tapes from his old bands, and, of course, his Polaroid collection – which was what he'd returned to claim. He shuffled across the loft to the wall which was still covered with his shots and began pulling them down recklessly. He stuffed them by the handful into a trash bag he had tied to his waist.

Devlin spoke up first. 'Hey, Gavin. What's up?'

'Oh, lots. Starting a new band, working the piers again,

235

going to the doctor. Did I tell you I got the gay cancer? Imagine that. I must be the only straight guy in the world who caught the gay cancer. Did one of you two put some stray drops of gay in my needle?' Gavin couldn't seem to stop laughing.

'Gay cancer' had been dotting the local news for several weeks. It sometimes cropped up in the paper, but rarely. There'd only been a few hundred cases reported around the country, mostly in New York and San Francisco. Jayson hadn't read much past the headlines. It seemed like such a random disease – like regular cancer. But he had to admit that it was curious that Gavin, whose only tie to homosexuality was letting himself be blown by men for money down by the piers, would come down with it. He wasn't actually gay. Did that mean it was something you could catch? It was impossible. Cancer wasn't something you caught – like a cold. It all had to be some strange coincidence.

'What's new with you lovebirds?' Gavin cackled.

Jayson spoke up – more than anything to stop Gavin from continuing to talk and laugh. His voice was so thick and gravelly that it was painful to listen to.

'I think you were still around when I went to L.A. I filmed a TV show there . . .'

'That's so cool, pal!' Gavin interrupted, still chuckling at nothing. 'When's it on?'

'Most likely it'll premier in the fall . . .'

'Oh, right! That show you taped like *Dynasty*. That was great, man . . . I remember that.'

Jayson was confused momentarily. He realized that Gavin had mixed up what Jayson was saying with the silly little summer project he'd filmed in Oconomowoc last year – *Dallasty!* Was it really only last summer? It seemed so incredibly long ago. 'No, no, this was a real show that I filmed with Helen Lawson.'

'La Lawson! I love her!' Gavin shouted, too loudly. 'Man, I wish I had a Polaroid of her. She cracks my shit up. Do you think you could get a picture of her for me?'

'Sure,' Jayson said, more to keep Gavin happy than as an actual promise. He remembered how hurt he'd been that Gavin had disappeared from Oconomowoc so long ago without taking a Polaroid of him. Franck had explained then that Gavin took a photo of everyone he'd ever met, to keep a piece of their souls, but Gavin had never taken one of Jayson. He still hadn't, in fact.

'Ah-ha!' Gavin shouted. 'Here's the little fucker!' Gavin discovered his ancient Polaroid camera underneath one of the grimy blankets. 'Man, I've missed this.'

Jayson wondered what Mariette Hartley and James Garner would think if they knew that a crazed junkie was using their product as his exclusive medium.

'Okay, both of you,' Gavin continued, suddenly turning as serious as he was frivolous a second earlier. 'I guess I'd better get a shot of you two before I die.'

Now it was Jayson and Devlin's turn to laugh. Nervously.

'You're not going to die,' Devlin said. 'People with cancer go into remission all the time. You're going to have a kid soon!'

237

'There's no remission with the gay cancer,' Gavin said. 'Not a single faggot has made it. And I'm pretty sure I'm not gonna escape it either just because I'm straight. Now you two stand together.'

Devlin and Jayson nervously walked over to one another and stood side by side.

'Good, good. The light's good there.' Gavin took a few shots with them standing next to each other. Then a few more after Devlin put his arm around Jayson. 'Now look like you two guys actually love each other,' Gavin said, holding up the camera to his mottled face.

Like *we love each other*, Jayson thought. It was an idea that had been bothering Jayson for weeks. Did he love Devlin anymore? Was his initial infatuation with him merely an extension of his childhood crush? Or was it just because Devlin had been so protective of him when he was alone and lost in the city? They had so little in common anymore.

It was Devlin who finally pulled Jayson toward him.

'That's better. Now kiss him, Butter Bean.'

'No, that's okay,' Jayson stalled. 'Just get our faces.' Jayson felt Devlin's grip on him loosen.

'C'mon. Just one kiss,' Gavin pleaded. Jayson was about to give one final protest when Gavin's voice broke. 'All I see are broken people,' Gavin said. 'I've forgotten what love looks like.'

Again it was Devlin who made the first move by pulling Jayson around so that they were face to face and wrapping his arms around him. This time Jayson wouldn't resist. Gavin's plea was too heartfelt. He remembered the night of the Homecoming Incident, when Gavin, Franck, Tara, and Willie were all laughing along with him as they careened away from the scene of their greatest caper, bouncing in the backseat of their beat-up old chartreuse Ford Maverick, the same rusty old Ford Maverick that was now abandoned somewhere on Broome Street. Jayson also remembered how kind Gavin had been in taking him and Devlin home when they were homeless. How Gavin had almost nothing to share, but scrounged up a packet of hot chocolate for the shivering pair.

Fate had changed so much for all of them in such a short time. And Gavin had gotten the very shortest straw of them all.

Jayson was now looking up into Devlin's amber eyes. Devlin smiled and, with the smile, came his famous dimple.

Their lips met the way they used to, but without the usual spark. At the same moment, Gavin's Polaroid flashed.

Only a second later, the door to the loft opened for the second time that afternoon.

'*What the fuck are you doing here?!*'

It was Toni. She and a man Jayson didn't recognize were standing in the doorway. '*I told you never to come back here,*' Toni bellowed at Gavin at the top of her lungs.

'Oh Christ,' Jayson muttered. He just wanted to get back to *The Ropers*.

Toni made a move toward her trusty blowtorch, but

stopped in shock when Gavin turned around to face her with his gaunt face marred by dozens of sores.

'Hey Toni,' Gavin said. 'Don't worry, I was just packing up some stuff. I'm leaving again. No need to torch me. I'll be dead soon enough.'

Toni was as speechless as Devlin and Jayson had been. Gavin gathered up the trash bag into which he'd tossed a few hundred of his thousands of Polaroids and strung the camera around his neck.

'You can keep the rest of the pictures,' Gavin said to them. 'I'm not strong enough to carry them.'

'Let me take a picture to remember you by,' Jayson said to Gavin, suddenly feeling overwhelmed with sadness. With his upcoming move to L.A., this might be the last time he ever saw Gavin.

Gavin chuckled.

'Thanks, pal, but I don't think I have a soul to steal.'

Gavin held out his hand toward Jayson, but Jayson just lifted his hand in a weak wave 'goodbye.' Gavlin shuffled toward the door, straining to carry his bag of Polaroids – his entire life in a garbage bag. On his way past Toni, she grabbed his arm and pulled him into a tight hug. Jayson was shocked. He'd resisted Gavin's hug because on the news he'd heard that hospitals were quarantining anyone who showed up with the dark purple lesions that covered Gavin face and arms.

'I'm Gavin. Nice to meet you,' Gavin said to the man still standing next to Toni.

In the chaos of Toni's arrival, Jayson forgot that Toni had brought someone with her. The short, round man recoiled at Gavin's sore-covered hand.

'*Boo!*' Gavin shouted, suddenly leaning in toward the man, causing the stranger to jump backward into the wall. Gavin just chuckled and pulled the door shut behind him.

'Butter Bean . . . Devvie,' Toni bellowed as soon as Gavin disappeared down the stairwell, I'd like to introduce you to my newest fiancé, Sal Castellari.'

The man was busy pulling the collar of his jacket up over his face, while also trying to subtly pull down the brim of his bright red fedora.

What little of the man's face Jayson could make out seemed vaguely familiar. The salt and pepper mustache . . . the triple chin . . . the eyebrows that extended out from his face further than his nose.

Why was he hiding his face?

'Um. Hello, boys,' Sal muttered softly, as if trying to disguise his voice slightly. His voice. His higher-than-normal tenor voice was somehow familiar to Jayson, too. He glanced over at Devlin.

Devlin stood frozen, wide-eyed. When the unaware Toni turned to take off her coat and hang it up on the hook by the door, Devlin grabbed Jayson and whispered through his clenched teeth: '*It's the Sneezer Geezer!*'

# *Twenty-four*

**After the awkward 'introductions'** between Sal, Devlin, and Jayson, the four of them spent no more than an hour together before Sal made an excuse about an 'urgent art auction matter' and dragged Toni off with him.

The short time they were together was spent touring the loft and the other abandoned floors in the building. The Sneezer Geezer made up some excuse about being interested in old architecture, but Jayson knew that it was really just an effort to stay away from Jayson and Devlin. It was obvious that Sal recognized them just as they recognized him. But Jayson stuck to his mother and Sal like glue. At one point during the building tour, Jayson got a noseful of dust, and had a sneezing fit. Sal glared at him menacingly.

Sal made it a point never to leave Toni's side, so neither Jayson nor Devlin had a chance explain to Toni what they knew about Sal – namely, that he was one of the flamingest queens in the city.

But before Sal was able to make his escape with Toni,

Jayson was able to slip a note in Toni's pocket that read: 'CALL PAYPHONE!!! URGENT!!!!'

The second Toni and Sal left, Devlin hurried to their filing cabinet room and began stuffing clothes in a trash bag.

'What are you doing?' Jayson asked.

'He saw me. He knows me,' Devlin answered.

'So?'

'He's going to go straight to the police.'

'I think you're paranoid.'

'Look. We don't know what he's up to with your mother, but whatever it is, I'm sure he doesn't want us messing it up. And it'll be harder for me to get in the way if I'm stuck in jail.'

'He's not going to turn you in,' Jayson laughed dismissively.

'You want to take that chance? You want me to be here in an hour when the news vans show up? Do you want to try to explain why, on the week before the upfronts – the week before you finally get what you've always dreamed of – why you live with a fugitive gay prostitute?'

'But you're not! Stop!' Jayson tried to take the trash bag Devlin was stuffing away from him. Devlin pushed his hand away.

'Look,' Devlin said, staring Jayson directly in the eye. 'You've been a shit to everyone since you got back from L.A. I've been trying to ignore it. But I'm not a damn stooge. I've been exactly where you are right now, Jayson. You're not the first person to get a lucky break.'

If Jayson could have taken back everything he'd said or not said in the last two and a half months he would have stuffed it all back down his throat until he was ready to throw up. He'd had no idea that Devlin had been patiently putting up with him. He'd been consumed with thinking it was the other way around.

'Don't go,' was all Jayson could say as the tears starting backing up in the corners of his eyes.

'I don't have a choice. This is probably better for both of us. You've got a fresh start. I haven't found mine yet.'

'But I don't have anyone else.'

'You have a lot of people. The problem is that you don't want them.'

Jayson winced. Devlin was right. He didn't know what else to say.

'Will you let me know you're okay?'

'When I figure out where I'm going, I'll call you when I get there.'

'But, I might be in L.A.,' Jayson said.

'Well then, Butter Bean, I don't think you'll much care what I'm up to.'

With that, Devlin tied a knot in the top of the black plastic bag and leaned over to give Jayson a kiss on the forehead – just like he had that first day in New York, when Jayson was all alone and scared of his new surroundings.

'I don't want you to go,' Jayson said one last time as Devlin pulled at the heavy metal loft door.

'But you don't want me to stay, either,' Devlin said. 'And *that — Jayson with a 'y' —* is a problem you've got to figure out yourself.'

'You promised you'd always take care of me,' Jayson said.

'And you promised you'd never give me up for fame,' Devlin countered.

'But I won't! I *need* you. I couldn't have gotten this far without you.'

Devlin stepped out the door, turned around, shook his head 'no' and said — softly: 'It wuuuzzzzn't me.'

The next week went by with neither Toni nor Devlin calling the payphone outside of the loft. The weather had been unseasonably warm, so Jayson slept right under the open window nearest the phone in case it rang. Tara was his only company, but she was so tired after she came home from school that she usually just sat down in her nest of blankets and flipped through the six channels they could get on Jayson's huge TV.

'Get me a Grape Crush,' Tara yelled to Jayson sitting in his perch under the window. 'I can't get up.'

Jayson plodded over to the reclaimed refrigerator that Toni had found on the street and installed. He found an Orange Crush inside and brought it to Tara.

'I said *grape*,' Tara said.

'It's all we have. You'll have to go shoplift more.'

'I'm seven fucking months pregnant,' Tara replied. 'It's not like I can stuff the bottles down my top anymore, now can I?'

Tara seemed even larger than most pregnant women Jayson had seen. She hung out with a group of classmates in a similar condition. The school's Home Ec teacher had even suggested starting an after-school mommies club until she was informed that if she did, the Reagan White House would cut off the school's funding.

'Have you gone to the doctor yet?' Jayson asked. Once she revealed to the school that she was pregnant, the school nurse set up an appointment with a free pregnancy clinic on the Lower East Side.

'Why the hell would I go to the doctor?' Tara asked, with her usual unwarranted incredulity. 'I'm pregnant, not dis-eased.'

Secretly, Jayson was worried about her health. If Gavin could get gay cancer from having guys blow him, then could Tara have gotten gay cancer from him? He was, though, like everyone, including the newscasters, too uninformed about the whole thing to raise it with her. He doubted she would do anything about it anyway. Tara seemed to live her whole life with a death wish. Or at least an 'I don't care if I die' wish.

Jayson sank down in the big pile of blankets next to Tara. It reminded him of the summer nights he would share the giant beanbag chairs with her and Trey in the Wernermeiers' basement. Evidently, it reminded Tara of the same thing.

'Trey's really been bugging me at night lately,' Tara said. 'I can't get a decent night's sleep.'

Jayson knew this already. He was having a hard time

sleeping since Tara's increasingly frequent nightmares about Trey caused her to shriek for help at all hours of the night.

'It's just the pregnancy,' Jayson said, 'I read in *People* magazine that Cindy Williams barely slept a wink during her entire last trimester.'

'Was her brother kidnapped too?' Tara asked.

'Trey wasn't kidnapped,' Jayson clarified. 'He ran away.' Jayson half expected to hear Willie shouting his usual protestations all the way from the Upper East Side.

'That's what *you* say, queerboy,' Tara sighed, turning her attention back to the television.

'What are we having for dinner?' Jayson asked.

'Beats me,' Tara said, 'That's your department. I'm pregnant.' Tara used her pregnancy as a sort of permanent 'get out of jail free' card.

'I don't think there's any food.'

'Well, then, someone's going to have to go steal some. And that someone is the someone in this room whose uterus isn't at full occupancy.'

Jayson hadn't realized how interdependent their little freak show had been until it started to disband. They were the perfect ensemble cast – like *M\*A\*S\*H* or *Mary Tyler Moore*. Without Devlin around, they hadn't had a hot meal in a week. Without Toni, there was no one to kick their asses out from in front of the television to fix a leaky pipe, or clean the syringes off the doorstep, or rig up some sort of scrap part dishwasher. Even Willie had had his place in their bedraggled troupe as a sort of comic relief. Tara's role was to always call things like she saw them, whether you wanted to hear it or not.

'So are you going to get food?' Tara asked again. 'Or is it physically impossible for you to do anything without a live studio audience?'

'Shut up,' Jayson said, unexpectedly stung.

'C'mon everybody!' Tara continued, waving her arms at an imaginary audience in the darkening empty loft. 'Let's give our star a hand for singlehandedly feeding himself!'

'Fuck you.'

'After this commercial break,' Tara continued with her monologue, undeterred, 'we'll watch our hero take a breath, and maybe, if we're lucky, *exhale!*'

'Don't give me shit,' Jayson fired back. 'I'm not the one who got knocked up by a junkie who's dying of . . .' He caught himself.

'Of what?' Tara asked.

'Of drugs,' Jayson lied.

Luckily, before Tara could push the subject anymore, the phone outside rang. Jayson leapt up from the blankets and raced for the stairway. He took the stairs five at a time, jumping off every landing as if it were a trampoline. He reached the phone on the seventh ring.

'*Hello,*' he said, out of breath.

'Hello?' said a female voice on the other end of the line. It wasn't Toni or Devlin. Jayson slumped onto the payphone with disappointment. 'Is William Devlinson available?'

*Shit.* He forgot that without Devlin, he had no 'agent.'

'Uh, no. um. Not right now,' Jayson stammered. 'I mean, he's in the john.' Jayson winced, embarrassed by his poor improv skills. 'Can you hold on a second?'

Jayson stood on the sidewalk, cupping the receiver with his hand while he tried to figure out what to do next. A lone junkie was on a stoop halfway down the street, swatting around his head at invisible flies. He brought the phone back up to his face.

'This is Mr. Williamson,' Jayson said, doing his best to lower his voice to approximately the same tone as Devlin's. 'May I help you?'

'This is Margaret Adams, Executive Producer for Light Dancer Productions,' the professional voice on the other end of the line began. 'I'm calling in regards to your client, Mr. Jayson Blocher.'

'Blocher . . . Blocher . . . *ah yes,* Jayson Blocher, the Picky Prince. He filmed a pilot with you.' Jayson was starting to get into his imitation of Devlin's imitation of an agent.

'We're calling to let you and Mr. Blocher know that the pilot for *Lights Out!* has been picked up by CBS.'

Jayson covered the receiver again and shrieked so loudly that the imaginary fly-swatting junkie stopped hallucinating for a moment and shrieked back. Jayson went back to the phone.

'Well, that's wonderful news,' Jayson said, clearing his throat. He spent the next half hour attempting to negotiate contract points. He had no idea how to proceed, so he simply decided to say 'yes' three times for every 'no.' It seemed to work, and he and the producer proceeded to 'nail down' everything from salary requirements to travel preferences. Toward the end of the call, the producer requested Jayson's presence at the network upfronts scheduled in New York for two days from now, and then to fly to L.A. for a press junket with 'Ms. Lawson' later that same evening.

*Network upfronts,* Jayson thought to himself giddily. He had been quite possibly the only first grader in America to know what network upfronts were. And now he was attending them – as a star.

'Why yes, yes,' Jayson assured the producer, 'my client will be thrilled to attend.'

Jayson hung up the phone and shouted as loudly as he could toward the open window five stories above his head.

*'Hey Tara!'*

*'I'm pregnant. Not deaf, asshole,'* came the predictable response.

*'They picked up the pilot!'* Jayson shouted back.

*'Congratufuckinglations. Now try to go pick up some egg rolls from the trash behind Wok & Roll.'*

Jayson sat down on the stoop. His cheeks hurt from the grin that had been frozen on his face since the phone call began. All the other complications in his life had disappeared in an instant. They seemed very quaint now, like anecdotes he could use on the press junket. He would do his best to sound bittersweet about it all during interviews – his 'troubled youth, spent on the cold, harsh streets of New York City.' The public ate up bittersweet.

# Twenty-five

'**You'll go out first,**' Helen Lawson shouted into Jayson's ear over the loud applause filling Radio City Music Hall. 'They always put the fresh meat toward the front of the case.' They were standing in the wings, and suddenly she gave him a shove out onto the stage. The phalanx of flashbulbs clustered at the foot of the stage exploded in his eyes.

'Ladies and Gentlemen!' the network VP announced from his podium at the other end of the stage. 'Meet Jayson Blocher! Star of *Light's Out!*, premiering this fall on Monday nights at eight-thirty!'

Over Jayson's head, an enormous screen made of individual tiny colored light bulbs blinked to life with a two-story-tall close-up of Jayson as a sulky teen and future American dreamboat. It was the scene from the pilot in which Helen Lawson's character explained that he'd have to throw his Walkman away now that he was part of the Amish community. On the screen, his character sneered at her and asked if he really had to.

'Yep,' Helen's character said. 'The only thing that runs on electricity out here is me caught in a lightning storm.'

The audience laughed hysterically along with the laugh track. The entire upfront presentation show was orchestrated to pump up the adrenaline of the media reporters in the audience. Everything was bigger and better and louder, from the gigantic TV screen to the network's swelling 1982 Fall Premiere Week theme song: 'Great Moments for You on CBS.'

*'Shoo Fly, Schmoo Fly!'* Jayson's enormous flickering image shouted at Helen Lawson's character while cocking an eyebrow. The audience exploded. That would be his catchphrase, Jayson decided. *Shoo Fly, Schmoo Fly!* He could already envision teenagers around the country yelling it at their parents. Jayson turned back around from his own image to look over the vast audience of middle-aged white media men bursting into Pavlovian laughter.

*'And here's America's favorite funny woman . . . Helen Lawson!'* the VP continued.

*Please God,* Jayson thought, *please let Helen not be drunk. Or at least not shout out something racist.* Jayson turned robotically, with the plastic smile he'd been practicing since birth, and gave a warm round of applause and a slight bow of deference to his co-star – the equally plastic-grinning Helen, as she walked out onto the stage to join him.

The crowd rose to their feet in unison at her entrance, as if suddenly filled with the Holy Spirit of Hollywood. Helen looked out over the sea of faces and clutched her hand to her chest in the standard Hollywood patronizing gesture of *'Me? All this for me?'*

When she reached the center of the stage, Helen put one arm around Jayson and pulled him close. As the applause began dying down, she leaned over, still smiling, and whispered into his ear with her scotch-and-soda breath. 'Don't fuck this chance up, Half-pint. Hollywood has fewer comebacks than Christianity.'

Jayson chuckled at the particularly 'Helenesque' advice.

Helen clasped his hand in hers and made an overly dramatic bow. He followed her lead.

Bow. Clap. Smile. Acknowledge audience. Clap again. Jog offstage waving.

It was just that simple.

Toni had been right all those many months ago – maybe for the only time in her life: all he needed to do was find the applause and stand in front of it.

# Twenty-six

**As the network's limo** turned onto Wooster Street, Jayson was finishing up his mental checklist to make sure that he'd packed everything for that evening's flight to L.A. The limo had been instructed to take him to the loft to gather his bags before proceeding to JFK.

'I can't make the turn,' the limo driver said. 'Street's blocked.'

Jayson leaned forward and squinted through the windshield. Halfway down the block there was a giant pile of junk, like a hastily arranged garage sale in front of his building. It was all stacked up on itself in the middle of the cobblestone street, reaching almost as high as the second story of the warehouse.

*Shit.*

Jayson bolted from the car and ran down the street. Toni was sitting on one of the orange floral kitchen chairs that had been hauled from Wisconsin to the loft, and now down to the street.

'What the *fuck* is going on?' he demanded as he closed the

distance between them. Tara was seated on the stoop folding up random pieces of clothing, and Willie was scavenging
around the edges of the immense pile as if he expected stray
pieces of food to tumble out of it.

'Good news, Butter Bean,' Toni said, unfazed as usual by
Jayson's histrionics. 'We're moving uptown.'

'What?!' Jayson said, finally reaching her.

'We're all moving into Sal's townhouse,' Toni explained,
busily trying to glue together a small broken vase in the shadow
of the vast pile of junk.

*'I'm not going anywhere! I'm moving to L.A.!'*

'That's sort of contradictory, Butter Bean.'

'I mean I'm not moving to Sal's place and neither are you.'

'Well you might be half right, but my half is moving to
Sal's,' Toni said. 'Tara, Willie, and I are just waiting for the
trucks Sal arranged.'

'I'm gonna ride in a truck!' Willie boasted to Jayson.

'Why didn't you call me?' Jayson asked Toni, 'I put a note in
your pocket to call me!'

'What note? I didn't see any note. At Sal's place, the maid
does the laundry.'

'You can't move in with the Sneezer Geezer,' Jayson said
urgently.

'Who?'

'Sneezer Geezer. He used to be one of Harley's clients.
He's a big fag.'

'Well he wasn't a fag when he was fucking me.'

*Fucking her,* Jayson thought. Wait a second. Toni never slept with anyone unless they were . . .

'*You married him?!?*'

'You know the rules, Butter,' Toni replied. 'If you want to finger Toni, you put somethin' on Toni's finger.' She held up her right hand and waved a gold ring at Jayson.

'This can't be happening. Why on earth would he marry you?'

'A less secure woman might be insulted by that.'

'He's slept with every chorus boy on Broadway.'

'So? Maybe he likes to get sung to sleep,' Toni shrugged. 'It's not like I haven't explored my own lesbianese nationality.'

Jayson was exhausted by the discussion. Besides, it didn't really even affect him. If his mother wanted to marry a gay man who got turned on in public during flu season, fine. He had a plane to catch.

'I'm not going. I have to fly to L.A. in two hours. Where's my suitcase?'

Tara interrupted.

'I left that upstairs. I knew you needed it.'

'Well thank you,' Jayson said, grateful for the small miraculous favor.

'Uh-oh,' Tara said. She was staring at the far end of the street. 'I smell bacon.'

'Goddammit,' Toni said. Two NYPD cars and a Fire Department sedan were slowly advancing down Wooster toward them.

'You're blocking the entire street,' Jayson said, 'Did you think no one was going to have a problem with that?'

The cars rolled to a halt in a line in front of the vast junk pile. The officers sat inside their car for a minute, radioing something into their CBs. Finally, they all got out of their cars simultaneously. They huddled together for a moment. One of them was carrying something in a large black bag. They began walking toward them.

Jayson shuddered at what could potentially happen given Toni's notorious track record with authority.

'Afternoon, officers,' Toni said. 'Nice day for causing trouble, isn't it?'

Every muscle in Jayson's body clenched in fear.

'Anybody inside the building, lady?' the shortest and fattest of the men asked Toni, pointing up at their old warehouse. As he was the only man dressed in a tie and shirtsleeves instead of a uniform, Jayson figured he must be a detective or something.

'Nope,' Toni declared. 'I ran the last of them off with my blowtorch. That isn't against the law, now, is it?'

The officer chuckled. 'Not in this neighborhood, it isn't,' he replied. 'But I wouldn't try it on Park Avenue.'

'Damn, that's probably where they need a good blowtorching the most,' Toni said. The detective laughed with her.

Led by the detective, the group of officers walked over to the abandoned warehouse's stoop. Tara scootched over a little to let them climb the front steps.

'You'll have to move off the stoop, miss,' the detective said apologetically to Tara. As Tara descended, he motioned for the officer with the black duffel bag to approach.

It took two officers to lift out the heavy contraption of chains and metal from the duffel bag. Jayson couldn't figure out what they were doing. Were they going to make repairs to the rusted out wrought iron stoop, or the fire escape hanging by a thread from above? Only when one of the officers looped the heavy chain through the handles of the double metal door did Jayson realize what was happening.

'Wait! Stop!' Jayson shouted running over to the stoop. 'I've got my bag inside there!'

'Sorry kid,' the detective told him, catching Jayson by the elbow as he tried to run up the steps.

'I have to get my bag out of there! I'm supposed to go to Hollywood in an hour for my press tour with Helen Lawson!'

The group of officers all laughed together, infuriating Jayson further.

'I *need* . . .'

The stout detective cut him off. 'Look. I'm sorry. I got an order here to seal up this building. The owner declared it unoccupied and dangerous.'

'What owner?' Jayson said. The detective shuffled through the packet of official looking documents he'd rolled up and shoved into his polyester back pocket. As long as they'd squatted in the warehouse, Jayson had never seen a soul come by claiming to have any connection to the building. *All* their neighbors in the surrounding buildings were artists and drug addicts who squatted in the empty factories and warehouses that populated SoHo. In fact, the city had recently instated 'Loft Laws' which gave the squatters the right to stay in the buildings that they'd improved over the years – sometimes decades. No longer could a landlord come in and kick out the people who'd invested the time and money to make the building habitable, and then turn the gentrified building into high-priced condos.

'Says here,' the officer read off one of the sheets of paper, 'that the owner is a Mr. Salvatore Castellari. Owns all the buildings on this block, according to this.'

'That's my husband!' Toni said. Again the officers laughed in unison. The idea that this woman, dressed in a flannel shirt and torn sweatpants guarding a pile of junk in the middle of the street could be married to the man who owned half the buildings in SoHo was ludicrous.

And Jayson had to agree – but for different reasons.

'Ma. That's why he married you,' Jayson said to her as soon as the officers turned back to securing the building.

'But he already owned the building, why would he need to marry me?'

'Because he needed you to move out voluntarily. There was no way to force you out legally. It's the new loft laws. They can't evict squatters.'

'Then why is he sending the moving trucks?'

As he watched Toni's face fall, Jayson softened his voice.

'There are no moving trucks coming, Ma.'

Toni took the vase she'd been busy repairing and hurled it against the sidewalk on the far side of the street. Jayson, maybe for the first time in his life, felt sorry for her. She'd never once, in all her marriages, been taken for a ride by a man. They'd always pursued her for her. She was Toni Blocher: a barrel of fun and a handful of happy. Eventually her men couldn't keep up and she had to trade them in. But however explosive the endings may have been, all parties walked away even in the end, always the better for having been invited to the circus.

But this time Toni got took.

Jayson hated what he saw in his mother's face. Defeat. It was something he'd never seen before, and it made her look old and tired. Sal Castellari had promised to make her an artist, an honest-to-God artist. With shows. And sales. And dignity. Unlike Jayson, Toni had never been vocal about what she wanted in life. But Jayson finally realized, as he watched his mother's face crumble on the sidewalk, that maybe the one thing she wanted was a little respect. He knew that she didn't regret a single unconventional action in her life – from her teen pregnancy, to her many marriages, to her fluid sexuality. But underneath it all, Jayson realized, what was missing was just a little goddamn respect from the world. And she'd been duped into thinking she'd found it.

'We'll sue the fucker!' Tara said from the sidelines. 'You're his wife after all. Half of this is yours, now.'

Toni stood, and gently folded up the lawn chair she'd been sitting on.

'I'm not going to sue anyone,' she said. 'How could I sue someone? I don't have a penny to my name. I don't even have a mailing address.'

Jayson had never seen his mother this passive. It was unnerving.

'Well then what the hell are we going to do?' Tara said. 'I'm not sleeping here on these steps. I'm fucking pregnant.'

'Yes, I know,' was all Toni said. But she didn't make a move. She just stood there in the middle of Wooster Street in front of a pile of every belonging she'd collected during her thirty-three madcap years of life.

Willie picked up on the tension.

'Where's the truck?' he asked nervously.

'No truck ride today, Willie Prader,' Toni said quietly. 'No truck ride today.'

'What if . . .' Tara started before Toni interrupted her.

'I think maybe, Tara, that it's time for you to go back to your mom and dad.'

Tara look stunned. Pregnant or not, there was no way she was going back to the house where her mom talked to a Jesus who lived in the microwave.

'Why don't we both go back?' Tara said. 'We'll live in your house.'

Toni chuckled a little. 'I haven't paid the taxes on that house in three years. If we hadn't left for New York when we did, we'd have been hauled out of there by the sheriff on New Year's Day.'

Now it was Jayson's turn to be stunned. His mother, brother, and pregnant best friend were homeless.

From its parking spot at the end of the street, Jayson's limo honked its horn. *Fuck.* The driver knew the schedule. If they didn't leave for JFK now, they wouldn't make Jayson's flight in time.

Jayson didn't know what to do.

'That's my car,' he said to his mother. He hesitated a moment. 'I, um, have to go.' His mother gently stacked the folded lawnchair she'd been sitting on onto the pile. 'What are you going to do?'

'Watch you get in your car, I guess,' answered Toni.

'Will you be okay?'

'When have I ever not been, Butter Bean?'

*Right now,* Jayson thought. But he couldn't wait any longer. He knew Toni would come up with something. She wouldn't let a pregnant Tara and his retarded brother be homeless for even one night. She'd come up with some scheme. She always did.

'Okay, then,' Jayson said. 'I gotta go.'

'Then go already, would ya? I got two and a half kids to take care of here. I don't need you suckin' on my tit too.' She tried to smile, but only made it halfway.

From the back seat of the limo, Jayson turned around to wave to his mother, but she was facing the other way, staring at the huge pile of her past. The last thing he saw as the car took the corner was Toni's head sinking into her hands.

# Twenty-seven

'**Don't you have any bags?**' Helen asked Jayson as they stood next to the baggage carousel in LAX.

'Um, no. I, um, planned on going shopping here.'

Jayson was too ashamed to relate what had happened just before he left New York – how all his family's belongings were in a pile on Wooster Street. He sat next to Helen in first class for the entire six-and-a-half-hour trip to L.A. and never once let her know that he'd just left his entire extended family homeless on the curb.

Instead he'd regaled her with stories of her *own* past. He remembered more guest-starring Helen Lawson appearances than Helen herself did. He could recite entire lines of flirty comic dialogue between her and McLean Stevenson from her *Match Game* appearances five years ago. She, in turn, kept him laughing with increasingly scandalous tales of behind-the-scenes Hollywood as she drank her way across the country. By the time they touched down in L.A., he'd all but forgotten the drama he'd left behind.

Walking with Helen through the airport, he couldn't help

but notice how many eyes craned to watch her simply go down the concourse. This was what being a real star was like, he thought. And soon it would be happening to him, too.

Struggling, he carried her four bags to her limo waiting by the curb.

'Jesus, Mary, and Darkie . . . don't you people come inside to help anymore?' Helen yelled through the window at the limo driver, who wasn't in fact black but Indian. He started to protest but Helen shut him up by clenching her hand in a Black Power fist and telling him, 'I was just kidding. Lighten up, brother.'

She gave Jayson a quick boozy hug, and he nearly swooned. Dozens of people were watching him – *Jayson Blocher* – get hugged by Helen Lawson.

He was exhausted by the time he reached the Bel Air. The car would be back to pick him up promptly at seven in the morning to take him to the studio and production offices. There, the entire cast would assemble to discuss 'next steps' and get their itinerary for the rest of the day's press events. Having nothing to unpack, he fell instantly into bed and slept fitfully through the night. What he was so easily able to forget while conscious haunted his dreams from the moment he closed his eyes. He dreamt about his mother, Willie, and Tara wandering around SoHo in the middle of the night, while Tara occasionally screamed out for Trey.

In the morning, he awoke, quickly washed out his underwear in the sink and blew them dry with the hotel's hairdryer. He was ecstatic to begin his first day in his new city. He decided that during the weeklong press tour, he would ask someone in the production company to secure him an apartment. Somewhere in West Hollywood, he thought. He'd done the budgeting in his head, and though he probably wouldn't receive a paycheck for a couple of weeks, surely some landlord would allow him to move in on credit. He was about to be the star of a network sitcom, after all.

A production assistant met him at the studio gate.

'Mr. Blocher?' the young woman asked. She looked a little like Tara – only tidied up, dressed in preppie clothes, carrying a clipboard, and not pregnant.

'Yes, that's me.' It was odd being called 'Mister' by someone probably five years older than he was.

'Why don't you come with me?'

The girl and her clipboard escorted Jayson across the lot to the production offices. She walked so quickly and efficiently that Jayson had a hard time keeping up with her.

'Have a seat in here,' she said, opening the door on a cute, red-tiled bungalow that looked like it served as a boardroom for the production team. The room was empty save for a pitcher of water in the middle of the table. From its cloudiness, it looked like it had been a while since it had been refreshed. Jayson sat down at the table and waited for more people to arrive.

After about a half an hour he began getting anxious . . . and a little angry. He was the star of this pilot – well, co-star.

Why the hell was he being kept waiting alone in this confer-
ence room? He opened the door of the bungalow and peered
out across the studio lot. There was no one else around. He
decided to explore. He knew a driver had been ordered to pick
Helen up roughly the same time he was picked up, so she must
be here somewhere.

He crossed the parking lot to the large soundstage where
they'd filmed the pilot, and opened the side door beneath the
red light that flashed during filming. The set was dark, and
it took a moment for his eyes to adjust. He heard a group of
people talking in low tones somewhere to his left.

He made his way over to a group of producers, directors,
Helen, and assorted crew members sitting around the table
where they'd had their first read-through of the script.

'Hey!' Jayson said, suddenly furious at the production
assistant for having initially taken him to the wrong room.
'Here you all are. Some girl put me in some weird boardroom
across the lot,' he laughed.

No one else laughed. In fact, they were dead silent.

Finally the director spoke up.

'Uh. Jayson. Hello there. We, uh, just needed a minute to,
umm, look at some paperwork before we, ah . . .'

'Criminey Rickets, Francis,' Helen chimed in over the
director's nervous stuttering. 'You're stammering like one of
Jerry's kids on a pogo stick.' She turned to Jayson. 'Follow
me, Half-pint.'

Helen stood up and walked over toward Jayson.

'What's going on?' Jayson said, finally realizing that something *was* going on – something they didn't want him to know about. Maybe they were planning some sort of surprise for him, he thought. Maybe they were going to surprise him with his own dressing room . . . or more lines. Maybe they were meeting with Helen to tell her that they were going to give him equal billing with her.

Helen put her arm around Jayson and walked him to her dressing room.

'Well, Half-pint, sometimes you can look at a glass and say it's half full. Other times you can look at a glass and say it's half empty. And sometimes, like right now, you're sucking down a big old tumbler of piss.'

Jayson had no idea what she was talking about.

'Siddown,' she commanded, pointing toward the mauve sofa against the wall of her dressing room. She shut the door behind her. 'You want a candy?' she asked handing him a bowl of the same stale sugarless hard candies she had in her dressing room for the pilot.

'What's going on, Helen?' Jayson said, ignoring her offer. His voice cracked with nerves. 'Is something wrong with the show?'

'Not so much the show, queery. Much more with you.'

'What did I do?' Had they heard about his mother? Did she find some way to call them? Could they have found out that he came from a family of crazies he'd left homeless on the curb to starve to death? He'd just have to explain. They'd understand. Who wouldn't understand? He'd made the only sane choice. They'd have done the exact same thing.

'Again,' Helen said, '. . . not so much *what* you did, but *who*.'

She tossed the rolled-up paper that she'd been carrying onto the coffee table in front of Jayson. He picked it up slowly. It was the *National Enquirer*.

'Page nine,' Helen said.

Jayson slowly turned to the page. He flipped past a story about Joyce Dewitt being abducted by aliens. Then Tom Bosley's alleged Siamese love twins. A preposterous interview with someone claiming to be Nancy Reagan's psychic. And then he reached page nine.

Which was three quarters covered by a photo.

A photo of Jayson.

And Devlin.

Kissing.

The headline on the opposite page screamed in 72-point type: Runaway Gay Child Star Hooker Sweet on Picky Prince! The subhead followed: America's Sweetheart Candyman Goes Ga-Ga for Gay Fugitive.

Jayson couldn't even begin to read the short accompanying article. He was fixated on the pictures – Gavin's pictures! Gavin's Polaroids of the two of them hugging and kissing in the loft.

Jayson's hands began to shake. The middle section of the paper dropped to the floor.

'I don't know how they got these,' he started.

'Doesn't much matter now, Half-pint,' Helen replied lighting a Pall Mall. 'The only thing that matters now is how high you hold your head.'

'I could say they're fake,' Jayson said. His mind was spinning. Mostly he was trying to figure out a way to turn back time and un-take the pictures.

'Doesn't matter. Everyone's seen 'em already. That's all that counts. Like those infamous shots of me, Paul Lynde, Roy Cohn, Barbara Walters, and the zucchini . . .'

'But it's nobody's business,' Jayson stuttered, reaching.

'When you're in this business, everyone is in your business. Somebody didn't like you and sold the pictures. Probably didn't even get that much for them. It's page *nine* for Chrissake.'

'But . . .'

'Jesus, Half-pint. You got more butts than a West Hollywood bathhouse on double coupon day.'

'What about the show?' Jayson asked. 'What am I supposed to do about the show?'

'Well, that's an easy one. You're not going to do anything about the show. The show's over. For you at least.'

The blood was rushing to Jayson's ears, throbbing with every racing heartbeat. He could barely hear Helen.

'Look, kid,' Helen said. 'This is rotten luck. No doubt. There's no way to plop a maraschino cherry in it and sip it. You gotta chug this hooch and walk out of the bar.'

Jayson didn't even bother trying to hold back the tears.

'So just tell me what you need right now,' Helen continued. 'Tell me where your family lives again? Do you want to get the hell out of here? I'm not good for much, but I've got a lot of practice with getaways. Do you want me to put you on a plane? Get you home?'

*Home.* With that Jayson broke down completely. He told Helen everything. About coming out after watching *Phil Donahue* when he was five; about his secret crush on Trey and him running away; about his Prader-Willi brother who ate out of garbage cans. He spilled everything about Gavin the drug-addict traitor, Franck the erstwhile prankster, and Tara the pregnant teen half-twin who was plagued with nightmares about her missing brother. It all kept tumbling out, uncontrollably – Sal Castellari who tricked them all, and Harlande his movie-star father who let him down. And Devlin, whom he truly loved and ultimately chased off. And Toni – his certifiable mother – who was straight, then lesbian, then not, and now homeless for all he knew. And how he couldn't stomach the idea of going back to all that. He wouldn't. He would throw himself off the Hollywood sign before he went backward again.

Jayson was pouring his life story onto Helen Lawson's lap. And she let him. It was the longest stretch of time that Helen 'La' Lawson had ever gone without speaking. He finally finished only because he could no longer get a word out between his sobs.

Helen leaned back and lit her third cigarette in ten minutes.

'Well, Half-pint. That's quite a potboiler,' she said, inadvertently exhaling a perfect smoke ring.

'I'd give up anything,' Jayson said tearfully, *'anything,* just to start over.'

'No can do, kiddo. You can't change the script after it's been filmed.'

She kicked both of her feet up onto the coffee table between them.

'Now I'm not one to give advice – if I had any good stuff, I'd use it on myself. But what I *do* know is that you're stuck in the show you've been cast in. You can't recast midseason, kill characters off, and start with new ones. So your family is crazy. So am I. So are you. So what?'

Helen took a long drag on her Pall Mall before continuing.

'Big deal – you're a fruit and now everyone knows it. It happens. You're not the first. You won't be the last.'

Helen pulled a flask out from underneath a magazine on the coffee table and took a swig.

'I just want to do everything over,' Jayson sobbed. 'Do everything a different way.'

'Impossible, amigo,' Helen declared. 'The universe wrote the script, and cast us in our roles. It was all planned out for us before we left our mothers' hoo-ha.'

Helen looked Jayson directly in the eye.

'That's just the way it is, Half-pint. You can't just trade in one way for another way,' she said, leaning forward and blowing smoke and scotch into his face. 'Nope. You can't trade in one way for another way.'

She picked up the bowl of stale sugarless candies. 'Here. Have one of these nasty things. I'm trying to get rid of them before my diabetes goes completely away.'

Through his tears Jayson looked down at the unappetizing candies. He remembered how the creepy Unsinger used to force Jayson to barter for them at the end of each 'rap session.' How he used to have to 'trade in one way for a better way.' Well it didn't work that way. Helen 'La' Lawson just confirmed it. Unsinger had always used Trey as the perfect example of what Jayson should strive to be. Jayson should be athletic, like Trey. Jayson should make more friends, like Trey. Jayson should come to church, like Trey. But Jayson *wasn't* Trey. Could never be like Trey. And, anyway, Trey turned out just as fucked up as Jayson had. *Trey* didn't trade in one way. *Trey* was a runaway.

Jayson froze.

Trey didn't trade in one way.

Trey din't trade in one way.

*Trey din't – Trey din't run 'way!*

'Oh God.'

'Whassamatter Half-pint? You're whiter than Loretta Young.'

'Helen, I need that plane ticket.'

# *Twenty-eight*

**Jayson prayed she'd be there** at the gate. The message he'd left on her answering machine was vague and rambling. If he explained too much she might not believe him. And he needed her to believe him.

Jayson left the jet way and scanned the gate area. *Shit.* She didn't show up.

'Hey, Butter Bean, next time try looking down.'

Franck was standing almost directly in front of Jayson. He'd forgotten how tiny she was. His memory of her knocking out the three football players made her much larger in his mind. Plus, he hadn't seen her in almost a year. He'd probably grown an inch, at least.

He reached out and enveloped her in an inescapable bear hug.

'Easy, pal,' she said. 'I'm still a cripple you know.'

Jayson laughed – for the first time in months it seemed.

'We have to go to Oconomowoc,' Jayson said. 'Tonight.' He grabbed her hand and began race walking toward the exit.

'Are you going to tell me why at some point?' Franck asked, her cane tapping the ground as quickly as Jayson led her.

'Let's just get in the car and drive.'

By the time they reached Unsinger's house it was nearly one o'clock in the morning. It was on the far northern outskirts of Oconomowoc, away from the lakes in the middle of the flat, endless farm country. Unsinger lived in an old farmhouse that had once belonged to his grandparents, in the middle of hundreds of acres of farmland. They saw the porch light shining from over a mile away.

Jayson couldn't shake a strong sense of unease, but he didn't know whether to attribute it to his hunch about Trey's whereabouts, the uncertainty about the fate of his mother, Willie, and Tara, or the disastrous tabloid article that had ruined his chance of stardom less than thirty-six hours ago. Or maybe it was simply being back in Wisconsin again that made him feel a little queasy.

Having heard Jayson's story, Franck turned off her head-lights about a quarter mile from Unsinger's house. His drive-way alone was almost that long. She coasted in neutral until the car came to a stop.

'Okay,' Franck said. 'You stay here.'

'I'm not staying in this car.'

'Look. This is your crazy idea. I don't need you getting reckless trying to prove your point.'

'But I *know* I'm right. Unsinger was *obsessed* with Trey. Plus Tara had all those nightmares,' Jayson explained.

'Oh right,' Franck said facetiously. 'That's one of the first things we learned at the police academy: Dream-ology.'

'Plus,' Jayson continued defending his theory, '*you* were the one who told me that Willie had been missing at the same time Trey disappeared. Willie *saw* Unsinger take Trey. I'm convinced. That's why he was so adamant whenever we mentioned that Trey ran away.'

'Then why haven't you asked Willie what happened?'

Jayson flushed. Confirming his hunch with Willie had been Jayson's first idea too. Except that there was no way to reach him . . . or his mom . . . or Tara.

'I couldn't reach them on the phone,' Jayson replied, which wasn't a lie. It was more of a Helen Lawsonesque truth. 'Let's go,' Jayson said, trying to change the topic. 'There's only one way to find out if I'm right.'

'Look, drama queen. Just stay in the car. Let me look around a little bit, and if I see anything suspicious, I'll get a search warrant first thing in the morning. Okay?'

Franck waited for a response. Jayson set his jaw.

'I said, "O*kay!*"' Franck repeated.

'If I say "no" you won't go look, right?'

'Exactly.'

'Fine.'

'Good,' Franck said. She reached up to the ceiling of her pickup truck and yanked out the bare wires on the dome light before she opened her door so they wouldn't turn on and give them away. *Lesbians think of everything,* Jayson thought.

There was just enough light from the quarter moon for Franck to pick her way toward the farmhouse but not enough light for Jayson to see Franck's progress once she got beyond fifty or so feet from the truck.

After ten minutes or so, Jayson began growing impatient.

*This is stupid,* Jayson thought. *I was the one who figured this out. I should be there when Trey is rescued.*

Jayson imagined how the rescue scene would play out in the eventual movie of the week. Trey would no doubt be tied up in a farm chair, probably with a bandanna gag in his mouth. If it were a nighttime soap, he might even be shirtless.

*Fuck it,* Jayson thought. *If I'm going to get a starring role in this, I at least have to be there when it happens.*

Jayson quietly opened the passenger side door of the truck and slipped out. He wished he had a jacket. He wished he had any clothes other than the same ones he'd been wearing since he left New York. It was almost June, but the air still had the chill of early spring. The corn had only recently been planted in the surrounding fields, and in the dim moonlight the rows seemed to stretch on forever, as if nothing existed on the entire flat earth except the white farmhouse a hundred yards away.

He crept along the gravel drive as softly as he could. As he got closer to the house, he grew increasingly frightened. Given the late hour, all of the lights were naturally out. The small yard around the house was manicured perfectly – in keeping with Unsinger's military mindset, Jayson thought. The house itself seemed equally attended to. There were no crooked shutters, no broken spindles on the porch railing.

Jayson stopped and listened to see if he could hear Franck. He still hadn't spotted her. He heard faint sounds coming from around the back of the house. He squinted in the darkness and felt his way around the corner.

It was pitch black in the backyard. A large maple tree blocked the scant moonlight and Jayson became disoriented. There were sounds somewhere near the ground just ahead of him. He knelt down, and heard a tiny whisper. It was Franck's voice.

*'I heard you. Say something else. Quietly. I'll find you.'*

Jayson couldn't hear exactly where Franck's voice was coming from. He inched forward in the darkness.

*'Here. I'm down here,'* came the soft reply.

It was Trey.

Unmistakably Trey. Even though it was the most silent of whispers, Jayson knew it was Trey.

*'Stay still. I'm unlatching the door.'* That was Franck's voice. Jayson squinted at the darkness in front of him and could barely make out Franck's silhouette pulling open the cellar bulkhead door, and disappearing down the steps that led to the basement. At least with Unsinger's attention to detail, the hinges on the metal bulkhead were well oiled. Even only twenty feet away, Jayson couldn't hear any of her movements. All Jayson could hear was a slight breeze through early summer weeds in the miles of fields around him. He had to

know more of what was going on. He could help if necessary. Jayson inched forward until he was at the top of the bulkhead steps.

He was going in.

He reached out to hold something for balance as he took the first step into the basement's inky darkness. He grasped what he thought was a railing of some sort.

Only it wasn't.

It was the handle on one of the open bulkhead doors.

The metal door crashed shut, nearly knocking him completely down the stairs.

The sound of clanging metal was deafening. The only thing more explosive was the light turning on in an upstairs window. The light spilled out the window and flooded the yard.

Jayson bolted back up the short flight of stairs and ran out into the backyard. He was halfway around the front corner of the house, racing back toward the truck and safety. But there was a twitching in his chest that made him stop.

He couldn't leave Franck and Trey behind the way he'd left Toni and Tara and Willie in New York. Actors that desert a hit show to break out on their own almost never succeed. He was stuck with the cast he'd been given, and for the first time in his short life, he realized that he would rather die defending them than attempt yet another spinoff.

Jayson ran back to the back of the house. One by one, the lights inside the house flashed on, seemingly brighter than the sun. He heard footsteps – Unsinger's – pounding through the house. Jayson flattened himself against the siding between windows, trying to make his way back to the bulkhead without Unsinger spotting him through the window.

'*WHO'S IN MY HOUSE?!*' Unsinger's voice rang out. '*I'VE GOT A GUN.*'

Jayson could trace the sound of Unsinger's footsteps as they ran through all of the upstairs rooms, then the downstairs. One by one, each window of the house lit up.

Jayson finally reached the darkened mouth of the basement bulkhead at the same moment it exploded with light. Unsinger had made it to the basement.

Jayson heard Unsinger's racing footfalls pound down the interior stairs.

'*I KNOW YOU'RE DOWN HERE! DON'T THINK YOU CAN HIDE!*'

*Fuck.*

Jayson's mind raced. He didn't know what to do. Should he run back to the truck to try to get help? Would Unsinger kill Franck before he could return?

Jason dropped down to the ground and peered down the steps into the now well-lit basement.

From what he could see, the cellar was some sort of bedroom – it was decorated like the bedroom of a 1950s high school football player. There were purple and yellow Oconomowoc High School pennants hung all over one wall and a shelf full of glittering trophies on another. On the far wall there were black-and-white team portraits, under which stood a table with a row of old OHS football helmets.

This was Unsinger's high school bedroom, either meticulously preserved, or meticulously re-created.

Out of the corner of his eye he saw Franck and Trey, crouched behind what was either the water heater or the furnace. Trey was wearing purple sweatpants and an OHS football jersey. He looked fine. Other than a 1950s buzzcut exactly like Unsinger's, he didn't look that much different than he used to look when Jayson hung out with him and Tara in the Wernermeier basement rec room. Nothing seemed that unusual, except for the fact that they were crouching in fear, and that Franck was clutching one of the larger football trophies as a weapon.

Then he saw Unsinger. He looked bigger than ever, wearing a ripped T-shirt and boxer shorts. In his right hand, he held his Child Protective Services–issued pistol, and he was stealthily making his way closer to where Franck and Trey were hiding. Franck slowly stuck her head out to peer around the water heater.

Except that she was looking the wrong way.

'HE'S COMING FROM THE OTHER DIREC . . .' Jayson started to yell just as Unsinger lunged at the unsuspecting Franck. Before she could turn toward him, Unsinger swung the butt end of the pistol across the back of her head. Franck sank to the ground as if her bones had all melted at once.

The second after he'd knocked out Franck, Unsinger turned toward the open bulkhead. He glared, squinting up into the darkness at the top of the bulkhead. Jayson had given away his location by yelling his warning to Franck and Trey.

Unsinger made what sounded like a growl before springing toward the bulkhead stair. Jayson turned to escape, sprinting for the darkness of the fields beyond, when he heard a crash and a loud yelp.

He turned back to see that Trey had tripped Unsinger, and now the two were locked in a violent struggle on the floor. Even with Trey's athletic physique, Unsinger still had nearly a hundred pounds more bulk on him, and quickly had Trey pinned on the floor.

'Why?' Unsinger was asking – almost pleading – with Trey. '*Why are you doing this to me? You have everything here. The trophies. The varsity jackets. It's all yours now. Why would you leave? If you leave it's all over. You'll have to join the army. And you'll go to Vietnam. You don't want to go to Vietnam, do you?*'

Jayson couldn't believe what he was hearing. Unsinger was trying to turn Trey into himself. His high-school self. His pre-Vietnam self.

If Trey couldn't overpower Unsinger, Jayson thought, then there was no way in hell that he could. He took off running for the truck. His only choice was to go for help.

He only made it about halfway across the backyard before he stopped, frozen. His heart collapsed into his gut.

Franck had the keys.

'I KNOW YOU'RE OUT THERE, FAGGOT,' came Unsinger's voice bellowing from the basement behind him. It would only be a matter of time before he found a way to restrain Trey and begin searching for Jayson. 'YOU WON'T GET FAR. YOU WON'T EVEN MAKE IT TO THE END OF THE DRIVEWAY. I DIDN'T KILL THIRTY GOOKS WITH BAD AIM.'

Jayson scanned the darkness for someplace to hide. There were no trees or shrubs for miles in any direction. The cornfields surrounding the house were barely shin high. Jayson would be spotted the instant Unsinger turned on any outside light.

*The garage.*

Jayson spotted it about a hundred feet off to his right. It was a detached wood frame building, probably as old as the farmhouse itself. He sprinted across the yard and ducked around the opposite side of the structure. He peered around the corner back toward the house. Was Unsinger still in the basement? He had no idea. He could easily be somewhere outside already. Camouflaged. Stalking Jayson. The thought of trying to hide from a Vietnam vet successfully was almost enough to make Jayson give up. This wasn't turning out like any detective show he'd ever seen. The bad guy had all the advantages. It was hopeless – only a matter of time before Jayson was caught. And then what? Would Unsinger kill Franck and him? No one had any idea that he and Franck were there. Nobody had any idea what state Jayson was in. Unsinger could get away with a double murder. That didn't happen on TV. Ever.

For the first time in his life, Jayson didn't feel like he was on television.

He felt reality. And he didn't know what to do.

There's no such a thing as reality TV.

Jayson started to cry. He felt limp. Exhausted and hopeless, he fell back against the garage for support.

The wall behind him gave way.

It was a door: The back door to the garage.

Maybe, just maybe there was a lock inside the door. He could buy a few more minutes of precious life to ponder everything that had gone so very wrong.

He crept inside the garage. As dark as it was outside in the barely moonlit night, it was even darker inside the garage. Jayson tried to find a hiding place somewhere amid the chaotic piles of junk and tools. . . .

*Tools!* Tools could be used as weapons! How many guys in movies had he seen whack someone with a tire iron? It was his only hope. He dropped to his knees and started feeling around for the heaviest, most solid thing he could lift. Everything seemed to be in a tangle on the floor. He couldn't determine what anything was in the pitch black. He frantically began digging through the impossible pile of pick-up sticks.

Then he felt it.

And he yanked as hard as he could.

Jayson ran back out the garage door and into the night with his prize in his hand. When he reached a drainage culvert at the edge of the cornfield, he dropped to the ground. The minute he hit the dirt, he saw the porch lights flick on.

They were even brighter than he imagined. They must have been floodlights. Jayson held his breath and slowly raised his head just barely high enough to spot Unsinger circling the house, looking out across the brightly lit fields for Jayson. He ducked back down just as Unsinger turned the corner of the house looking in his direction.

'C'mon, Jayson. What's the point of hiding? It's just delaying things.' Unsinger wasn't yelling anymore. He voice sounded calm, and reasonable, almost like when he used to sit with Jayson and Willie at the picnic table in their backyard. *'You can spend a little time with your friend Trey. You'd like that wouldn't you? You want some candy? Everybody wants candy.'*

Jayson felt around underneath him until he found a rock the size he needed. When Unsinger had his back toward Jayson, Jayson quietly stood up.

*Please God,* Jayson thought, *just this once – just one time – help me throw like a boy.*

Jayson wound up and let loose. The tennis-ball-sized rock lobbed through the dark night sky and came down exactly on target: the wooden clapboard side of the garage.

Jayson crouched back down just as Unsinger turned toward the origin of the noise – the garage. Unsinger sprinted toward the outbuilding, screaming into the black night: *'ALRIGHT YOU ROTTEN MOTHERFUCKER! TIME'S UP!'*

Unsinger ran up to the same door that Jayson had closed moments ago. He paused a second, leaning into the doorway, and shouted into the interior of the garage. He raised his pistol and the click of it cocking ricocheted across the fields.

*'THE CANDY MAN'S HERE!'*

Jayson held his breath. The hundred feet between them felt like inches. *Just step inside, Unsinger, step inside.*

It seemed like hours before Unsinger finally decided to enter the garage.

Jayson counted to ten. He wanted to be sure that Unsinger was far enough inside.

*. . . Eight-Mississippi–Nine-Mississippi–TEN!*

Jayson stood up, took the remote control garage door opener from his back pocket, aimed it toward the white wooden garage, and pressed the big center button.

WHOOOOOOOMPHHHH!!!!

Beautiful bright orange bits of flaming debris drifted down from the sky all around him, landing in the dewy grass like thousands of small candles – thousands of small candles that had just a second ago been assembled in the shape of a garage. And in the shape of Philip Unsinger.

Jayson finally let himself exhale, and as he did so, he released his clenched fists. From one hand dropped the garage door remote control – the remote control that caused a tiny spark as it clicked the overhead garage door opener to life.

From Jayson's other hand dropped the length or rubber hose that had been, up until a moment ago, the connection hose to the propane fuel tank in Philip Unsinger's garage.

'Roll credits,' Jayson said into the cool Wisconsin night.

# *Twenty-nine*

**Naturally,** the first thing Franck did after regaining consciousness was cold-cock the doctor who was shining a penlight into her pupil. She'd been out for nearly eighteen hours. And Jayson had only left her side twice, each time to talk with detectives about what had happened at Philip Unsinger's. The police were waiting to release anything to the media until they were sure of exactly what had transpired the evening before. Since Franck was still enrolled in the police academy, they seemed overly protective of whatever information got out.

Once the newly conscious Franck realized that she was in Oconomowoc Memorial Hospital, Jayson reminded her of everything that had occurred. She recalled fuzzy bits and pieces, but most of the evening was a blur to her. When he reached the point describing how he'd rigged Unsinger's death in the exploding garage, Franck smiled and mouthed, *'Toni would be proud,'* before slipping off into more drug-induced sleep.

While Jayson knew that Trey was somewhere in the same hospital, he didn't have the courage yet to seek him out. There was a part of him that was still afraid he'd blame Jayson for the events leading up to his kidnapping. He'd learned from a nurse that he'd had a couple of ribs and his leg broken in the scuffle with Unsinger, and that they would likely keep him in the hospital for at least a week for 'observation.' Jayson knew from the countless true-life crime newsmagazine shows that Trey would likely need to be 'deprogrammed' after having been kidnapped for so long.

Finally knowing that Franck would be okay, Jayson went out into the hospital hallway. He didn't know where he was going. He had no place to go actually. But he needed to walk around to sort out the jumble in his mind. He was exhausted, but kept declining the nurses' offer of a place to sleep.

He was at the vending machine near the emergency room trying to decide between a 100 Grand bar or Cheetos when he felt a tap on his shoulder.

'Hey, Jayson.'

It was Tom Wernermeier. Before Jayson had a chance to respond, Tom reached out with his thick German arms and enveloped him in a crushing bear hug. Jayson buried his face in Tom's shirt. He could smell the fresh-cut grass and lake breezes in its folds. They stood in a mutual embrace for nearly a full minute.

'I don't know what else there is to say right now,' Tom said when they parted, 'except thanks. But that seems so small.'

'I didn't know if I was right. It was just a hunch,' Jayson said.

'Well, it was the right hunch,' Tom said.

Jayson peered around Tom at the waiting area. Tom noticed.

'She's not here,' Tom said. Jayson was embarrassed to have been caught looking for Terri. But Jayson couldn't help but be wary of her possible presence. She'd always been a bad omen for him. 'She's run off with some religious group,' Tom explained. 'To Waco, Texas . . . or "Whacko," as I call it. They've cut her off from all contact. There's no way for me to reach her.'

'I'm sorry,' Jayson said.

'That's okay,' Tom replied. 'We all had different ways of dealing with it.' Tom reassuringly cupped Jayson's cheek in his beefy hand. 'Have you told Tara that you found Trey? Should I call her?'

Jayson flushed. Eventually he would have to tell someone the truth: that he had no idea what had happened to Tara, his mother, and Willie; that, in all likelihood they were squatting in some other building . . . or in a shelter . . . or camping out in Central Park.

'I, uh,' Jayson began, 'I was in L.A. . . . it's kind of hard to get hold of them. They, umm, had to move out of . . .'

Suddenly there was a loud bang from outside the emergency room doors. Given the recent drama, Jayson first thought it was gunfire, but quickly realized it was just a vehicle backfiring. The loud pop was followed by a squealing engine noise, which was followed by a loud rattling as whatever it was rolled to a stop just outside the double glass doors. Then the yelling started.

'*We've got an emergency here! Jesus Christ, let's see some action, people!*'

A clutch of orderlies raced to the door toward a voice that was all too familiar to both Jayson and Tom.

A second later, the emergency room doors slid open and Toni came racing in, shouting orders at every person she laid eyes on. She was followed by a grinning Willie who was munching on a Snickers. Willie was followed by Tara, who was being pushed in a wheelchair by an orderly. As always when Toni was around, it felt like someone had pushed the fast forward button on time and space.

'*Contractions at thirty seconds,*' one of the orderlies shouted as a nurse rushed over to take over the wheelchair.

'*Let's giddy up into those stirrups people,*' Toni shouted. '*Are you all on a goddamn Sanka break or something?*'

Then she spotted Tom and Jayson. As someone whose entire existence proved the theory of random chance, Toni didn't seem the least surprised to see them.

'Well, hello there, Tom. You look good. Hardly grandfather material at all. How was L.A., Butter Bean?'

Tom quickly embraced Toni, and then followed her and Willie as they raced to catch up with Tara – who was being wheeled hurriedly into the emergency room. Jayson broke into a jog to catch up with the group.

At the entrance to the operating room, a petite nurse held up her hand to stop them from entering.

'If you think you can stop this convoy, honey,' Toni said,

pushing past her, 'you might want to pick out which emergency table you want to wind up on.'

When they all got into the room, the befuddled doctors and nurses had no time to deal with the prohibited guests. All attention was fixed on Tara, who was calmly asking that if she was too late for an IV, could someone please get her a joint.

'Crowning,' the doctor said, peering between Tara's legs. 'Forceps.' A nearby nurse handed the shiny steel implement to him.

'Motherfucker, this is a bitch,' Tara groaned, typically underwhelmed by the miracle at hand. 'Oh, hi, Dad!'

Tom walked over to hold his daughter's hand. He cradled her head against his side. Toni stayed off in the corner. She pulled out a Newport and began to light it.

'You can't smoke in here,' one of the nurses scolded her.

'Really? Then what would you call this?' Toni replied, drawing on her freshly lit menthol and exhaling a smoke ring. Jayson walked over next to her.

'How the hell did you get here?' Jayson asked.

'By the skin of my teeth, of course,' Toni replied. 'Traded some junkies my whole pile of trash to get the Maverick started. They really are a determined lot if you give them stuff to pawn for dope.'

'You drove all the way home?' Jayson asked, incredulous.

'Well, nearly all the way home,' Toni replied. 'Tara's dam burst somewhere around the South Side of Chicago. Thought we could make it over to Tom's to pick him up, but Tara just kept pushing.'

'Tara's tummy hurts,' Willie helpfully tried to explain to Jayson.

Suddenly, Tara let out a loud yelp.

*'Goddamnsonnofabitch!'* Tara shouted. *'What the hell is happening down there? Is there some sort of roadblock?'*

'Head's clear,' the doctor said calmly. 'Keep pushing.'

Tara bore down again, wincing.

'It's a boy!' the nurse said as the tiny red being emerged between Tara's knees.

Tom leaned over and gave the sweaty Tara a long kiss on the top of her blonde head.

*'Great,'* Toni joked. 'Just what the world needs. Another goddamn man.'

'Wait,' the doctor said as he passed off the baby to one of the nurses, 'there's another one coming.'

'What?!' Tara asked, exhaustedly.

*'Assistance!'* the doctor called. The nurse whisked away the first baby and another stepped up beside the doctor.

*'Oh God . . . if there's more than two, I'm sending one back,'* Tara huffed, groaning.

'Crowning . . .'

'You can do it,' Tom whispered into the top of Tara's head.

'Uhhhnnnn . . .' Tara grunted.

'And . . . a *girl*. It's a girl,' the doctor announced less than a minute later, handing off another bloody bundle to the nurse.

The nurses went about cleaning off the two babies, and handed them back to Tara, who held one in the crook of each arm. She looked down at them and smiled.

'Do you have names picked out?' one of the nurses asked holding her clipboard.

'This one is called Tony,' Tara said, nodding at the boy. 'And this one is called . . .' she paused, looking down at the girl 'Jayye . . . J-A-Y-Y-E . . . two "y"s.' She looked up and winked at Jayson. 'For extra flair.'

The group huddled around Tara.

'Good job, girl,' Toni said. 'Now, of course, comes the hard part. It ain't easy being the perfect mother.'

Jayson tried valiantly not to roll his eyes.

'And now,' Tom said, 'I think I'm going to go give the good news to your brother.'

Tara and Toni turned to stare at him with wide-eyed amazement.

Only Willie seemed unfazed. He picked up a half-empty cup of Jell-O that had been left on a tray just outside the door and licked at the inside.

'*Trey din't,*' he said softly, as if to himself, '*Trey din't run 'way.*'

297

# Thirty

'You awake?'

The hospital room was lit only by the various colored bulbs on the medical equipment and the bluish light from the television mounted on the wall which was tuned in to *The Dukes of Hazzard* – Trey's favorite.

Trey turned his head toward the room's door.

'Hey Jay-Jay!'

Trey's grin dissipated any anxiety Jayson had about seeing his friend for the first time since the Homecoming Incident. Trey pushed a button on the remote connected to his bed and it slowly raised him to a sitting position. His torso was wrapped completely in bandages.

'You hurt bad?'

'Not so bad. They're just keeping me in here to make sure I didn't go nutso.'

'Did you?'

'No,' Trey laughed. 'I keep tellin' em that I wasn't the crazy one – Unsinger was.'

'I'm sorry about it all,' Jayson said, looking down at the tile floor.

'Why? You *saved* me.'

Jayson hadn't really thought about that. He'd been too busy blaming himself for making Trey's life miserable.

'I was horrible to you,' Trey said. 'And still you came and saved me. I still don't get how you figured it out.'

'Willie saw you. He was foraging for food near the bike path. He must have seen the whole thing happen.'

Trey rubbed his temples. 'Man, I barely remember. Unsinger was sitting in his car at the entrance to the bike path and he called me over. He'd heard about the Homecoming business – about the stupid kissing thing. Then he started telling me to take one of those nasty candies. He started screaming at me when I wouldn't – something about trading in something for some other thing. I started to ride away, but he wigged out. I think he hit me with the same gun he whacked Franck with.'

'I was horrible to you too,' Jayson said. 'I'm sorry. The Homecoming thing wasn't my idea though.'

'Doesn't matter. That was nothing,' Trey said. 'Comparatively speaking, of course.' He gestured toward his bandaged chest with the hand that wasn't in a cast. Jayson fell silent. He didn't know what more to say. He had a million questions about what had happened to Trey at Unsinger's house, but figured they were best left to professionals. Like Dr. Joyce Brothers.

'So, um, you weren't, um, treated too, uh . . .' Jayson stammered.

'No, the creep didn't rape me or nothin',' Trey sighed. 'He just had some weird hangup about the war, and how it ruined his life. But don't tell anyone that yet. I want to keep 'em guessing so I can have a few more days where they give me anything I ask for.'

Jayson laughed. 'You know you're an uncle?'

Trey rolled his eyes. 'I heard. Dad told me. He said you also had a big year . . . *Devlin Williamson?*'

'Yeah,' Jayson chuckled. 'I'll tell you about everything when you feel better.'

They fell into a long, but comforting silence. They each had plenty to tell the other – too much, really – but Jayson was satisfied simply being in the same room with Trey again. They had never really spoken that much. Some of Jayson's favorite memories were of sitting quietly next to Trey on the Green Bay Packers beanbag chair in his basement. And while he wouldn't have traded in a moment of the past year, it was nice to just *be* with Trey again. Like the old days.

Their silence was interrupted by the loud screeching of the General Lee's tires from the television. They looked up at the set.

'This is the episode where Boss Hogg robs his own bank, and Uncle Jesse mortgages the farm to bail him out,' Jayson explained. 'It's a rerun.'

'Not to me. I haven't seen any of my shows. I missed the whole goddamn season of television.'

Jayson's eyes lit up. 'I can help with that!'

Forty-five minutes later, Trey drifted off to sleep just after Jayson finished his recap of the previous season's *Magnum PI* story lines and right before he started in on *The Fall Guy*'s.

# Thirty-one

**The evening was one** of those perfect early summer evenings by the lake – just cool enough to keep the mosquitoes at bay, but warm enough to sit outside without jackets.

Toni, Willie, and Jayson were sitting at the picnic table set up between the two yards – the same picnic table where Unsinger and Jayson used to hold their 'rap sessions.' Tom was a few feet away, cooking dinner for them on the grill, and Tara sat on the grass nearby with one twin on each breast.

As Toni predicted back in New York, the Blocher house had been boarded up and posted with NO TRESPASSING signs by the County Tax Department. The violet and lilac house was scheduled to be auctioned off sometime later in the month. Toni, Jayson, and Willie were crashing at the Wernermeiers' until they decided what to do next. Jayson was sleeping in Trey's old bedroom while he was still in the hospital, and he woke up each morning staring into his old bedroom window, empty, not twenty feet away.

'Someone should get a plate of food ready to take to Franck and the girls,' Toni said.

'I'll do it!' Willie volunteered.

'I got it, Willie,' Jayson said patting his brother on the back.

'The burgers'll take another five minutes or so,' Tom announced from behind the grill. Jayson started putting a plate of various mayonnaise-y salads and chips together for Franck, who was stationed down at the end of Lac LaBelle Drive along with a half-dozen of her lesbian colleagues from the Waukesha County Sheriff's Department. They'd all parked their cars across the roadway to keep the dozens of news vans and satellite trucks out of camera range of the Wernermeier and Blocher houses.

Trey was scheduled to return home from the hospital tomorrow, and everyone from the local news to several national newsmagazine shows wanted to capture scenes of his homecoming which had been made possible by the 'Picky Prince, ex-boyfriend of fugitive child star Devlin Williamson.' It was all just too sensational to be true. Reality, Jayson had realized, was often the least believable script.

Jayson had dragged the old black-and-white TV up from the Wernermeiers' basement and set it on the driveway. He wasn't embarrassed to admit that he was captivated by the coverage of his own story.

'Hey, Jay-Jay, look!' Tara called out. She was sitting on the grass next to the driveway with one twin on each breast. Without any free hands, she nodded her chin toward the TV. 'Your boyfriend's on TV, queerboy.'

It was Devlin. On television. On Jayson's favorite new show, *Entertainment Tonight*.

The young host, Mary Hart – whom Jayson had previously known from *Days of Our Lives* – was interviewing Devlin via satellite. She was in L.A. while he was speaking from the *Entertainment Tonight* studios in New York. The lighting was shadowy and serious, as it always was whenever *ET* featured a controversial topic. Of all the strange events of the last month, this was the one Jayson was least prepared for. He'd fallen asleep each night desperately trying to puzzle together where Devlin might have gone after disappearing. As far as Jayson knew, Devlin was still a fugitive, which made the possibility of tracking him down even more difficult. Devlin was the only person Jayson had yet to apologize to for his diva-like behavior over the last eight months. Now, here he was: on the TV set from the Wernermeiers' basement. The same TV set on which he'd first laid eyes on Devlin Williamson.

'How will you prove your innocence?' Mary was asking Devlin, in her usual breathily serious tone which sounded more like she was imitating serious news journalists than being one.

'I don't have to prove my innocence, Mary,' Devlin said, with practiced celebrity sincerity. *'It wuuuuzzzzzn't me!'*

Mary laughed. Devlin chuckled at his own joke as well, his dimples appearing on cue to melt America's heart.

'And what's next for Devlin Williamson?' Mary continued.

'After my name is cleared, I plan on returning to cooking

school.' Mary laughed again, this time, apparently, at the idea that a former celebrity could ever learn another trade. Or maybe she was just laughing because she laughed at everything any celebrity said. Jayson didn't think that Mary Hart would hold down this job for very long.

'My boyfriend likes my cooking,' Devlin continued.

Mary kept laughing, although now a little more nervously. She was no calm, collected Phil Donahue when it came to homosexuality. While Devlin was talking, the interview cut away to show the pictures that had appeared in the *National Enquirer.* Gavin's pictures. Jayson's and Devlin's faces were blurred in the kissing shot. Apparently, showing a gay kiss on TV was the one thing Mary didn't find entertaining.

'It's been reported,' Mary continued, 'that your boyfriend – who some might recognize as the Picky Prince – is a hero now.'

It was Devlin's turn to chuckle now. 'Yes, that's him. I'm very proud of all he's accomplished.' Devlin beamed. Jayson almost went up to the TV screen to kiss the dimple like he used to.

After a few more minutes of clips from *Disorder in the Court*, and some inane celebrity questions about spirituality and old costars, the trumpet blasting *Entertainment Tonight*'s theme song swelled and the show cut to commercial.

'Who was that?' Tom asked.

'That's Devlin,' Tara answered, 'the love of Jayson's life.'

'He looks good,' Toni added. 'Hardly recognized him

without a scarf and hat. You can borrow the Maverick anytime when you want to head back to New York to see him.' Characteristically, the fact that Jayson had never driven a car in his life hadn't crossed Toni's mind.

Jayson stared out over the lake as he waited for Franck and her friends' burgers to finish cooking. A few sparkles of the season's first fireflies were twinkling underneath the low hanging branches on the shore. Seeing Devlin finally cleared away the chronic uneasiness he'd been plagued with since returning to Wisconsin. Now he had a plan again. Or at least the first step of one. He would go back to find Devlin and start over again in New York. But first he had to get his mother and brother settled into a new home. They couldn't stay with the Wernermeiers forever. Not with Trey coming home, and the new twins.

Toni, who had been going through the immense stack of mail that had accumulated in her long absence, tossed an envelope in front of Jayson.

'Something for you, Butter Bean.'

The pink envelope had an L.A. postmark on it, and was marked in the upper left-hand corner with a simple, cursive, H.L. It also smelled faintly of scotch.

*Helen?* He tore open the envelope.

Inside was a folded note card with Helen's initials embossed on the cover. When he opened it up a folded-up check fluttered into his lap. He opened it up. PAYABLE TO JAYSON BLOCHER: THE SUM OF $24,587.

Half-pint,
Took six scotches, but I finally remembered "Oconomowoc."
After the ninth, I could even pronounce it well enough to make
the maid look it up.
Anyway—found Harley on death's door in Rock's guesthouse.
The gay cancer is killing the fruits out here faster than
a heavy frost.
Anyway, his last words were: "Let go of my goddamn balls Helen,
and I'll give you the money I owe Jayson."
Love on the rocks,

Helen 'La' Lawson

Jayson couldn't believe it: *his commercial money!*

He could pay off the back taxes on their house. Toni and Willie would have a permanent place to live again, right next door to Tara and the twins. And there would still be enough money left over for a plane ticket back to New York. First class, of course.

His excitement fell, though, when the realization that his father was dead sank in a little deeper. Whatever trouble Harley had caused him, he'd still taken Jayson in and taken care of him as best as he was able. Maybe Devlin had been right. Maybe Devlin and Jayson were Harley's karma insurance. They were his true charity that made up for his scam. Jayson hoped so. He raised his bottle of Diet Squirt skyward and quietly hummed the first few notes of 'Sunrise, Sunset' from *Fiddler on the Roof.* Not only had it always been the closing song of Harley's sing-alongs, it had also been one of Harley's signature songs when he played the part of Tevye in the road show — the road show were he met Toni. And drunkenly fathered Jayson.

'Burgers up!' Tom shouted from the grill.

Jayson tucked the check safely in his pocket. He'd tell Toni about his plans later. Better yet, he'd simply take care of paying all the overdue bills himself — as he always had.

Tom plopped six burgers onto the buns that Jayson held out on a platter. Jayson placed them and the salads on a tray and walked with them down the driveway out to the street.

As soon as he turned west onto Lac LaBelle Drive, the news crews that were assembled at the end of the street spotted him. They surged forward, causing the phalanx of uniformed lesbians to shout orders calling for them to back off.

*This should make some great B-roll news footage,* Jayson thought. *'Picky Prince Hero Serves Dinner to Lesbian Cops.'*

He stood up straight, and held the dinner tray out in front of him proudly, while imagining the soaring crane angle of the scene that would one day surely be the closing shot in the Movie of the Week about his life.

*Wait, no,* he thought further. *This would be the shot right before the first commercial break. There was still plenty of plot left to go. This was still just the beginning.*

The news crews' powerful television lights clicked on, flooding Jayson's face. But he didn't blink.

Jayson walked ahead, smiling widely, directly into the blinding lights – not able to see where he was going, but absolutely certain of what lay ahead.

# Acknowledgments

**Let's start with Brent,** who, for whatever reason, hasn't fled. Your tenacity is equaled only by my devotion.

People for whom I'd buy presents if I were decent enough to remember their birthdays: Moe-sy O'Brien, Stephanie Fraser, Andy McNicol, Carrie Kania, Jeannie O'Toole, Jennifer Cooke, Maya My-My, Laura Fegley, Mick Castagna, Pat Patrick, Anna DeRoy, Jeffrey Taylor, Aaron Hicklin, and a whole lotta Harper Perenniallians whom I've come to consider my friends.

Then there are Jaime, Armistead, Clive, Maria, Danielle, and Hillary – whose talents have taught me the true meaning of envy.

These people are the best invisible friends a guy could ever have: Christopher Nicholas Fields, Peter Benj Wright, Danielle Duffy, Alan Berquist, Lizzie Pea Romenesko, Lance Kandler, Mee Ae Caughey, Colin Matthew Cowden, Bethany Hansen, Katie Dunlap, Hanish 'HAN' Vanc, Lesley J. Merola, Craig Beyerinck, Pam Dunlap, Bryan Morgan, Alison Schaal, Leslie Carleton, Rose Borggraefe, Bryan K. Moody, and Julianne Moore, seriously.

*Josh Kilmer-Purcell*

And, lastly, my grandmother Katie, who held me on her lap to watch *MatchGame* together. Our favorite was Brett Somers – who taught us that booze, wit, and a brightly patterned blouse are all you really need to fill in life's blanks.